praise for m. malone

"Just what you need right now. It's low on angst, the writing is... beautiful and the love story is sweet but also very steamy...I just love everything about this one!"
—Sil, *The Book Voyagers* on RITA® Winner *Bad Blood*

"I am now officially in love with the Alexander family. There was so much about this book that worked for me. I loved the romance between Jackson and Ridley. They had fabulous, explosive chemistry. I loved that Jackson works and lives the music industry. When he sang his song to her, I honestly melted."
--Smitten by Reading on *One More Day*

"Ridley and Jackson explode with passion... this is a pure romance! A sweet and sensational couple and I can't wait to find out what happens in their future. Malone has a winner with The Alexanders series. Please keep them coming!"
--Joyfully Reviewed on *One More Day*

"Malone does an exceptional job ... showcasing how two very different people can fall in love."
--- 4 stars, RT Book Reviews on *The Things I Do for You*

"Nicholas is perfect leading man material..."
-- 4 stars, Romance Junkies on *The Things I Do for You*

"Ms. Malone does an excellent job of taking an unconventional way of coming together and developed it into a true love story. The sexual chemistry between the hero and heroine was off the charts."
--BookKraze Reviews on *The Things I Do for You*

"The book is full of great characters - my favorite had to be Jackson - he is sweet and sexy yet cautious with his heart...The story is well written with plenty of twists. I can't wait to read the next installment of the Alexander brothers."
--Fairy Tale Ending Reviews on *The Things I Do for You*

just one thing

just one thing

M. MALONE

Just One Thing © March 2017 M. Malone

Editor: Daisycakes Creative Services

CrushStar Romance
An Imprint of CrushStar Multimedia LLC

ISBN-13: 978-1-938789-34-2

just one thing

just one thing

Bennett Alexander is a scientist, an inventor and speaks four languages but the intricacies of dating are something he's never mastered. If only love could be like one of his lab experiments; start with a hypothesis, control the variables and then test until you find a solution.

Katie Mason is everything he is not. Warm, funny and beloved by his entire family, she's also a single mother desperate for a job after a painful divorce. With her help, Bennett decides to run the most important experiment of his life. Katie will be the control and with her help, he will test how to modify his behavior. With Katie as his teacher, they embark on a series of unorthodox dating lessons. Soon she has him doing the craziest things from going on fake dinner dates to reading fantasy novels to having...fun.

From what he can tell, there's just one thing wrong with his experiment – the fact that Katie seems to like him exactly the way he is.

one

PALE STREAMS of sunshine slanted through the windows and angled over the metal worktables. Outside several birds chirped, trilling a merry duet. It was as perfect a spring day as could be had in southern Virginia but Bennett Alexander didn't notice any of it. All of his attention was directed to the microscope in front of him.

"Perfect. Absolutely perfect," he mumbled and scribbled his observations on the pad of paper next to his hand.

There could have been an earthquake going on outside and he wouldn't have noticed. Not when he was in his favorite spot doing his favorite thing.

Learning.

A high-pitched shriek finally pulled his attention from his research. Stretching his arms overhead, he rolled his shoulders to release several hours' worth of accumulated tension as he moved closer to the window.

His brothers were engaged in a spirited game of football along with their women. Although after watching for just a few seconds it was clear the game was less about competition and more about giving his brothers ample opportunity to tackle the girls.

A strange sensation rose in his chest as he watched his younger brother Nick grab his wife around the waist and lift her off her feet. Raina squealed but laughed heartily as they both fell to the ground. The football tumbled to the side, forgotten, as she threw her arms around his brother's shoulders and kissed him. A second later, his brother Elliott appeared and grabbed the football off the ground and ran to the other side of the yard, holding his arms above his head in victory. His fiancée Kaylee cheered while his youngest brother Jackson and his wife, Ridley, watched them indulgently.

Bennett turned from the window, swallowing down the tickle of longing he felt. For years he'd accepted the fact that while he was extraordinarily gifted in many areas, there was one subject where he would never excel.

Flirting.

The strange rituals of courtship between men and women were the one subject that he had never been able to master. He was awkward and always had been. He'd long accepted that he was one of the people that functioned better solo and it was illogical to focus on an area he had no aptitude for. If he hadn't figured it out after thirty-two years, then it wasn't going to happen. It was better to spend his time on the things that he understood, like his research.

He walked back over to his worktable. The gloriously perfect soil sample on the slide was the culmination of months of experimentation and testing. His family's farming co-op was constantly looking for ways to increase yield without sacrificing the quality of their crops. His parents had given him complete leeway to develop soil, fertilizer and innovative farming techniques to make it happen.

Some people hated the tedium of testing but he found it soothing. Everything about science was calm. Logical. Why couldn't life be like an experiment? Things would be so much easier.

If you do this, *then* you will get a certain result.

Observe and note the results and adjust how you proceed accordingly. No one expected to have perfect results in the lab.

His gaze fell to the square piece of paper on the center island. It was heavy cardstock with that curly, metallic lettering that was really hard to read. But even his terrible eyesight couldn't miss it. He'd been nominated for an award. Which meant he would have to attend the awards ceremony.

He sighed.

Since he'd been ignoring his mail for the past month, his mother must have put it there so he'd see it. Ignoring things that he found uncomfortable was his usual way of navigating a world that was often baffling and many times humiliating. But his mother had already seen the invitation and if he knew anything about Julia Alexander it was that she wanted her children to be happy. She couldn't understand that he was happy here, just as he was.

Alone with his work.

Alone with his thoughts.

Alone.

It was how he'd always been, even in the midst of a large extended family. But she wouldn't understand that. His eyes strayed over to the window again where he could still hear the faint sounds of shrieking and laughter.

He was starting to understand it less and less himself.

Frustrated, his hand shot out and knocked the invitation to the floor. It made him feel ridiculous to have this sense of dissatisfaction with his life when he had achieved so much. He had a PhD in Molecular Biology, spoke several languages fluently and was in the process of filing for his tenth patent.

He didn't need anything else.

Bennett turned back to his work, ignoring the sun shining through the windows and the noise outside. He took note of where he was stopping so he could pick things back up after getting something to eat. He'd exceeded the recommended time between meals on too many occasions lately and was starting to lose weight. For optimal health it was important to maintain a certain muscle-to-fat ratio. Anyone who worked as many hours as he did, inside the lab and around the farm, couldn't afford to lose valuable time to sickness.

Maybe he would even go to the main house and have dinner with his parents. He hadn't done that in a while and it would make his mother happy. Over the years, his parents had done the best they could with him, despite the fact that they'd never really understood him. Although he often felt like an octagonal peg in a family of circles and squares, they'd always loved and encouraged him. He honestly couldn't ask for better.

Satisfied with his decision, Bennett started packing away the samples. He'd just clean up and then get going. Maybe he wouldn't even tell them he was coming. His brothers always teased him about being buried in his work. He'd show up for dinner as a surprise and for once prove them wrong.

———

IT WAS time to face the facts.

She'd been ignoring it for months but as she looked down at the various bills scattered over her dining room table, Katie Mason had to finally admit that she was in way over her head.

"Are you even listening?"

"Yeah, Mari. I'm still here."

Katie adjusted her phone between her shoulder and her ear. Her sister Marilyn was complaining yet again about their mother. She smiled. It was probably petty but it was nice to know she wasn't the only one her mother criticized. The only one who escaped their mother's eagle eye was their older brother Nelson, who could do no wrong.

"Then she asked if I needed help cleaning since my windows were dirty. I mean, who has time to clean windows every season?"

"Sheila White does," Katie replied.

They both laughed. Their mother loved to tell them all about how she'd managed to keep their father happy and their house clean with no problem. Katie had long ago given up trying to meet her mother's high standards. It was one of the few perks of divorce. She'd already failed so completely in her mother's eyes that she didn't bother to nitpick so much anymore. Katie figured she was probably already considered past redemption.

"Whatever," Mari grumbled. "Did you sign up for that dating app I told you about? I heard it's really good."

Katie didn't bother asking who her sister had heard that from. Her sister was an incurable romantic. Mari thought all her problems would be solved by finding a new boyfriend. Katie couldn't get too annoyed at her persistence, after all romance had always come easily for Mari. Her sister was happily married to her high school sweetheart, Dennis. They didn't have children yet but were enjoying *practicing*, as Mari liked to say.

Katie thought it was good that they were taking their time. Her sister was three years younger at twenty-four and Katie felt she could use the time to mature before becoming a mother. Instead Mari used the time to hound her siblings about their dating lives. She had been telling Katie to "get back out there" ever since the divorce was final. Both of her siblings were worried about her being alone, not that her brother would ever say it, but Katie doubted that going on a date with some random guy was the answer.

"Um... sure I did."

"No, you didn't. I don't know why you won't at least try it. You deserve a hot guy that makes you lose your good sense. Don't you want a guy with a sexy ass? I want that for you, Katie."

Katie picked up one of the bills on the table. PAST DUE was stamped on the front. Just like the one beneath it and the ones beneath that one.

She was drowning in bills and had no idea what to do.

"Right now, I'm just focused on keeping my head above water. Not on a guy with a sexy ass."

It was no wonder that her ex-husband had looked so smug when they signed the divorce papers. Don had willingly given her the house and now she understood why. He knew she hadn't worked outside the home in years and wouldn't be able to keep up the payments.

If she didn't get a job that paid well soon, she and her children would be out on the street.

Okay, that was a little dramatic. No matter how bad things got, her friends would never let her end up on the street.

Mari sighed. "Do you need money? I might be able to help."

"No. I'm going to figure this out on my own."

There was a light knock on the door before it opened. She smiled when she saw who it was. As usual, her closest friend always seemed to know when Katie needed her.

"Let me call you back, Mari. Someone's at the door."

Her sister grumbled. "This conversation isn't over."

"I love you, too." Katie hung up just as her friend Ridley stepped into the room.

Ridley Wells Alexander was married to her neighbor Jackson. Despite being a famous producer, he was also a really nice guy and (when she'd first met him) a single father to two young boys. She'd been thrilled to see him fall head over heels for Ridley when she came to town. It wasn't hard to understand why. Ri was as sweet as could be.

"Hi, are you busy?" Ridley's eyes scanned over the pile of envelopes spread across the table.

Katie's first instinct was to hide them, especially since so many carried the embarrassing PAST DUE stamp. However, she'd been hiding how bad things were for months. At first she'd thought that Don would come back or grow a conscience and pay his child support. However as the months passed and things got worse and worse, she'd started ignoring things out of self-preservation.

But it was past time for that now. She couldn't bury her head in the sand any longer because before long the bill collectors were going to come and take that, too.

"I'm just going through some bills. Come on in. Do you want some lemonade?"

Katie started to rise but Ri waved her off and then settled

carefully in the dining room chair next to her, one hand resting on her rounded belly.

"I'm just fine. Please don't get up. I've already had plenty to eat and drink today. Probably too much."

"You look beautiful as usual," Katie replied as she always did when Ri groused about her pregnancy weight gain. She remembered all too well feeling like a cow when she'd been pregnant with each of her sons but Ri hadn't even gained that much weight.

Ridley's twin sister was a well-known model and since they were identical, Ri had the same long, willowy frame, golden skin and curly dark hair. Today Ri had bundled hers on top of her head in a sloppy bun that somehow still looked amazing.

Katie patted her hair. She'd pulled her shoulder length tight curls up into her usual bun. Don had hated it when she cut her hair but with two young kids, it had seemed like the practical solution. She glanced over at Ri who was the step-mother to two kids and pregnant with another and somehow still woke up looking like a goddess. She sighed.

"So what is all this?"

Ridley picked up one of the envelopes and then glanced over at Katie. When she didn't make a move to stop her, Ri thumbed through the stack of bills, her sharp eyes taking every-thing in. When she got to the bottom, she let out a soft sigh.

"Oh, Katie. How bad is it?"

"Bad. I've already burned through all my savings and we're barely scraping by each month. Honestly, I'm not sure what to do."

Ridley looked like she wanted to say something but clamped her lips shut. Both Jackson and Ridley had offered her financial help before but Katie had quickly shut that down. She wasn't anyone's charity case and besides, that would only be a temporary solution, anyway. If she took their money, things would be okay for a few months but then what would happen after that ran out? She'd be right back in the same position.

No. She had to figure out how to earn her way out of this mess on her own.

"I'm so sorry. We had no idea things were this bad," Ridley said.

"Yeah."

There was really nothing else to say so Katie gathered the envelopes up and wrapped them in the rubber band she'd been using to keep them together. She glanced over at the digital clock in the kitchen. The boys would be getting home from school soon and she needed to be ready to meet them at the bus stop.

"There has to be something we can do," Ridley said. "The same skills that relate to taking care of children have to be translatable to other industries."

Katie shook her head. "I only wish. That's why I started doing the summer camps, remember? It was the only thing I could do to earn money, even before Don left. Taking care of kids is all I've ever done."

Ridley looked thoughtful. Then her eyes swung over to Katie.

Uh oh.

Whenever her friend had that look in her eye, it usually resulted in some sort of crazy plan. For such a sweetheart, Ridley could be a bit of a troublemaker.

"What? Why are you giving me that look?"

"Nothing. I mean, I just had an idea." At Katie's nod, she continued, "Kaylee used to be an administrative assistant and the way she described it sounded like taking care of men who are nothing more than overgrown babies. I bet you'd be great at that!"

Katie thought about it. "I don't think it's that simple. You have to know how to do office stuff. I can type but not as fast as I used to back in school."

"Well, you can brush up on that. I bet we can download one of those typing programs and you'll be up to speed in no time. And I know that you make great coffee and have no problem keeping a million details straight. You remember all the kids' allergies, likes, dislikes and favorites like it's nothing. I bet you'd be the best assistant ever!"

Ridley grinned, looking quite pleased with herself. Katie smiled. Her friend was one of the most optimistic people she'd ever met. The sky could literally be falling and Ridley would just assume it was leaning down to kiss you hello. Even though she didn't share her friend's benign view of the world, it made her feel better to know that someone else could see the positive.

"I'm not sure about being the best assistant ever but I'll settle for someone just giving me a chance."

"Oh don't you worry about that. We'll get someone to give you a chance." After a little groan, Ri pushed up from the table. She waddled over to the front door. "As a matter of fact, I know exactly how to get the ball rolling. Come with us to dinner at the Alexanders' tonight."

Suddenly Katie understood exactly what Ri had in mind. Jackson's parents, Julia and Mark Alexander, were pillars of the community and knew pretty much everyone in town.

Including all of the business owners.

Her heart soared at the possibility of finding a way out of this mess. For the past year, she'd struggled to do it all on her own, raising her children, working, keeping the house up and trying to hold together the pieces of her shattered heart. It had been important for her to do things on her own, if for no other reason than to prove that she could.

Never again would she be that naive, impressionable girl who believed that love was all she needed. She would stand on her own two feet. But pride wasn't going to keep food on the table and she'd been raised to believe in the power of family. Community.

Pride be damned. It was time to accept a little help from her friends.

———

A FEW HOURS LATER, Bennett lifted his head and blinked a few times. Damn it, he'd been about to go up to the main house for dinner and he'd gotten distracted. *Again.* He stood abruptly, his knee colliding with the edge of the work-table. It took a moment for him to catch his breath after the pain subsided and that was when he heard the noise that had broken his concentration in the first place.

His phone was ringing.

Not many people had his number to begin with so it probably meant he'd forgotten something important. *Again.* He gripped the back of his neck in frustration.

It was one thing to make a decision to change but actually doing it was an entirely different matter. The ringing stopped only to start again a minute later, the annoying noise only pushing his frustration even higher.

After he finally located his cell phone in the front pocket of the coat he'd been wearing that morning, he answered with a terse, "Hello."

"Finally! I've been calling and calling. I was about to send out a search party."

His friend Olivia's voice brought a smile to his face. She was one of the few people that could have that effect on him. He supposed it made sense because she'd been his first friend back in kindergarten (before alienating all the other children by refuting the widely held belief that babies came from kissing), his first kiss (the summer after sixth grade), and his first date (the prom). She'd been his first in a lot of ways, although not in the way people usually assumed. The thought brought an unexpected blush, making his cheeks uncomfortably hot.

"Oh, hey Boo." He could almost hear her annoyance at the nickname even over the phone.

"How many years have to pass before you stop calling me that?"

He chuckled. "It's instinct now. I will forever associate peek-a-boo with my Olivia."

"Whatever. I've been trying to reach you. What's up with you ignoring my texts?"

"Sorry. I really meant to call you last night but I'm in the middle of testing the newest iteration of my soil. I started reading my notes from the last phase of testing."

"Of course. The last time we spoke you'd decided to alter the nitrogen levels again, right?"

Bennett relaxed as the conversation turned to his newest formula. He could talk about his research for hours and never get bored. Especially when he was on the cusp of a breakthrough.

"You sound really excited, Ben. I hope this new batch is the one."

Bennett was momentarily paralyzed by a wave of insecurity. There was so much riding on this research. He didn't want to think of what would happen if his newest theory didn't pan out.

"It has to be. The changing weather patterns have really messed with our crops in recent years. We need soil that's robust enough to gain us maximum yield this coming summer."

Talking to Liv was always so easy. Even though she wasn't a scientist, she was remarkably clever. She understood the basis of his research and was an excellent sounding board when he needed to bounce ideas around. She also understood when he tended to zone out in the middle of conversations. Something he was grateful for when he realized he'd done it again.

"Bennett? Hey!"

"Sorry. I'm still here."

"Your mom said you've been nominated for a Mentor Science award! That's awesome."

He glanced behind him at the invitation on the floor and bit back a curse. "Yes, I just got the invitation to the awards ceremony. Wait, you talked to my mom?"

Her warm laugh carried over the line. "Well, you weren't answering your phone as usual. So I figured Julia could at least make sure you were still breathing!"

He wiped a hand over his face. It was a running joke with his friends and family that he could get so lost in his research that they often weren't sure if he was dead or alive sometimes.

"Great. So that's why she put the invitation out for me to see. I was wondering why she bothered. Social gatherings have never been my favorite thing."

"Um, well she did that because I asked her to. I was hoping that you'd take me as your date."

His mouth fell open. Was Olivia asking him on a date?

"I was just thinking that we don't get to spend nearly enough time together these days, you know? And I can talk to everyone for you when you get nervous."

His heart was beating so hard that it was difficult to hear himself think. Olivia had always been there for him and she'd covered for him in social situations more times than he could count. Her parents and his ran in some of the same social circles so they'd grown up attending a lot of the same events. It had seemed natural for them to attend those events together since they would have both been there anyway. This, however, was different. Bennett couldn't even put his finger on exactly why other than it just *felt* different.

"That's true," he said finally. "I'm no good at this kind of stuff but you always cover for me."

"I don't mind covering for you, you know that. So, it's a date! I'll call you later. Bye!"

Before he could even respond, he heard the soft click and dead air. He slipped his phone in his pocket as he considered the strange conversation. People were always a mystery to him but this behavior was strange, especially for Olivia. She'd seemed in a terrible hurry to get off the phone, like she didn't want to talk to him any longer but that didn't make sense because she was the one who'd called him.

Why would you call a person if you didn't feel like talking to them?

He sighed. There was something that he was missing, a puzzle piece that he knew the shape of but not what it looked like or what it meant. Much of his life was like a puzzle, different parts fitting together in ways that he couldn't under-stand or replicate.

He wasn't good with words and his awkwardness was a weakness that he constantly had to compensate for. Olivia was the only one who'd ever seen past all that and treated him like a person instead of an oddity. She was the only one outside of his family that he was truly comfortable with.

Almost like a girlfriend.

Bennett stilled at the thought. It was impossible of course. He was just thinking that way because of the scene he'd witnessed outside earlier. Normally his solitude didn't bother him but after watching his brothers fall in love one by one over the past few years, he'd have to be made of stone not to feel a little lonely. Since Olivia was his closest friend and also happened to be a beautiful woman, of course he'd start to wonder.

But the more he wondered, the less ridiculous it seemed. Until finally he had to ask himself, why *couldn't* Olivia be his girlfriend? Given how many years they'd known each other, she knew him better than anyone else. She was used to all of his strange silences and social mishaps. All things considered, she was the woman most suited to him there probably was.

The longer he thought about it, the more he liked the idea. They would go to the ceremony together and then afterward they could spend some time alone. They would talk and she could see all the ways he'd changed since high school. He was a different man now.

He just had to make her see that.

THE DOOR to the laboratory opened and Bennett smiled as his sister-in-law Ridley walked in. Or he should say, waddled in. He knew better than to comment on it though after seeing the way she'd pinched his brother when he'd mentioned it.

"Hi, am I interrupting anything? Nothing is going to blow up if I come in, right?" She glanced around warily.

Bennett chuckled. She'd interrupted him once before while he was mixing something and there'd been a minor chemical reaction. It had scared Ridley though. For her to venture out here there had to be a good reason.

"No, nothing is going to blow up. Here have a seat."

He stood and pushed his stool to the other end of the worktable so she could sit down. Although pregnancy wasn't a foreign concept by any means (he did have three younger siblings and a slew of cousins), it still made Bennett exceptionally nervous. Pregnant women just seemed so delicate, like there were a million factors waiting to go wrong at any moment. Which made being around pregnant women nerve wracking on any given day but especially when it was Ridley.

He adored his sister-in-law, not only for saving Jackson from himself but because she brought so much happiness to his family as a whole. She'd given his parents the daughter they'd always longed for, was a wonderful mother to his two nephews and had fit into their family like she'd always been there. She even tolerated his strange behavior with a patience unmatched by the rest of his family. She always seemed interested in what he was working on and didn't expect him to be like everyone else.

Which was why this pregnancy was so particularly stressful. If anything ever happened to Ridley it would devastate them all.

"Did Mom send you out here?" he asked.

Ridley shook her head. "No, I just wanted to see what you were up to. It feels like I haven't seen you in ages."

Bennett rubbed his hand over his hair. He had been working pretty doggedly the past month. Without his assistant to keep track of things, his usually orderly existence had become a bit haphazard.

"My assistant got a teaching fellowship to Oxford. So I'm trying to manage by myself. There are just so many details that I'm not used to keeping track of."

He wasn't exaggerating either. John Wilson had been the perfect assistant. He'd hired him originally as a graduate student. John had needed a job that wouldn't interfere with his classes. Bennett had needed someone who could keep track of all the pesky details that came naturally to everyone else. Like when to eat and whether or not he needed a haircut. But over the past year John had become like his right arm. With his science background he'd been able to help Bennett with his testing and kept his notes organized.

Ridley put a soft hand on his arm. "No wonder you look so lost. I mean, it's great for him that he got a fellowship though."

"Yes, it is. That's why I recommended him for it."

"You recommended him even though that meant you'd lose your assistant?" she asked incredulously.

He nodded slowly, not sure why Ridley would find that so surprising. John had been a fine student and would likely go on to have a promising career. He'd been determined to develop formulations for pesticides that would be safer and less expensive to produce. Bennett was extremely proud of him.

"Yes, of course. He was a very bright student. I believe he'll do great things in the world."

She grinned at him then. "You're a good guy, Bennett Alexander. But then I already knew that."

Unsure of how to respond to that, Bennett just nodded. Then he jumped to his feet when she struggled to stand.

"Oh, it's fine. I can get up. It just takes me a minute with this belly, that's all."

Even though she didn't want his help, Bennett hovered behind her uncertainly, ready to offer a hand if she stumbled. It was a miracle to him how she managed to stay upright while carrying around the basketball-shaped lump under her shirt.

"Anyway, I hope I'll see you at dinner. I know you usually don't have time to come but yeah ... anyway."

"I'll be there. I was planning to come today anyway but I got distracted earlier."

Ridley's face lit up. "Oh good. I know everyone will be really happy to see you."

She stopped at the door. "Bennett? Have you already hired another assistant? Or did you have someone in mind?"

"No. I haven't had time. But I suppose I'll have to eventually. Why?"

"Oh nothing. Just wondering." She smiled again, her face the picture of innocence.

Bennett wasn't sure why but he suddenly wondered if going to dinner was such a good idea. He'd heard his brother complain that Ridley could be a bit of a meddler and fancied herself a matchmaker but he'd never seen it firsthand. His brother was probably exaggerating anyway. From what he could tell, Ridley just liked fussing over everyone because she wanted them all to be happy.

What was the harm in that?

Besides, there wasn't too much she could do to meddle in his love life considering that he didn't have one. Unless she could somehow manage to get Olivia to see him as her perfect match. In fact, maybe he would ask Ridley for help. If she liked matchmaking, then she probably wouldn't mind giving him a few pointers and there really wasn't anyone else he could ask.

"Yes, I am going to dinner. Would you mind saving me a seat? There's something I want to talk to you about tonight."

Ridley looked curious but didn't ask any questions. Just watched him with a little smile on her face that made him feel very much like a bug under a microscope.

"Sure thing. I'll save you a seat. I know exactly what you need."

———

KATIE TOOK a deep breath and then let it out slowly as her youngest son ran past her for the hundredth time.

"Matthew Hosea Mason. Come back here and put your shoes on, right now!"

He skidded to a halt but not in time to avoid colliding with her. Katie grabbed him so he couldn't run off again and then held him on her lap while she wrestled his shoes on. Her oldest son, Hunter, stomped down the stairs carrying a soccer ball and what looked like a plastic snake.

"Uh uh, no way. You're not taking that plastic snake with us and playing pranks on everyone."

Hunter's face fell but he put the plastic snake on the edge of the couch. That was when she noticed the small stain on his T-shirt. Katie hung her head. If she sent him upstairs to change it, it would be another ten minutes before he came back down. They were already late as it was. Maybe no one would notice it? It wasn't that big and it was on the hem.

"Okay, everyone to the car. I'm sure Ms. Julia is wondering what is taking us so long."

The boys ran out the door and raced to the car. Over their squeals of *I'm first! No, I'm first!* Katie managed to lock the front door while carrying the peach cobbler she'd made that afternoon. It hadn't seemed like it would throw them that far off schedule when she'd decided to make it but as usual, she'd underestimated how long it took to get the kids cleaned up and under control.

Ten minutes later, they pulled into the long drive leading to the Alexander-Bennett Co-op. She'd heard the story from Jackson before about how his parents had joined the farmland they'd each inherited and then built a home right in the middle of it. It almost sounded like a fairy tale to her, to find someone who was so perfectly matched that you could actually work and live together. But the Alexanders made it look so easy.

As soon as the car was parked, Hunter took off his seatbelt and pushed open his door.

"Look! I see a horse!"

Before Katie could even respond, Hunter took off at a run across the yard. She sighed.

"Hunter, wait for us please!" she called out to him as she got out of the car. When there was no response, she hurried around to the other side of the car and made short work of getting Matthew out of his booster seat. He scrambled down, eager to follow his brother. The first time they'd come here she'd been so worried they'd get into something but Julia had quickly reassured her that the farm was used to wild little boys running around.

It was hard to imagine Jackson and his brothers being the age her sons were now but she bet it was a lot of fun. Just thinking about it made her miss her own siblings. Nelson traveled so much because he was a musician. He was living in London now. Mari actually lived close to her mother in Barbados but over the years, she'd gone home less and less because Don had always complained about the expense. She talked to her family on the phone frequently but it wasn't the same as being there.

It hit her at the strangest times, this feeling of homesickness. She missed the food, the dancing and the sense of belonging. Most of the people born in this part of Virginia carried a faint southern accent but it was nothing like home. There were times she picked up the phone and called her mother just to hear the lyrical rhythm of the accent she'd grown up with instead of the flatter American sound.

Katie grabbed her purse and the covered pie plate from the passenger seat of the car before walking in the general direction the kids had run toward. She was already late so she didn't bother worrying too much. Instead she took the opportunity to enjoy the view. The Alexander farm was acre after acre of rolling land so green it practically sparkled. In the distance several large red barns broke up the vista, looking postcard perfect. There was a large tractor in front of one of them. She sped up her steps. Even though the farmhands who worked here were used to little boys being around didn't mean they weren't in the way. Katie didn't know a lot about farming but she figured springtime had to be a pretty busy season for them.

"Hunter? Matthew?" She turned around to go back the way she'd come and slammed directly into someone. The pie plate in her hand smashed against the front of her shirt and it startled her so much that she fell, landing hard on her backside in the dirt.

"Oh my god!"

"I am so sorry!"

She looked up from the ground at the tall man standing over her. Silhouetted against the sun she could barely make out his face but she didn't need to see his features to know who he was. No one else around was that tall or had that voice.

No one except Bennett Alexander.

The oldest of the Alexander siblings, he was the one she'd seen the least. The others spoke about him like some kind of mystery. He'd been called many things in her presence: strange, brilliant, different and antisocial. But the one thing no one ever called him was the word that Katie thought every time she saw him. Magnetic.

"Hi. I didn't see you."

She could have kicked herself for the obvious statement. Of course she hadn't seen him. No one bumped into someone else on purpose. But Bennett didn't seem annoyed at her clumsiness. He knelt next to her and picked up her handbag which had landed in the dirt next to her.

"That was my fault. I was on my way into the house for dinner and I wasn't looking where I was going either. Besides, it looks like you got the worst of it." He looked down at her shirt pointedly, where the peach cobbler was now smeared all over.

Katie's shoulders drooped. "So much for dessert I guess."

Bennett made a sound that could have been a laugh. She snuck a peek up at him. He was the palest one of his family and had a smattering of small freckles across the bridge of his nose. She'd never noticed before this but his eyes were hazel, a blend of green and gold and brown. A flush went through her when she realized she was staring at him.

And he was staring back.

"I should probably get cleaned up." Then she remembered the reason she'd been walking back here in the first place. "I just have to find my sons. They ran back here because they saw a horse."

Bennett nodded to something over her shoulder. She turned to see Hunter and Matthew trailing behind an older man who was leading a horse slowly across the wide yard toward them.

"Hey Grady. I see you found two new farmhands." Bennett spoke easily to the other man so Katie figured he must be one of the men who lived and worked on the farm.

Grady grunted out a response and stopped walking. He tipped his hat in their direction.

"Just taking old Ellie here for a little exercise. The boys have been keeping us company. I told them if they're good at dinner then they can help me brush the horses down later if they want."

Judging by the wide smiles on both of their faces, her sons definitely wanted to.

"Thank you. I think they'd love that."

She stood gingerly, happy that at least nothing more than her pride was bruised in her fall. "Come on boys, let's go inside and say hello to everyone."

For once they didn't protest, just waved goodbye to Grady who led the horse back the way they'd come. Katie followed behind them as they chattered happily to Bennett about the horse. To his credit, he listened patiently and didn't seem at all annoyed by their questions.

She glanced down at her shirt and groaned. It was even worse than she'd thought. Hopefully Julia wouldn't mind loaning her a T-shirt.

———

BENNETT WATCHED as Katie squared her shoulders like she was going into battle and stepped into the house. She'd been embarrassed. He wasn't adept socially but even he could tell that.

He'd seen her around plenty of times and knew that she was one of Jackson's neighbors but he'd only spoken to her casually a few times. In the moment when she'd looked up at him from the ground, looking so lost and alone, he'd wished he knew her well enough to make her smile. But his jokes usually fell flat and he definitely didn't want to make it worse, so he'd kept quiet.

Luckily her sons were keeping up a steady stream of

conversation as they walked into the house. Bennett was used to the kinds of noise that little boys generated since Jackson's two sons spent so much time with his parents.

When they entered the dining room, everyone else was already seated. His mother's face lit up when she saw him.

"Bennett! I'm so glad you're here, sweetie." She got up from the table with her arms open for a hug but she stopped when she caught sight of Katie behind him.

"Katie, dear. What happened?"

He could almost feel the other woman's embarrassment. It was coming off her in waves and the fact that everyone else at the table turned around to see what his mom was talking about probably didn't help.

Bennett gestured at the pie Katie was holding. "I wasn't looking where I was going as usual. Katie happened to be in the way."

His mother frowned at him and he realized how rude that sounded. Damn it, he'd done it again. Whenever he tried to explain things they always came out wrong.

"Not that she was in my way. She was where she was supposed to be. *I was in the way.* That's what I meant."

Katie cleared her throat. "Would you mind if I borrowed a shirt, Julia?"

His mother put a gentle arm around her shoulders. "Of course I don't mind. Let's go find something for you." She took the smashed pie plate and handed it to Bennett. "We'll be right back."

Bennett looked around, confused as to why she'd given the pie to him. Was he supposed to throw it away? That seemed logical to him but he'd learned long ago that his logic didn't coincide with everyone else's. Maybe his mom was planning to save some of the non-smashed portions of the dish.

To be safe, he put the pie plate on the counter and then washed his hands in the sink. Afterward, he walked into the dining room. His father rose from his seat at the end of the table and shook his hand. He got a fist bump from Jackson and Ridley waved. She was seated across from her husband and there were two empty seats next to her. His brother Eli and his fiancée, Kaylee, were seated next to Jackson.

After nodding hello to everyone, he sat next to Ridley, angling slightly to fit his long legs under the table. When he leaned back, he could see the small card table his mother used to seat the children in the corner. His nephews, Chris and Jase, were already seated and eating chicken fingers. Katie's two boys sat with them and played with the plastic superhero figures that his mom kept on hand to entertain her grandsons.

His mom returned then with Katie trailing behind her. She was wearing a plain blue T-shirt now with the Co-op's logo on the front. When she saw that the only empty seat was next to him, she glanced around.

She probably didn't want to sit next to the weird guy who'd bumped into her and then made it sound like it was her fault. He couldn't exactly blame her for that.

Julia took her place at the opposite end of the table from Mark, winking at his father as she sat down. Katie slid into the seat next to him wordlessly.

After saying the blessing, Julia started passing the dishes down the table so they could all serve themselves. Bennett held out his plate and accepted a slice of the ham that his father had just carved. Everyone was quiet for a few minutes as they filled their plates and Bennett used the time to observe Katie from the corner of his eye. She filled her plate but turned every so often to check on her sons sitting behind her who were by now happily munching on chicken fingers and macaroni and cheese.

When he turned around, he caught his mother's eye.

"So it's a pleasant surprise to see you here, Bennett. I didn't think we'd see you until summertime. You haven't been answering your phone," Julia scolded gently. "I miss John already. He at least would pick up the phone when I called!"

Bennett winced. "Sorry. I've been a little distracted lately. I'm going to hire another assistant. As soon as I find the time."

Ridley suddenly turned to look at him. "Oh, you need an assistant!"

Stunned, Bennett just nodded. Ridley sounded surprised but hadn't they just talked about that earlier? He thought back frantically, cataloguing everything he'd done between then and now. It wasn't unheard of for him to lose whole days when he was in the middle of a project but in this case he was quite sure they'd just had that conversation a few hours ago.

"Yes, I do. Remember, I told you that John got a fellowship—"

"That's such a coincidence because Katie is looking for an assistant job!" Ridley cut him off and then leaned back in her chair to look at Katie on the other side of him.

Katie paused with her fork halfway between her mouth and the plate. She blinked several times before nodding. "Well, yes. I am looking for a position."

Ridley rubbed her hands together. "This is perfect. Bennett should hire her. She's awesome, very good with details and she even has experience with botany."

Bennett wasn't entirely sure what was going on but he got the definite sense that Ridley was up to something. He glanced across the table to where his brother Jackson was shaking his head at his wife. There was an awkward silence and Bennett realized Ridley was waiting for him to respond.

Katie spoke up then, breaking the tension. "Ri, I'm sure Bennett already has a list of people he's considering for the job."

"Actually, I don't."

Katie's mouth fell open slightly. "Oh. Um, okay then."

Again, Bennett had the sense that he'd committed some social faux pas that was just outside his understanding. Everyone at the table seemed slightly uncomfortable and he could tell there were several nuances that he wasn't aware of going on. His shoulders lowered.

Was it any wonder he preferred to spend so much time alone? It was exhausting, second-guessing every interaction looking for all the ways he'd screwed it up. Maybe he should have come by after dinner was over and taken a plate back home.

"I've been in the middle of testing some new soil samples. That's why I've been so distracted lately. Also Olivia called earlier." He threw that in there because he knew how much his mother loved Olivia.

"Oh good. She called here a few days ago looking for you since you weren't answering. Such a sweet girl. What is she doing these days? Alberto is always so vague when I ask about her."

Bennett shrugged. "She's managing a nightclub, I think. You know Olivia. She never stays in the same place for long."

He definitely wasn't getting into the reason why Olivia and her father had such a strained relationship. That wasn't the kind of thing you brought up over dinner. Or ever. And it was one of the only things in the world that made Bennett angry enough to become physically violent.

Yes, it was best if his parents never knew anything about that. That situation was a prime example of why he'd always kept to himself. He'd seen the way people treated each other, even people who claimed to love each other, and none of it made sense to him. Olivia had made one mistake and her family had disowned her. If that was being normal, maybe it was best if he didn't try to assimilate too much.

The stress of being social hit him all at once and suddenly all Bennett wanted was his laboratory. It was the one place he actually felt in control, like he knew what he was doing. After dinner, he'd just slip out.

No one would even miss him.

three

KATIE WANTED to strangle her best friend. Well, not really since Ridley was too dang adorable even when she was meddling but she would at least hug her extra hard the next time she got her alone.

What had she been thinking to say all that stuff at dinner?

She glanced over at her friend who was currently picking up the remains of the food from the kiddie table. As soon as Julia left the room, Katie put down the plate she was holding and cornered Ridley.

"What was that at dinner? And why did you say I know about *botany*?"

Ridley shrugged. "You've helped me with my landscape designs plenty of times. That's the same thing, right?"

Exasperated, Katie didn't even bother correcting her. Although she was pretty darn sure that knowing the names of a few types of flowers didn't count as experience with botany. That was the least of her concerns at this point.

"Ri, you totally put him on the spot. I'm sure he wants someone with experience."

Ridley carried the plastic plates from the kids' table into the kitchen. Since Julia was there hand washing several wineglasses they let the conversation drop. Katie had no illusions about what Ri was up to and she definitely didn't want to discuss it in front of Bennett's mother. Surely the woman knew her son was quite a catch but that didn't mean she wanted her daughter-in-law scheming to marry him off.

Just because Ridley thought she'd be a good match for him didn't mean Julia would agree. Most mothers probably wouldn't consider a divorced mother of two as the perfect catch for one of their sons.

Once Julia left to put the clean wineglasses away, Ri whirled toward her. "Just play it cool. He needs an assistant and you need a job. As far as I'm concerned this is the perfect solution for everyone."

Katie glanced out the window over the sink. The boys had raced outside as soon as they'd finished eating to go see the horses. Mark had gone with them since his grandsons wanted to see the horses, too. She never worried about the boys' safety here. It was such a relief to be able to relax for once instead of constantly being on alert and trying to keep them out of trouble. And despite how much attention she gave them, she could tell they still craved a male role model in their lives.

Don had always been too busy to spend much time with them and ever since the divorce, his visits had been sporadic at best. Matthew didn't seem to notice his father's disinterest yet but Hunter did; she could tell. There was nothing in the world more disheartening than watching her son figure out that his father would much rather be doing something, *or someone*, else than being with his kids.

"Maybe it would be okay. If I worked here, the boys could

spend more time with Mr. Alexander and they really need that. Hunter especially really needs a positive male role model around."

Ri hesitated and then asked softly, "Have you heard from him?"

When Katie shook her head, Ri hugged her. "I'm sorry. You and your boys deserve so much better."

The hug was a little too close, making all the tender, delicate parts of Katie feel as raw and exposed as the day her husband told her he was leaving her for someone else. For just a moment, she was tempted to sink into the embrace and bawl her eyes out but doing that wouldn't change anything. It would just give her red eyes, a stuffy nose and make her friend feel sorry for her. Her pride was about all she had left at this point so she straightened and put on the biggest, brightest smile she could muster.

Even if it was fake, it was better than wallowing in misery.

"It's his loss, really. They're such good boys. So full of love and so eager to give it. He's missing out on all of that. As for me, I'm just focused on starting fresh."

Ridley gave her a knowing look, like she could tell Katie wasn't as strong as she was pretending to be. But in the end, her friend understood all about starting over. She'd come to New Haven at the lowest point of her life and ended up finding the love of her life.

Katie wasn't expecting that kind of miracle. She'd blown her chances at the fairy tale when she'd chosen the wrong prince to ride off into the sunset with. All she could hope for was a stable job so her boys could stay in the home they'd grown up in.

She just hoped she was able to catch a break before the avalanche of bills caught up with her.

———

HE'D FINALLY FOUND his opening. After his father had accompanied the boys outside, Bennett had figured he could tag along and then just make a detour to his laboratory. Since he'd converted one of the existing barns into his laboratory and personal living space years ago, it was on the way to the stables anyway. It was perfect.

Or it would have been if Jackson hadn't cornered him before he could make his escape.

"Hey, Bennett! Wait up."

Cursing internally, Bennett paused and turned. Jackson clapped him on the shoulder so hard it felt like his spine bowed.

"I just wanted to catch you before you went back to work. About dinner, Ri didn't mean anything in there. She's just antsy waiting for the baby to come."

Bennett almost wanted to laugh. Ridley really did have his brother wrapped around her little finger. Luckily she was a good woman, not the kind to take advantage of that kind of power.

"I know she wasn't trying to be pushy. She's just looking out for her friend. No harm done."

"Oh, she was trying to be pushy. She's always pushy when she wants something. I kind of like her that way, if you know what I mean."

Jackson's dark chuckle told him exactly what his little brother meant by that.

"I get it. But either way, it's no big deal. I was just going to head back and get some more work done."

"Cool. I know you're busy." Jackson pulled him into a quick hug and then turned to leave but not before Bennett caught the faint look of disappointment on his face.

Man, it was a killer to know he was constantly hurting the people around him. And for what? All because they'd committed the crime of wanting to spend time with him?

If there was a way to let them know that the lack was in him, not in anything they'd ever done, he'd do anything to find it. He just wasn't wired the same way they were. He stayed away, not because he didn't want to spend time with them, but to protect them. It was easier this way all around. Solitude was safer.

No hurt feelings, no miscommunications. Just him and his work.

Exhaustion rode him hard as he pulled open the back door. Then he stopped short when he saw Katie outside talking to one of her sons. He recognized the little boy's posture. He was in trouble and getting an earful. As the oldest of four, he'd recognize that stance anywhere.

"When you take something from your brother, you're not thinking about his feelings. You're only thinking of yourself. That's not fair, is it?"

When the little boy shook his head, she placed a hand on his head.

"I know. Now go apologize. We'll be leaving in fifteen minutes, okay? Make sure you apologize to Mr. Alexander for your bad behavior, too."

Once Katie stood, the little boy raced off and she paused when she saw Bennett in the doorway.

"Sorry. Let me get out of your way."

As she moved to the side, Bennett followed her with his eyes. She really was a nice woman. Patient, kind and understanding. She corrected her son's behavior with a calm, steady kind of strength. Exactly the kind of woman who could whip any man into shape.

When he didn't pass, she peered up at him curiously. "Are you okay?"

"Does it bother you that you have to correct his behavior?"

The look she gave him was half *What the hell?* and half *What do you think?*

"Of course not. I'm his mother. Teaching him what's appropriate is part of my job."

"Do you ever get frustrated with them? Teaching someone how to behave sounds like a twenty-four hour job."

"It is. That's motherhood though." She regarded him silently for a minute and when he didn't say anything else, she tipped her head to the side. "Um, this conversation is really weird."

"Might I ask a favor?"

"Sure."

"Could you forgive the weirdness of this conversation because I'm truly not trying to cause offense? I just need help and I think you're the person who can help me."

Katie's expression closed up just that fast. She sighed and then tugged at the ends of her hair. The shiny, dark coils fascinated him. They looked soft and the pattern was fascinating. Every curl twisted around itself like a double helix, the pattern reminding him of a strand of DNA. He wondered what they felt like.

Yeah, like he'd ever know that. He was socially broken but

even he knew that putting your hands on a woman was grounds to get slapped.

He tuned in just in time to catch the tail end of what Katie was saying.

"Listen, all that stuff Ridley was saying before ... You don't have to ... She's just worried about me. No one expects you to hire some random woman to be your assistant."

Fascinating. Despite the fact that she'd barely completed a full sentence, her worry and affection for her friend came through clearly. She was scattered and nervous and the exact opposite of everything he usually required in an assistant.

Which made her perfect.

"Don't worry about it." He turned to leave and just before he left he realized that he hadn't actually responded to any of the things she'd said. Yet another thing he hoped she could train him out of over the next few weeks.

"Oh yeah, I'll see you on Monday morning."

"For what?"

"Your interview."

———

LATER THAN NIGHT, Jackson watched Ridley complete her nightly skincare ritual from his perch on their king-sized bed. It was his favorite way to end the night. After years of being a widower, you'd think the sex would be what he'd missed the most but no ... the tiny details that no one else paid attention to were his favorite things. He loved to watch his adorable wife putting on lotion and shaving her legs and brushing her teeth.

Until the one you loved was taken away, you didn't realize

how valuable those quiet, common moments were. It was an honor to watch the one you loved doing normal, everyday things. He could watch Ridley breathing and never get tired of the sight.

After she finished, she cut off the light in the bathroom and climbed beneath the covers next to him. When her back made contact with the mattress she let out a loud groan.

"Tired?"

"Exhausted. But it was a good night. I loved having everyone all together."

Her comment made him think back to that disastrous dinner. Even though his older brother hadn't made a big deal of it, Jackson could read him like a book. There were few things Bennett hated more than being put on display or being pushed into something he didn't want to do. Despite being the youngest brother, Jackson had always felt a curious protectiveness for Bennett. He was different but in a brilliant way and he didn't like to think of him being manipulated. Even by someone with good intentions.

"About dinner tonight ... I thought we talked about this."

Ridley didn't even bother to pretend that she didn't know what he meant. Instead she just rolled onto her side so she could see him without lifting her head.

"But look how well it turned out for Nick and Raina. And Eli and Kay. Everyone should be thanking me. Clearly I'm gifted at this."

Jackson was determined not to smile at her brazen statement, even though he really wanted to.

"Ri, you booked Kay and Eli into a room together when they weren't even dating yet. He spent the night on a cot on the floor."

"Well, that wasn't what I intended but that just proves your brother is a gentleman. Although, all he did was delay the inevitable. Love cannot be denied."

"You seriously think that pushing Katie at Bennett is a good idea? He's not exactly a people person."

Ri wrinkled her nose. "I know but I just think he seems lonely. He needs someone to draw him out of his shell a bit. Katie is perfect for that. She can handle any social situation and loves parties. All the stuff he hates, she can deal with."

"This has a really high probability of blowing up in your face. And I'm reserving the right to say I told you so."

Ridley grinned suddenly. "I accept the challenge."

Jackson pulled her closer, pressing a kiss to her forehead. For just a moment, they remained like that, breathing the same air. Then he felt her hand trail down his bare chest and settle at the waistband of his sweatpants. He normally didn't wear anything to bed but lately he'd been wearing sweatpants or shorts.

"Do you want to stay up for a bit? I'm pretty sure the kids are already asleep so we don't even have to be that quiet." She bit him gently on the throat and Jackson stiffened, all the blood in his body seeming to land in the same place, the erection currently trying to work its way through layers of cotton to get at her.

As his blood raged and his hormones surged, he bit his lip and willed his body to listen to a higher power for once. It took a few moments but once he was more in control, he pulled back slightly and then clicked his lamp off, leaving them shrouded in darkness.

"Actually I'm kind of tired. Let's just go to sleep."

He could feel the shock emanating from her; it coated his

skin like a film. Seconds later, her hands left his body and he heard the rustle of the sheets and blankets moving around as she got comfortable. In his mind he could picture her curled up with her hands tucked beneath the pillow, her spine curved forward like she was protecting herself from a blow.

Which was what he'd just given her, right? It might not have been physical but he could tell the rejection had hit harder than any fist ever could. Even knowing that ... he couldn't.

"Okay. I'm tired, too. Good night."

He registered the gentle kiss against his cheek before she turned over to face the wall.

four

MONDAY MORNING, Katie went through the usual steps of getting her kids dressed, fed and on the school bus with an extra pep in her step. As soon as the bus pulled off, she jogged back to the house and raced up the stairs. After a quick shower, she stood in her closet surveying her choices with a critical eye.

Intellectually she knew that what she wore probably wouldn't make that much of a difference. Bennett didn't seem like the kind of guy who would even notice that sort of thing. However, it was the first time in quite a while that she'd been excited about something. She was going to dress to fit her mood and to make herself happy.

By the time she left an hour later, she was dressed in a fitted blue pin-striped skirt and cream blouse, her neck adorned with a single strand of pearls. She'd kept her makeup simple and her shoes had only a low heel but the outfit made her feel professional and in control. It was only through her friend's dogged persistence that she even had this chance, so she definitely wasn't going to screw it up. She needed all the mojo she could get.

As she drove carefully through the quiet suburban streets, Katie gave herself a pep talk. Maybe she didn't have that many skills but she was a hard worker and took pride in that. There were other people with more experience, sure, but she was going to bring a fresh perspective and an enthusiastic spirit. Hopefully that would be enough to convince Bennett to give her the job.

Over the weekend, she'd gone through her bills one more time and honestly the situation looked worse at second glance. She needed this.

After parking in the long drive, she walked up to the front door and rang the bell. Usually she just walked in but this situation called for a more formal approach. Especially since she wasn't sure if Bennett had told his parents to expect her for this interview. When he'd said it, it had seemed like he'd been doing it as an afterthought, a concession to make his adored sister-in-law happy. She'd be lucky if he even remembered she was coming today.

"Katie! What are you doing out here on the steps? You know you can just come right in." Julia held the door wide for her to come inside. Katie stepped past her into the cool interior of the house.

It was strange to see it so quiet. She'd only ever been here when the whole family was around and the entire place was awash with people and noise and life.

"Bennett asked me to come back to interview for the assistant position. Is he here?"

Julia looked shocked but recovered quickly. "That's wonderful. I'm sure you'd be perfect for the position. But if you're here for Bennett, you're in the wrong place. He's in the converted barn around back. The first one."

Julia led her through the family room and into the kitchen, then to the back door. They stepped out onto the back deck and Katie shielded her eyes from the bright morning sunlight. Julia gestured across the wide expanse of the yard to the closest red barn.

"Just go right on in. The door should be open. Bennett is an early riser, always has been."

With that, Julia went back inside, leaving Katie on the porch alone. She descended the steps, noting with satisfaction that the farm was bustling with activity. One of the ranch hands rode by on some sort of small tractor and tipped his hat to her as he passed. She continued across the yard, the heels of her shoes sinking slightly into the soft grass. When she reached the barn, she raised her hand to knock and then dropped it just as quickly. Cursing herself for being a coward, she wiped her suddenly sweaty palms on her skirt.

She'd been around the Alexanders so many times but it had never been a matter of life and death before. If she didn't get the job she wasn't sure how she'd pay the mortgage. With a quick shake of her head, she banished the thoughts. Dwelling on her dire financial circumstances wasn't going to convince Bennett to hire her. If she wanted this job, she was going to have to prove to him that she could handle it. That wasn't going to happen as long as she stood out here feeling sorry for herself.

Determined not to waste any more time, she knocked once and then opened the door. Her mouth immediately fell open and a part of her wanted to step back outside to make sure she was in the right place.

Whoa.

The barn was so quaint on the outside that she'd originally felt overdressed. But once you were inside, there was a totally different vibe going on. The inside had been completely renovated and was a modern scientific lab. The ceiling panels on one side of the building had been converted to skylights and there were little pods of plants growing beneath the streams of light revealed.

Katie leaned down to peer at the plant pod things. They were set up in rows on metal tables and every few minutes there was a soft hiss and a mist of water sprang up covering the whole area.

"Fascinating. It's a greenhouse."

She was careful not to touch anything even though she really wanted to pick up one of the little pod things to see what was underneath. Not only was it fascinating but also *really* intimidating. She wasn't even sure exactly what Bennett did for a living so why would he want to hire her?

From the way Ridley described him, he was some kind of intellectual prodigy, a brilliant scientist and inventor. She smoothed her skirt again and wished that she'd spent her time over the weekend reviewing science journals instead of brushing up on her typing. What if he asked her questions about his projects? She had no idea what any of these plants even were.

"You came."

The voice behind her echoed throughout the space and Katie jumped a little. She turned to see Bennett standing in the doorway across the room.

"Yes. Hello." When he didn't respond or move any closer, she gestured awkwardly toward the plants and then the skylights, desperate to fill the silence. "This is very impressive."

Apparently that was the right thing to say because his face lit up and he moved closer, dodging between the tables with the kind of certainty that told her he'd done it a million times. When he reached her side, he looked down at the rows of plants almost affectionately.

"Are you familiar with hydroponics?" he asked. "It seems counterintuitive but to create *better* soil, it's actually helpful to study how plants grow without it. It also helps me design solutions for parts of the world where soil conditions are poor."

It was so tempting to lie but she couldn't do it. He looked so excited and she wasn't going to build up his hopes and then dash them. If he hired her, it would be with full knowledge of exactly what she could and couldn't do. All she could do was hope he was open-minded.

So she clamped her lips together, wished for the best and then shook her head slowly. "Nope. I don't know anything about that."

"Botany?"

At the slow shake of her head, Bennett smiled. "So basically my sister-in-law is full of shit?"

That startled Katie into laughing out loud. "Pretty much. Are you angry?"

"No. We all start knowing nothing. The most important question is are you willing to learn?"

She nodded. "I'm a fast learner and I don't complain. I know being a mom isn't considered valid work experience to most people but if I can handle a baby that screams for twelve hours straight and another that pooped on me every time I changed his diaper, I think I can handle just about anything."

Bennett's face was blank for a minute and then his lips stretched into a smile so wide it looked like his face might crack.

"Good. That's good. Look, I have to go out briefly because I forgot I had an appointment this morning. But after I come back, we can figure out how to go forward. I'm going to need to train you in several areas, starting with caring for my babies."

He gestured to the little buds of plants growing on the tables and Katie realized belatedly that he was trying to make a joke.

"No problem. I'll hang out here until you come back. But I want to at least be helpful so point toward something that needs organizing."

Bennett looked behind himself sheepishly. "My office is a disaster."

Katie brightened. "Well, that's where I'll start. I'll see you when you get back."

He nodded and then walked past her. She walked to the other side of the room and opened the door he'd indicated. The desk in the middle of the room was empty save a small lamp and a laptop. A box sat on top of the filing cabinet with a single sheet of paper poking out.

Her mouth dropped open. "A disaster, huh?" She turned around to face Bennett and then let out a soft sigh when she saw that he'd already left.

"If this is his idea of a mess then I have a feeling I won't last long here."

She picked up the single sheet of paper and filed it in the folder with the current month's date. Then she sat in the office chair to wait.

———

BENNETT PARKED his truck on the private drive behind his laboratory. The entire time he'd been meeting with his old classmate he'd been aware that Katie was back at his place waiting for him. Although he wouldn't necessarily call it excitement, it had given him a curious feeling to think that she would be there when he returned.

He got out, not bothering to lock his vehicle, and then walked back into the building. Every time he entered, it never failed to make him smile, remembering the way this building used to look. The barns on their land were all original structures and this one in particular had been in dire need of repair. When he'd first asked his parents if he could have it, they'd agreed easily, probably thinking he would just replace the beams or something. No one had expected him to completely renovate the entire thing until it looked like something out of a sci-fi movie.

It was the place he felt most comfortable. Since he'd made sure to have the builders put living space on the second floor, it was also his home. He lived here, ate here, created here and slept here. Very few people broached his space, save his mother when she needed to reach him. So when he walked in and Katie turned around, he was unprepared for the blast of warmth he felt seeing her sitting at one of the worktables.

It should have felt weird to have someone in his space. Instead, it was nice.

"Hey! How was your meeting?" She closed the magazine she'd been reading and turned on the stool to face him.

Bennett put his keys on the peg near the door and then slipped his arms into the lab coat he'd taken off before he left.

"She was late."

Katie blinked. "Oh. But you weren't gone that long. That must have been a short meeting if it got started late. How long did you have to wait for her?"

"I was waiting for her roughly seven minutes."

"Well, according to Emily Post you aren't late until after ten minutes. After fifteen, you need to call and explain. That's the rule."

For someone who viewed the world around him as a wild west of sorts, it was a revelation that there were rules governing such things. Maybe the social scene wasn't as confusing and unstructured as Bennett had always believed.

Was it possible that he'd only had such a hard time dealing with others because he'd never thought to look up and learn the rules?

Katie blinked at him. "Are you okay? I mean, you don't have to listen to me. I understand if you were pissed about waiting around. I hate waiting, too."

Bennett smiled at her. "No, I'm not upset. I've just never heard that rule before."

"Really? My mom has always been big on etiquette. You wouldn't believe how many rules there are, down to how long you have to send out thank you cards after receiving a gift."

Bennett frowned. "You're supposed to send a card to say thank you? Why wouldn't you just say thank you when they give you the gift?"

Katie paused, her forehead crinkling in a way that Bennett found surprisingly endearing. It caught him off guard, this sudden attraction. He'd found women attractive before, of course, but it was strange to suddenly be attracted to someone that he'd known for a while. Granted, he was used to thinking of her as "Ridley's friend" instead of a beautiful woman but it was a shock to discover that she could be both.

"You know, I've never thought about it that way. I guess it does seem odd to send a thank you card instead of just saying it. Weird, huh?"

Still reeling from the sudden, and extremely inconvenient, blast of desire, Bennett shook his head and tried to recapture the thread of the conversation.

"It seems illogical, that's all," he finally muttered.

"Do things always have to be logical in your world?" she teased.

"Yes. Always."

Katie paused, her mouth forming a little pout. The motion drew his attention to her lips and he tried, he really tried, to turn away. After a few seconds he gave it up as impossible. With her richly colored skin, she stood out in the stark paleness of the sterile room like a rose in the desert. She had small, delicate features but there was something about her that spoke of strength. Then she looked at him again and he had to take a breath. It was her eyes. Her dark eyes weren't those of an innocent. She looked like someone who'd seen quite a bit in her life and wasn't afraid to face the bad stuff head on.

He could respect that.

"My need for logic and order is often at odds with the world around me. That's part of why I need you here. I spend a lot of time immersed in my work so I need you to be the one who interacts with the outside world for me."

She straightened, the teasing expression gone. "I can do that."

He doubted she really understood just how much interacting

she'd have to do on his behalf. There had been weeks at a time working on his last invention where he wouldn't have remembered to eat or take a shower if John hadn't been there. When he was working, his mind was completely absorbed in the process. The real world couldn't compete with the joy he found in his work.

"Bennett?"

When he looked up, she held his gaze. There was a resolve there that he hadn't seen before.

"I can't pretend to understand what you do here but I can tell it's really important. The way I see it, you need me to take care of all the boring, everyday stuff so you can focus on all the brilliant, science stuff. I can do that. So don't worry about anything okay?"

Bennett was surprised to find himself nodding. "Okay. Let me show you around properly then."

Katie stood eagerly, pushing the stool beneath the worktable. Bennett was suddenly overcome with nerves. Why did this always happen? He knew this lab inside and out so there was no reason for him to have stage fright showing it to someone else. Yet he was nervous all throughout the short tour he conducted.

He ended by gesturing toward the stairs leading to his private quarters. "And that's where I sleep. Any questions?"

Katie just regarded him with wide eyes. "No. Not yet anyway. Thank you for the opportunity. Sorry that your family sort of forced you into hiring me."

"No one forces me to do anything."

"Oh, of course not. I didn't mean to imply anything."

Now she looked uncomfortable again. He cursed his inability to read social situations the way his brothers did. He'd been trying to put her at ease and now she looked even more upset than before.

———

"SO, you don't have any questions?"

Katie glanced over at all the weird things on the tables and the chemicals lining the walls. She'd followed quietly as Bennett showed her the different areas of what he called "The Laboratory" and wished the whole time for a pad of paper and a pencil to take notes. Not that it would really help in the end since she only understood about half of what he was saying.

Honestly, she had so many questions that it would probably take him all day to answer them all but the whole reason she was here was to make his life easier, right?

"Just one. What time do you normally eat lunch?"

He looked surprised but gestured toward the refrigerator on the back wall. She'd already made note of the fact that there was a full kitchen because if she was going to work here, coffee was a priority.

"I order out a few times a week and then just eat the left-overs whenever. Sometimes my mom comes by and brings me food also. I think she worries about me."

"I'm sure she does. That's what moms do. Plus I'm sure she wants to help. She's crazy proud of you."

Bennett seemed momentarily startled by that statement but then he gave a little shake of his head before motioning to the office.

"You can fill out the employment paperwork and then get started."

Katie walked ahead of him into the office and sat in one of

the old wooden chairs in front of the desk. Considering how high-tech and modern the rest of the building was, it seemed strangely incongruous to find such old furniture in his office.

"These chairs are cool. Are they antiques?"

Bennett shrugged and then peered at the chairs. "I'm not sure. My father brought them over when I said I needed furniture."

"Oh. I just thought it was interesting that they look so much older than everything else."

"I suppose they are. But they're adequate to their purpose."

Katie laughed nervously. "Adequate. Yes, they are."

She read over each sheet as it was placed before her and signed in the appropriate places. Bennett then placed the papers in a manila envelope and set it on top of his desk before walking over to the bookshelf. He picked up the tablet on the shelf and held it out to her.

"The project notes for the development of our current soil additive have all been loaded on here. You have access to the shared folder that holds all of my current formulations and the resulting yields for the following year's crops. Familiarize yourself with those so you'll be able to assist when I'm ready to start testing the next phase."

Katie nodded even as her heart rate increased. She took a deep breath, hoping she didn't look as overwhelmed as she felt. What did she know about chemical formulas? It all looked like another language to her and she could only hope he didn't ask her to do anything more than hand him things.

"Thank you again for this opportunity."

He inclined his head and then motioned for her to follow him out to the main workspace. Katie slid onto the same stool she'd sat on before and placed the tablet carefully on the metal table. They had a tablet at home that her boys shared but she hadn't spent too much time on it. So her first order of business would be to make sure she knew how to use it properly. Her prior experience using a tablet wasn't going to help her much here, not unless Bennett wanted her to help him play Angry Birds.

"While you're reading, I'm going to review my most recent test results and make notes on what I would like to change."

Katie smiled, determined to put on a brave face. The whole reason Bennett had hired her was to appease his sister-in-law so she didn't want him to regret it. She might not have any experience but one thing she was great at was figuring out how to be helpful and she'd never had a problem working hard.

"You don't need to worry about me, Mr. Alexander."

Bennett grimaced and held up a hand. "Bennett, please. If you call me Mr. Alexander, I'll spend the entire time looking over my shoulder thinking my father is here."

Katie laughed. "Fair enough."

For the next hour, Kate opened the different apps loaded on the tablet. There was an app that allowed her to access the shared folder he'd mentioned before and she started reading the first file only to close it right away. It had been written in such complicated language that she figured maybe she'd better work up to that.

There was a books app that had quite a few research books in its library. Her favorite thing was looking through the photos in the device's Camera Roll. She supposed it must have been Bennett's former assistant who had taken the pictures because he'd captured not only the little pod things at various stages but also several photos of Bennett at work. He looked so serious, his brow crinkled in concentration while mixing various strange looking liquids together in a glass beaker.

She swiped through a few more pictures and then stopped on an image of Bennett caught with a rare smile on his face. He looked so happy and so young that it took her off guard.

"Everything okay out here?"

Startled, Katie clicked out of the pictures so he wouldn't catch her staring at a picture of him like a stalker.

"Yes, I'm good. Oh look at that; it's lunchtime."

Bennett blinked. "So it is. I think there are cold cuts and other sandwich stuff available. I'll be just a little longer."

Katie wandered into the kitchen and discovered that the refrigerator had been fully stocked. She pulled out a tray with thin cut deli meats and found mayonnaise and mustard. The mustard was full while the mayo jar was almost empty.

"Guess I don't have to ask which he prefers," she mumbled to herself.

It was quick work to make two sandwiches, mayo for him and mustard for her. She found paper plates in the pantry and then folded paper towels in lieu of napkins.

Bennett looked up in surprise when she entered his office and set the plate to his left. "You made me a sandwich? Thank you. You really didn't have to do that."

"Don't thank me yet. I guessed that you prefer mayonnaise but if that's wrong, you can have this one instead." She held up her plate.

"No, you got it right."

He picked up the sandwich and took a big bite. Satisfied that he was taken care of for the moment, Katie took a bite out of her own sandwich and walked back to the kitchen to rustle up some drinks. Again, it was easy to see what his preferences were because there was no soda at all, only almond milk, bottled water and orange juice. She grabbed two bottled waters.

When she walked back into Bennett's office, he was muttering to himself and patting his shirt pocket. He looked up and smiled his thanks when she set the water next to his plate and then went back to looking around.

"They're on your head," Katie said, amused by his bewilderment.

"What?" He peered over at her, his eyes slightly unfocused.

"Your glasses. That's what you're looking for, right?"

His hand reached up until he felt the frames sitting on top of his head. Then he smiled.

"Yes. That's exactly what I'm looking for."

He pulled them down and slipped them on his face. Then he picked up the tablet from his desk and stood.

Before he could get too far, she picked up the plate and held it out to him. "You should probably finish it now so you don't have to interrupt your work later."

He blinked at her a few times but then picked up the sandwich. After finishing what was left in a few bites, he sent her a small, satisfied smile.

"I have a feeling this is going to work out just fine."

Not the most effusive praise she'd ever received but nonetheless Katie was left feeling like she'd just gotten an A on a test.

five

THE WHOLE WAY home Katie thought about her strange first day. All she had done was sit around looking at a tablet and exploring the place but she guessed it wasn't so odd for a new employee to not have much to do. Bennett himself seemed at a loss as to what to do with her, too. If this job was going to work out, she was going to have to take the initiative and find ways to be helpful.

When she pulled into her driveway, she noticed the bus coming up the street. Wow, she'd only just made it. She was used to being at home and if she lost track of time, it was no big deal to just jump up and go get the kids. Now she was going to have to really watch the time and plan accordingly. It would be a huge adjustment to have to work around Bennett's schedule but this was the best job offer she'd had in ages. Close to home, flexible hours so she could be there for the kids and all she had to do was pick up after a nutty professor.

Easy as cake.

She stood at the end of the sidewalk and watched as a stream of little bodies piled off the bus. Matthew's blue backpack stood out from the rest so she saw him first. Then Hunter appeared behind him, talking a mile a minute. When they saw her on the sidewalk, they both ran to reach her. Matthew threw himself at her, almost knocking her off her feet. Katie squeezed him just as hard. It was hard to believe her little man was five now. This was Matthew's first year going to school and kindergarten hadn't been the easiest adjustment for him after being at home with just her for years. Hunter was seven and in second grade. So far his enthusiasm for school had rubbed off on his younger brother.

"Mom! You forgot my snack today so I had to eat pretzels." Hunter made a face.

Katie winced. Her son's teacher kept extra snacks for the kids who forgot to bring their own but the only options she had were pretzels and gluten-free crackers. Neither of which were Hunter's favorite things.

"Sorry buddy. I think it's time you start helping me get your backpack prepared every night. You're old enough now to take care of a few things on your own."

She ran an affectionate hand over his coarse dark curls, which were mussed and carried speckles of what looked like sand. There was no telling what he'd gotten in his hair on the playground.

"I can do it, Mom. Can I pack my lunch, too?" he asked excitedly as they entered the house.

Katie already knew why he was asking. Hunter was crafty and probably thought he could fill his lunch bag with as many snacks as he wanted if he packed it himself.

"You can assist, how's that?"

He grinned and threw his stuff on the floor. Katie sighed and pointed to the front closet. With mumbles and grumbles, both boys put their backpacks away along with their coats and shoes. They didn't hang the coats on the nails she'd hammered into the wall for just that purpose, instead throwing them on top of everything else.

Katie bit her tongue. She didn't bother asking them to pick them up. At this point she'd learned to pick her battles.

"Who wants a snack?"

After getting them settled with apple slices and peanut butter, Katie retreated to her room to change her clothes. Luckily, the boys were too young to notice details such as when their mom was dressed up out of the blue. She'd been careful to keep them in the dark about their precarious financial state. They deserved to just be kids and not worry about things like bills or whether their parents hated each other.

Stripped to her underwear, Katie sat on the edge of her bed and closed her eyes. She wasn't tired exactly but the strain of the past twenty-four hours was finally catching up to her. She couldn't relax until she was sure Bennett wasn't going to fire her although he'd seemed pleased with her work so far. Despite his awkwardness and blunt style of speaking, she liked him. There was no guessing with Bennett. If he didn't like something she did, she had no doubt that he'd just blurt it out.

Thinking of his strange way of speaking, she contemplating calling Ri and asking her about him. Although what would she even say?

Your brother-in-law is a little weird.

Gorgeous but weird.

And I kind of think I'm attracted to him?

No, she knew how Ridley's mind worked. If she even planted the thought, Ri would do everything in her power to throw her at Bennett, the poor man's wishes be damned.

After spending just one afternoon together, she already felt protective of him. There was something special about him, like he was untouched by the usual cynicism and ulterior motives that drove everyone else. He was blunt, sure, but at least he was honest. Katie would take harsh honesty over pretty lies any day. She'd seen the aftermath that pretty lies could leave behind.

The sounds of laughter and screeching filtered in from behind her closed door. It was time to get started on dinner before the kids started eating anything that wasn't nailed down. After pulling on her usual uniform of jeans and a T-shirt, her eyes landed on the manila folder Bennett had given her at the end of the day. It was copies of all her employment paperwork and his company policies. It seemed strange that he had policies when he was a one-man show but it was probably for legal reasons.

She opened the envelope and pulled out all the papers. To her surprise, the top sheet was a Job Summary and when her eyes landed on the number next to "salary" they almost bugged out of her head.

Was this some kind of mistake?

Katie wondered if Bennett had even bothered to update the paperwork after his last assistant left. This kind of salary went to people with education and experience, not pity-hires who only had experience making peanut butter sandwiches and wiping noses.

She mentally cut off that line of thinking. That was Don's voice in her head telling her that she wasn't cut out for much else and one of her New Year's resolutions was to squash that critical voice. Child care was a skill and she did have years of hands-on experience, just not in the field Bennett needed it in.

Damn, he really did need her help, didn't he? If he couldn't even update his employee paperwork before hiring someone new, then he hadn't been kidding about saying his office was a mess. Just metaphorically.

She would have to tell him, she decided as she shoved the paperwork back in the envelope. Katie wasn't the type who could sleep at night while taking advantage of someone. Although it was hard to believe he'd paid that kind of salary to his prior assistant. He'd described him as a graduate student so it seemed a little unbelievable that a student could command that kind of salary.

Maybe there's a reason the salary is so high, she thought. *He's probably the boss from hell. Maybe the reason his prior assistant left was because he wanted to escape.*

She shook her head. Her crazy imagination was always getting her in trouble. The job hadn't even really started yet and she was already imagining all the ways it could go wrong. She needed to just give it a chance and approach things with an open mind.

Considering that the alternative was losing her home and her pride, how bad could it be?

———

IT WAS A DISASTER.

Before today, Bennett wouldn't have thought there was that much damage one person could do in his lab. After all, he liked to think he ran a logical operation. Everything was in its place and well-labeled so as to reduce confusion. His prior assistant hadn't experienced any trouble following his written notes.

Katie, it turned out, defied the odds.

"Sorry!" she called out as she swept up the pieces of the petri dish she'd dropped.

He'd handed it to her and asked her to transfer the contents to the small aquarium on the east wall. Apparently he was supposed to warn her when a sample contained insects or worms.

"I really am sorry. You work with plants so I guess I should have known there would be at least some creepy crawlies involved. You'd think I'd be better at this after helping Ri plant so many things. I just wasn't expecting it to look right at me!"

Bennett lifted his head from the paperwork he was filling out. "It looked at you? The *worm* looked at you?"

She huffed slightly. "Well, it looked like he did."

"He? Earthworms don't have gender, per se. It's actually quite fascinating. Even though they're hermaphroditic, having both male and female sex organs, they usually still need a mate to reproduce—" He stopped talking at the horrified look on her face. "Although I suppose that isn't relevant right now."

"No. Not really." She knelt to position the dustpan to collect the mess. A second later, a soft giggle floated up from the floor. "I can't believe you know about the sex life of earthworms."

Bennett wasn't exactly sure why that was funny but he was glad she didn't seem offended by his random aside. He knew that was a particular failing, becoming intrigued by some side point and then losing the thread of the current conversation. Katie seemed to find it amusing rather than annoying at least.

"Well, I'll make sure to keep any live specimens I'm using away from you from now on."

Katie leaned the broom against the wall. When she came

back, she rolled up her sleeves and reached into the box containing the rest of the soil samples.

"Wait, Katie, you don't have to do that."

"Yes, I do. I'm your assistant. If looking at earthworms is what's required then I'll just have to get used to it. That's the job, right?"

She walked carefully over to the table across the room and placed each sample in a row where he'd indicated they should go earlier. The table was positioned to get only a certain amount of sunlight per day, mimicking the exposure the soil would receive if it was outside.

When she got to the last one, Katie let out a soft sigh of relief. "There. All done."

"You're a very hard worker."

She shrugged. "I was raised to be. My mom was a seamstress and she worked around the clock, especially after my dad died."

Bennett looked up at that. "I'm sorry to hear about that."

"It was a hard time. My mom loved him so much and for years afterward she just wasn't the same. It's almost like he took a piece of her with him when he left. It's one of the reasons I love visiting your parents. The way they look at each other—that's how my parents were, too."

"My parents are pretty special. Not everyone could raise four sons who are as different as we are without making any of them feel like they didn't belong."

Katie tilted her head quizzically. "Why would your parents think any of you didn't belong?"

"Not the others. They're all the model sons you'd want. Jackson and Nick especially were the popular, good-looking types that everyone else wanted to be like. Eli was more of a loner but he had the bad boy thing down pat."

"What about you? What was high school Bennett like?"

He couldn't hold back a soft snort of disgust. "Not that different than current day Bennett, unfortunately."

Her lips plumped up into a pout. *When had she moved closer?* Bennett thought.

"You know what? I think high school Bennett must have been pretty awesome. You're so smart. I wasn't like that. I mean, you can probably tell."

Now he was the one who was shocked. Katie was well-liked by everyone and she'd caught on to everything he'd shown her so far. When he was explaining the rationale behind why he tested his fertilizers on so many different soil samples, she'd immediately guessed that it was to mimic the many different soil conditions out there so his product would work anywhere in the world. He'd gone to school with people who wouldn't have understood that concept without it being explicitly explained.

"You're very smart, Katie."

When she didn't look convinced, he put his hand on her shoulder. Her eyes connected with his and Bennett was moved by how vulnerable she looked.

"I've been throwing technical jargon at you all day and you've kept up just fine. Other than your, um, interaction with our flirtatious earthworm."

She smiled then, slow and tremulous, and the sight of it sent a spark of heat that arced straight through Bennett with all the heat of a flaming arrow. He'd noticed that she was pretty the first time he'd met her; he was a man, after all. But her smile took her from merely pretty to knock out stunning.

"Oh, that's inconvenient," he whispered.

"Sorry, what?"

Now she looked hurt. Before he could even respond, she stepped back slightly and squared her shoulders. He'd seen her do that before, it appeared to be her way of getting herself together when she felt unsure. Oh god, had he made her uncomfortable by touching her shoulder?

"You don't have to say that to make me feel better, Bennett. I'm cool with who I am. I wasn't a straight-A student but I've always been great at keeping things organized and keeping up with details. Which is perfect since that's what you need!"

She finished with a bright smile that didn't even remotely resemble the first one she'd given him. This one didn't make her eyes sparkle or bring that slight flush to her cheeks.

It was a surprise to Bennett that he missed seeing the real one already.

"Believe me, I'm not the most tactful person out there. If I didn't think you were smart, I wouldn't say it. Hell, I'd have probably already told you the opposite without even meaning to."

That made Katie laugh and even though it was partially at his expense, he was happy to be the butt of the joke if it took that wounded look out of her eyes.

"You're blunt, that's true. But at least you tell the truth. Which reminds me, I meant to tell you that you made a mistake on my employment paperwork."

"I did?" Bennett wasn't sure how that was possible. He'd gone over it carefully before she'd arrived.

She blinked. "Well, yes. You didn't change the salary number. I figured you'd want to change it to reflect my experience."

"You'll be doing the same job so why shouldn't you be paid the same thing? Once you see how absentminded I really am, you'll probably feel you've earned every penny."

"Thank you, Bennett. I really appreciate it."

She sighed again and leaned closer. Suddenly the soft scent of her perfume was in his nose and the only thing Bennett could focus on was how soft her lips looked. She didn't wear lipstick, just some sort of shiny stuff that made it look like she'd just licked her lips. Then she *actually* licked her lips and he almost groaned aloud.

Was she staring at his mouth?

Her breath wafted against his cheek which was shocking enough to bring him back to reality. They were in the middle of the lab and she was likely unaware of the reaction her close proximity was causing.

Also he had an erection. Blushing, he pulled the sides of his lab coat together.

He had to get it together.

"I'm going to go upstairs and change. I think I got some ... um, soil on my clothes earlier."

Her face fell slightly. "Probably when I dropped the petri dish. I'm so sorry about that—"

"It's fine. Just finish notating in the log which soil sample is in which aquarium. Then you can leave early. We're done for the day anyway."

He almost knocked over his stool in his haste to get away from her. She nodded quickly and then turned toward the table with the soil samples but not before he saw the confused look on her face.

Bennett didn't blame her. He was in charge of his behavior and he didn't understand it either.

"SO, HOW WAS YOUR SECOND DAY?"

Ridley had waited until after dinnertime to call, which was showing considerable restraint for her friend. She'd called on her first day of work too and Katie had managed to get out of the conversation but she wasn't going to be able to put her off much longer. Ri was unrelenting when she wanted to know something.

Katie scrubbed at the same spot on the counter while trying to think of a tactful way to get out of the conversation. Once she'd gotten home, she'd been focused on getting her kids through homework and dinner. Seeing their sweet faces had calmed her a little bit. Her children were the only pure and real things in her world. Nothing else mattered.

But now talking to Ri was bringing it all back. The embarrassment and then the abject fear that she'd screwed up the best, *the only*, job she'd been able to find. Plus, it was frustrating to admit to Ri that she'd already screwed up by hitting on her boss.

She immediately thought back to the warm weight of Bennett's hand on her shoulder and how gorgeous and shapely his lips were. It had been a long time since she'd been on the receiving end of such intense concentration from a man. Even when she and Don had been dating, he'd never made her feel like she was the only thing on his mind. He'd always been slightly distracted, like there were so many more important things he had to get back to.

Bennett had made her feel like, despite all the important things he had going on, he hadn't wanted to be anywhere but there with her.

Matthew tugged on her sleeve so she balanced the phone between her ear and her shoulder so she could lean down to hear him.

"Mommy, can I have a popsicle?"

She nodded and pointed at the freezer drawer. He skipped off happily.

"Sorry, Ri. You know Matthew and his sweet tooth."

"I don't blame him. Popsicles were a lifesaver when I had morning sickness."

"How is Jackson doing?"

Ridley was quiet for a moment. "Ok, what's going on? The first day you dodged my questions saying it was too early to tell. Now you're just changing the subject. I guess that means you don't like working for Bennett."

Now Katie felt bad. Ri was a meddler but she always had genuinely good intentions. It wasn't her fault that Katie was a perv who was having dirty fantasies about her boss.

"Oh well, it was probably a long shot anyway. I know he's a little eccentric."

Katie frowned. She hadn't thought Ri would be one of the people who made Bennett feel like an outsider. It was easier now to see what he'd meant. She'd never noticed before how quick people were to label you if you didn't conform to society's social norms.

"He's not eccentric. He's *brilliant* and watching him work is fascinating. It's just a little intimidating."

"So you like it? That's great. I'm sure Bennett will teach you anything he needs you to know. He's such a sweetie so that's why I was hoping that you guys could help each other out."

Katie gave up on keeping her cool and let out a sigh as she gave up on cleaning and just leaned against the counter.

"He showed me how he tests his fertilizer and soil. I had no idea what a lot of it meant but he didn't mind explaining things again when I had questions. He didn't even get mad when I dropped his earthworm."

"Wait, his what? Is that a euphemism? Because being as tall as he is I'd expect it to be bigger than that."

Katie sputtered. "Ridley Alexander, I'm surprised at you!"

"No, you're not."

"Okay, no I'm not. But I'm talking about the earthworms he uses in the soil samples. He wasn't angry that I was a little squeamish about them. He even offered to do that part himself. That was really nice of him."

"Sounds like you like him."

"I—I almost kissed him today."

"*Whaaaat?* When did this happen? Tell me everything!"

Katie laughed at Ri's excited squeal. It reminded her of when she was in high school and would stay up late whispering on the phone with her girlfriends after their parents had gone to bed.

"It was a total mistake. He looked horrified and made an excuse about needing to change."

Katie cringed, remembering how quickly he'd run off. She wasn't even sure how that had happened. They'd been talking and then suddenly she'd found herself wondering what it would be like to kiss him. She'd probably scared the poor man with her intensity.

"I'm sure he wasn't horrified," Ridley protested. "Maybe just a little surprised. Bennett has always been shy."

Right. He was shy and she'd almost climbed him like a tree right in the middle of a workday. Katie sighed.

"He's just really handsome. I've always thought so."

"Is that right?" Ridley said.

"Don't pretend you didn't know that. You've been dying to find a way to push us together. You aren't fooling anyone, Ri!"

Ridley harrumphed. "Everyone talks down on my meddling but the way I see it, I'm two for two so far on putting people together with their perfect match. I'd go so far as to say I have a gift."

The thought of being a perfect match with Bennett made Katie lightheaded. He was so ... she couldn't even categorize him. He was more than just his achievements, despite what he thought. Even though he didn't socialize much, he was actually funny in a wry, understated sort of way. Sure, he tended to just blurt things out but he was a man who felt things deeply. She'd seen that when she'd told him about her father's death.

"I don't think we're a perfect match, Ridley."

Suddenly Katie was angry at herself for indulging in girl talk. This was how she always got herself in trouble, spinning romantic fantasies around everything. That was fine in the past when she was too young to know better but she was a grown woman now with very serious responsibilities.

"He's just a nice guy and I'm just a nice girl who really needs this job. Hopefully he won't fire me for inappropriate behavior."

After reassuring Ridley that she was fine, she got off the phone so she could start the long process of supervising the boys' bath and bedtime ritual. By the time she took a shower and climbed into bed herself, she felt like she'd just run a gauntlet.

That was when she noticed the red flag on her phone. She had a voicemail message.

Katie sat up immediately. No one ever left her voicemails anymore. Everyone just texted these days. She hit the button and crossed her fingers it wouldn't ask her for a password since she didn't even know what it was anymore.

Katie, it's Bennett. Can you bring groceries when you come in tomorrow? The standard restock list is on the shared drive. The instructions to access it remotely are in the employee policies and procedures packet. Thanks.

Once the message ended, Katie played it again, not even fooling herself that she needed to hear the information again. No, she was just shamelessly enjoying the deep rumble of his voice. Because that was exactly what she needed to hear right before going to bed alone.

He didn't sound angry about the almost kiss at all. In fact, from the sound of his message he apparently hadn't even noticed that she'd been insanely attracted to him.

Disgusted with herself, Katie turned the light off and then punched her pillow until it was the shape she liked. It had taken a while for her to adjust to sleeping alone and while she wasn't waking up in the middle of the night anymore, it was still strange to sleep all alone in the king-sized bed Don had insisted on. She blew out a breath and then flopped over to stare at the ceiling.

Sixty seconds later, she grabbed her phone and played the voicemail message again.

six

SOMETHING WAS UP.

Katie finished organizing the mail that had come in the prior day and wiped down the stainless steel table that Bennett had just finished working on. He hadn't asked her to assist this time and she thought it was really sweet that he was taking the effort to try not to give her anything that would scare her.

Then she frowned. It was sweet of him to try to protect her feelings but it was hardly going to help her prove her worth as an assistant. She really wanted to stretch her wings and get used to doing things outside of her comfort zone.

She'd always been the good girl, the one who followed the rules and tried to keep the peace. Not that there was anything wrong with that but it made for a pretty boring existence. Don had loved to throw that in her face, that she wasn't spontaneous. Well, no more. Things were different now and she would be different, too. She wanted to shake things up and make a difference in the world. Katie sighed. Nothing she'd ever done would be considered revolutionary or exciting.

"Can I help with that?" she asked when Bennett appeared holding several glass beakers.

She'd never tell him this but whenever he asked her to fetch one or the other, it always made her giggle because some of the liquids looked like Kool-Aid.

"No, I've got it. You can leave early if you want."

Frustrated, Katie slapped her hand down on the stainless steel table between them. "What gives? I know you only hired me to get Ri off your back but I can do more than sort mail."

"That's not true," Bennett said finally, after blinking at her in surprise for several seconds. "I didn't just hire you because Ridley suggested it. That was the catalyst, yes but I hired you because I wanted to."

Katie gave him a disbelieving look. "So far all I've done is grab a few things for you, clean up a little and sort mail. You don't need an assistant for that."

"You've been very helpful," Bennett countered.

"I'm a disaster. Try again."

"Um, actually ... I must confess to an ulterior motive." His eyes wouldn't meet hers all of a sudden and then he turned bright red.

Oh boy. Katie was starting to have an idea where this was going. This whole deal had been too good to be true from the start. Bennett had told her himself that he wasn't socially adept so he probably couldn't see just how screwed up approaching a woman like this was. Not to mention that if he was blushing like that, he probably had some weird fetish that he was going to spring on her. He was a good-looking guy even if he was a little odd so the only way he'd need to pay for sex was if he wanted her to do something pretty strange.

"You look like you're about to be sick," Bennett observed after almost a full minute of awkward silence.

Katie struggled to get her facial expression under control. Even if she was completely offended that he'd thought to hire her as a way to hit on her, this was still Jackson's brother. The Alexanders had always been amazing to her and she didn't want things to be weird when they saw each other in the future.

Or *weirder*, anyway.

There was no way things wouldn't be awkward when she saw him and she wasn't sure how she'd explain things to Ridley who adored her brother-in-law.

"I think maybe you've got the wrong idea about me. I need money but that doesn't mean I'm up for anything weird."

Bennett's eyes rounded. His mouth opened and closed a few times before he finally managed to speak.

"Wait, you think I brought you here as a *sexual* overture? I have no idea what in my statements or behavior could have indicated *that*."

Bennett looked truly perplexed. His confusion made it obvious that he hadn't been thinking anything of the sort which made Katie feel pretty stupid.

"Sorry. It's just when you said you had an ulterior motive, I assumed—"

"Actually this brings up a good point." Bennett interrupted. "I have no idea how the things I do or say are perceived by others. I make social missteps and cause offense quite regularly due to this. That's why I need you. To teach me."

"You want me to teach you how to be ... non-offensive?"

"*Normal*. I want you to teach me how to be *normal*."

"Um, okay." Katie sat on the stool at the counter. Her eyes

landed on the small plants growing under the clear domes. She looked around the room, taking in the string of chemical equations on the chalkboard across from them and the jars of strangely colored liquids in beakers on the next table. Suddenly she laughed.

"Actually that makes way more sense than, you know, the other thing."

Bennett smiled a little at that. "I saw you when you were disciplining your son that day. After dinner."

Katie nodded that she remembered. He'd asked her a lot of questions that evening, about whether she got frustrated correcting her children. It had definitely been a strange conversation.

"Well, it occurred to me then that mothers correct their children a little at a time. They're able to train them effectively because they're usually present to intervene when they behave inappropriately. That's exactly what I need."

"You need a mother? You already have a mother and she's amazing." Katie wasn't sure where he was going with this because Julia was practically the blueprint for the perfect mother.

"She is amazing. That's not what I mean. I need someone to watch my behavior and correct me in the moment when I misstep."

"Sorry but I have to wonder, wouldn't this have worked the first time when Julia was raising you?"

Katie crossed her fingers that he wouldn't take offense at the question. When he didn't say anything, she could have kicked herself. "Stupid question? Never mind."

"Don't ever be afraid to question things. That's the mark of a scientific mind," Bennett mumbled, sounding like he was only half-paying attention to the conversation. He stroked his chin a few times and then his lips moved silently.

Katie realized that he was talking to himself.

"Bennett, are you listening?"

"Hmm? Oh yes, I was just thinking about the fact that my mother's birthday is coming up."

When he noticed the look on her face, he shook his head hard. "See, this is what I mean! I drift off in conversation, go off on tangents and I need someone to bring me back to things. Anyway, where were we?"

"Wondering why you think this would work if it didn't stick the first go around when Julia was raising you?"

"My mother loves me too much to give me the harsh truth. She loves me as I am, even as strange as I am. She would never tell me something that she thought might hurt my feelings. But I need someone who can tell me the harsh truth."

"I don't want to hurt you either, Bennett. I like you."

Bennett gaped at her. "You do? Why?"

Katie laughed. "Um, you're brilliant and you're actually really funny sometimes. Maybe you just need to find more people who share your interests? Like, I don't know ... another scientist?"

Bennett gestured around them. "Look around. I want more than just this in my life. All I do is work and sleep and then wake up to work some more. But the only thing I know how to do is approach problems logically. Getting a tutor seems logical to me. I know this is unorthodox, but will you help me?"

Katie was pretty sure this entire thing had a high probability of being a terrible idea. But she discovered something about herself in that moment. She had a really hard time saying no to a handsome face and a sincere request.

"I'll help you. On one condition."

"What's that?" Bennett looked wary.

"You have to actually listen to what I have to say. If we're going to do this, it's not going to be easy and you're probably going to hate the things I suggest but I have to know you're serious about this."

He shrugged. "I dabble in genetic engineering of organic compounds. If I can do that then I should be able to handle this, right?"

———

BENNETT WATCHED Katie set up the workstation for his very first lesson on being normal. After she'd agreed to tutor him, they'd gone about the rest of the day as usual. He'd wanted to start right away but Katie said she needed some time to think about how to approach this.

He could understand that. Whenever he started a new project, he liked to take time in the beginning to be sure he truly understood the project goals and objectives. Maybe Katie was approaching him like a project. He wasn't sure how he felt about that but he had a feeling he'd have to get used to various indignities if he wanted to have even a shot of being with Olivia.

Strangely enough, thinking about her right then seemed wrong. Bennett couldn't pinpoint why but perhaps it was because he didn't like to think of changing himself for a woman. Like most people, he'd lived for years with the belief that the right woman would appreciate him the way he was. However as the years had passed, he'd come to see how foolish that kind of thinking really was. *Women only like you the way you are if you're naturally handsome, smooth and rich,* he thought.

He had two of the three down pat, he supposed. He'd heard many times that he was attractive and he'd definitely saved a lot of money over the years from his salary and the various inventions that he'd licensed to major corporations. But all of that didn't make up for the fact that he was seen as a bit of a weirdo.

He gritted his teeth, remembering the last time he'd heard that. Jackson's first wife had been talking about him, not realizing that he was in the next room. He'd never told his youngest brother what he'd overheard; what was the point after all? He couldn't deny that it was the truth since the person she'd been talking to hadn't objected to the characterization.

"Okay, I think I'm ready."

Bennett turned to see Katie standing at his elbow. Her eyes sparkled as she set the tablet he'd assigned to her on the table between them.

"I found a list of conversation starters online. I figured if we go over some ice breakers, it'll help you learn to make conversation."

Bennett pushed up his glasses, the first tickle of worry starting. He'd never been great at making conversation but perhaps it was best to start where he was weakest.

"Okay. I'm excited to start."

Katie touched the screen and then read the first topic. "The first conversation starter is 'Where did you grow up?' So you ask me."

Bennett felt incredibly stupid parroting back the words to her but he was determined to play along. "Where did you grow up?"

"I grew up in Barbados, just outside of Bridgetown."

When he didn't say anything, Katie leaned forward and whispered, "You're supposed to ask follow up questions. Or offer some information about you."

Bennett crinkled his forehead. "Oh, right. Tell me about Bridgetown. What's the median temperature there? Barbados is tropical so it must be a relatively mild climate?"

"Well, yes. I guess so."

"I bet the vegetation there is spectacular. Do you happen to know what the average rainfall is during their growing season? Typically I'm trying to prepare for drought but I've been meaning to investigate how our new soil additives would fare in a tropical region." Bennett patted his lab coat absently, wishing he had his phone or his own tablet with him so he could make a note of it. He must have left them in his office.

Katie reached across the table and grabbed his hand. The shock of her fingers closing over his jolted him out of his musing.

"Bennett! You're supposed to be thinking about me. Not rainfall."

"Oh right. Of course. Um, do you like the rain?"

Katie smiled. "Maybe we should try something else."

When she let go, Bennett flexed his fingers. Touching was always awkward but it hadn't felt that way when Katie touched him. He found he kind of liked the sensation. She had very warm hands.

"Let's try casual conversations instead. Like things you might chat about at the grocery store or while in a waiting room."

Bennett tugged at the collar of his shirt. He was afraid he was already failing this portion of the lesson because he couldn't understand why anyone would even want to talk under those circumstances. When he was grocery shopping he preferred to concentrate on his list so he didn't forget anything. He certainly didn't want to talk while at the doctor's office, otherwise he might not remember the list of concerns he needed to discuss with his physician.

Katie, however, didn't seem to think there was anything at all odd about talking to perfect strangers while engaging in vital tasks.

"Let's say I saw you in the grocery store. I might say 'Hello, Bennett. Lovely weather we're having today.'"

Bennett glanced outside. "Well, it's spring time so the weather is generally between fifty and seventy degrees and we're already past the rainy season—"

"*Bennett*." Katie shook her head.

"Sorry. Yes, we are experiencing seasonally appropriate weather today."

Katie covered her mouth with her hand. "This is going to be harder than I thought."

Bennett wasn't sure what to say to that.

After a moment of silence, Katie sat up straight. "Maybe we should skip the general chatting and get down to more meaty conversations. That might work better."

For the next hour, Katie led him through various social scenarios. She tried explaining how to gauge when people were interested in what he had to say by reading facial expressions. That was a bust. Every facial expression looked pretty much the same to Bennett. After all, how was he to know if a facial expression was a signal or the result of indigestion or something?

Polite conversation topics would have worked if they weren't all so dull. Did people really care to discuss their children's behavior, their lawn maintenance or whether the weatherman predicted a thunderstorm? He couldn't understand how anyone could stand talking about such inconsequential things. He thought the point of conversing was to gain information. He didn't gain any information at all by talking about what the weatherman had predicted especially since it was likely to be incorrect anyway.

It didn't help that he'd found himself distracted so many times by Katie's mouth. He found himself mentally tracing the little bow of her lips and imagining how soft they would be if he were to brush his mouth against hers. What the hell was wrong with him? He'd never been this distracted by a woman before.

Finally Katie turned the tablet off. "I don't think this is working."

He sighed. There was no way around it. Bennett was a bad student for the first time in his life.

He had to admit that he couldn't fault Katie's teaching. The things she'd tried to teach him, they were exactly the kinds of questions he heard on a regular basis so her research had been spot on. However, none of it addressed what he needed most, the *why* of it. Why did people have these conversations? It was difficult to play along in a scenario when you didn't understand the end objective for the other participant.

"Thank you for trying. Maybe I'm just not meant to gain mastery in this area. Perhaps I should stick to the lab." He tried to smile to reassure her. After all it wasn't her fault but his lips felt stiff.

How could he hope to convince Olivia that he'd changed when ... well, he hadn't?

Was he just doomed to be alone forever?

KATIE LOOKED AROUND THE LAB, unsure of what to do. None of the examples she'd used seemed to mean anything to him and she was honestly at a loss for how to move forward. How did you teach someone who didn't think the same way you did?

This reminds me of trying to deal with kids alone. She smiled. It often felt like her kids spoke another language and she was just doing her best to interpret it.

"What?" Bennett questioned when he saw her smiling. "I'd have thought you'd be running out of here by now."

"I don't give up that easily. I was just thinking this reminds me how I feel when my kids use some slang I've never heard of and I have to try to figure out the meaning. It's like learning a new language."

Bennett looked thoughtful. "Yes, I suppose it is. Perhaps that's why I thought this would be easier. I've always had an affinity for languages."

"Really? How many do you speak?" Katie had taken French in school but could only read some of it. She'd always been too self-conscious to practice speaking it the way she should have.

"English is my native, I learned French in school and then Spanish from the Reyes family that lives a few acres that way." He angled his head to the left.

"Wow, that's so cool—"

"And then I thought it would of course be useful to study Latin so I can read that, and German scientists have been doing fantastic things in recent years so I started studying German."

Katie's mouth dropped open. She'd known that he was

smart. Obviously, she thought looking around at the lab. But it was more than a little intimidating when he spouted off things like speaking multiple languages as if it was no big deal.

"Most people struggle to even learn one other language. The boys have a choice between French and Spanish at school but they don't offer anything else. I'm sure if Don were around he'd want them to learn French."

Bennett suddenly stiffened. "Yes, your husband, right?"

"Ex-husband. Extremely ex."

"Sorry. I thought I'd heard that but I didn't want to assume. That must be difficult. I didn't mean to bring up bad memories."

Katie shrugged. "It's okay. It's been more than a year now so I'm mainly adjusted to being alone. It's not like he was around much before anyway."

Bennett looked shocked. "He left you alone? Well, all facts pointed to him being a dumbass before but that confirms it."

Katie laughed. She hadn't expected Bennett to stick up for her but it felt good to have someone in her corner. Even though a lot of people said the right things when they found out, there was always an undercurrent of judgment, like they thought she must have done something wrong for her husband to leave.

"He's a doctor so he's pretty smart actually."

Bennett snorted. "I've met many dumbass doctors. It's entirely possible to have high aptitude in one area and be completely deficient in others."

Katie could definitely agree with that. Don had always looked down on her for her limited education but the man had often overdrawn his checking account until she took over handling the money.

"I'm mainly worried about my boys. I guess I always thought Don would be around to teach them the things I can't."

"There will be others who can do that. You're a great mom. I've seen that."

"Well, thank you. Coming from someone who was raised by Julia Alexander that actually means a lot."

Suddenly, Katie realized what was happening. Bennett was talking to her, easily and naturally, without any prompting. When she'd given him conversation topics, he'd faltered but when she asked about his educational background, he'd been fine. Could that be the key?

Communicate in the way he's comfortable with.

She started asking about his research and Bennett immediately launched into a detailed explanation of his latest batch of testing. She observed him while he talked, noticing that all the nervous tics he displayed when talking about anything other than science disappeared. He was completely comfortable talking about his work. He was in familiar territory.

Maybe that's all he needs, Katie thought. If he got some familiarity with popular culture then he should be able to talk about it just as easily as science.

"Bennett," she interrupted, "have you noticed anything interesting about the past ten minutes?"

He looked around, alarmed. "No, what's happened?"

She smothered a laugh at the suspicious look on his face. For such a smart man, he had very little faith in the world around him.

"You've been talking to me. We've had a very nice conversation."

Bennett just blinked at her and then slowly, a smile spread across his face. "Yes, we have. I didn't even realize."

"That's the way it should be. Making conversation isn't supposed to be hard. In fact, this has given me a totally new approach on how to help you."

He pushed up his glasses nervously. "It has? More practice drills?"

She shook her head. "Nope. No more drills. What you need is fun."

"Fun," he repeated blankly.

"Yes, fun. Maybe you've heard of it? This whole time I noticed how easy it is for you to talk about science but not anything else and I couldn't help but wonder: do you do anything else? You know, like, hobbies or something?"

By his stricken look, Katie could only assume the answer was no. Before he could say anything, she picked up the tablet. If she was going to help him, she needed to go in a completely different direction and she knew exactly where to start.

"We're done for the day, right?"

Bennett nodded absently. "Yes, I don't need anything else. Are we finished already?" He sounded relieved.

That wouldn't last long. Katie had a feeling that he wasn't going to like her new direction any better than the last one.

"For now. But I'm not done working. Once I'm at home, I'm going to come up with a list of ways to teach you to have fun. Then I'll send you homework assignments to complete."

"That doesn't sound so bad. At least homework is something I'm familiar with."

Katie didn't correct him but she had a feeling this homework was going to be a challenge. For the first time, Bennett Alexander was going to learn to do frivolous things.

seven

BY THE TIME Katie left work an hour later, she had a list of ideas to try to get Bennett out of his shell. It wasn't going to be easy. The man was naturally suspicious of anything that didn't seem logical or productive. She smiled, remembering his reaction to her question about hobbies. The poor man was probably going to need a drink to handle some of the things on her list.

The kids were a little more subdued than usual when they got off the bus. She'd noticed that Hunter in particular was very quiet. Katie gave them their snack and supervised their homework before she decided to call Ridley. Playing with the Alexander boys would definitely cheer the kids up and it would give her a chance to confer with Ridley about her "teaching Bennett to have fun plan." This kind of thing was Ridley's specialty.

Her friend didn't answer when she called so she hung up and decided to wait an hour. Knowing Ri, she was in the middle of whipping up some amazing creation for dinner. Katie opened her own refrigerator and sighed. Leftover spaghetti and meatballs would have to do. The boys were always starving within an hour of getting home which didn't leave much time for creating culinary masterpieces.

Her phone rang while she was heating up the leftover pasta. When she saw Ridley's name on the screen, she snatched it up. To her surprise, it wasn't Ri's voice she heard.

"Hi, Katie? It's Mara."

"Oh, hi! This is a surprise. Didn't expect to hear your voice."

Mara was an old friend of the Alexanders but had moved to New York with her husband Trent the prior year. Before that, she'd been a constant presence in Ri's house and Katie considered her a friend. Actually, Mara was one of the first people she'd confided in about her divorce. She was very easy to talk to and just a vibrant, fun-loving type of person in general. She'd always made their Girls' Nights more fun.

"Yeah, Ri asked me to call you back for her. My future sister-in-law is here with me and she's giving Ri a pregnancy massage. Can you come over? I'd love to see you while we're in town."

"That's actually why I was calling. I need Ri's advice about something but you're probably going to be a big help, too. I'm working as an assistant to Bennett now and he's asked me to help him with a ... special project. It's kind of hard to explain."

Mara hummed. "Now you have me intrigued. Hurry up and get here!"

Katie laughed and promised she'd be there within the hour. She packed the spaghetti in a box and called out to the kids. She could feed them at Ridley's house. They'd done that plenty of times before. Once she told them where they were going, the boys got their shoes and jackets on in record time. Twenty minutes later, they were happily eating spaghetti along with Ri's two boys.

Mara pulled her by the arm into the living room where Ri was lying on a table while Penny massaged her shoulders.

"Hey! Sorry I didn't get up. But I feel like jelly," Ri mumbled. "This pregnancy massage table is amazing."

Upon closer inspection Katie could see that the table had special cutouts to allow room for a pregnancy belly and to avoid putting pressure on the delicate chest area. Penny smiled and waved before turning to get more massage oil.

"Cool, right? Penny designed this modular massage table that can adapt for a variety of conditions, including pregnancy. This thing is fantastic. I'm so proud of her," Mara said.

Penny shrugged but didn't speak. Katie figured she was probably trying to remain quiet so she wouldn't jar Ridley out of the dreamlike state her friend was in. Katie and Mara got comfortable on the couch and talked quietly until Penny finished. A few minutes later, Ridley sat up looking completely relaxed.

"That was great, Penny. I didn't know how much I needed that!" Ridley climbed down from the table carefully before fixing her gaze on Katie. "Sorry I couldn't greet you when you came in. I was in another world."

Katie chuckled. "I could see that. It looked like you were on the verge of falling asleep."

"She actually did fall asleep for a little while there. Which is the ultimate compliment, by the way," Penny interjected before going back to packing up her supplies.

"So what's going on with you?" Mara finally asked. "You definitely sparked my interest on the phone. What kind of special project are you working on?"

Ridley took a seat on the other side of Katie on the couch. "Special project? What does Bennett have you working on? Nothing crazy I hope? He mixes all those chemicals in his lab and thinks that's totally normal so I don't think he perceives danger the same way we do."

Katie smiled thinking of all the random mishaps she'd already had in the lab. She'd been extra careful handling things since then. It would be just her luck to drop the wrong thing and end up blowing up the whole lab or something.

"Well, this is a project that I'm working on to help Bennett. It's a personal project."

Ridley smiled. "Personal, huh?"

"It's not like that. He's trying to be more social and asked for help. So I've been coming up with ideas to help him learn to talk to people."

Mara clapped her hands in excitement. "This is so cool. Kind of like *My Fair Lady* but in reverse."

"I guess so. Although it's weird trying to teach Bennett anything when he's pretty much a savant with everything else."

Ridley observed her with slightly narrowed eyes. She stared so long that Katie started to fidget under her gaze. Finally she couldn't take it anymore.

"What? Just say it, Ri. You think this is weird, right?"

Katie couldn't explain it but even though she wanted their help, she also didn't want anyone making fun of Bennett. She thought it was really brave that he was willing to put himself out there, even in spite of possible ridicule, to learn something new.

"No! I actually think it's sweet that he asked you for help. He has so many people he could have asked and yet, he chose you. You guys must be getting along really well."

Oh boy. Now Katie understood why Ridley was staring at her. Her friend thought every situation was a possible love connection. Then she thought about the picture she'd seen of Bennett smiling. Just remembering it was enough to send a flush of heat to her face.

Well, just because she was attracted to him didn't mean anything. He was handsome. Hell, the man was an Alexander so it would have been stranger if he *wasn't* good-looking. The whole family had been blessed with golden genetics. But that didn't mean anything was going to happen between them.

Ri finally gave her a break and reached over to the side table. "Maybe I can help. This should loosen him up."

Katie accepted the book her friend held out. When Mara saw the cover, she laughed so hard she almost snorted up a strand of her hair. Even Penny tried to cover her mouth to hide her smile.

"What? Why are you guys laughing?"

Katie examined the book cover. It looked innocuous enough, kind of boring actually. It was all black with the words *Silent Surrender* on the front. The author name wasn't familiar.

"Oh nothing. It's just the latest book craze." Ri blinked at her innocently.

With no small amount of fear, Katie cracked the book open and started reading. The beginning seemed pretty tame, just some guy in a meeting ordering everyone around. Then a girl came in and spilled coffee on him. Katie's mouth fell open as she kept reading.

The main character's thoughts about what he wanted to do to the girl were ... explicit. And sexy as hell.

"What is this?" Katie clutched the book to her chest when

Mara tried to take it from her. "You want me to give this to Bennett?"

The others finally lost it, exploding into laughter. Ridley wiped tears from her cheek before she could catch her breath long enough to talk.

"Could you imagine? The poor guy would probably have a heart attack!"

Katie bit her lip imagining Bennett reading something like this. Would he be offended or would he like it? She blushed again and tried to put that thought out of her mind. There was no way she was giving her boss a sexy book.

"Actually you guys just gave me an idea."

Mara's eyebrows flew up into her hair. "You're not actually going to give him that, are you?"

"Oh no. I would die instantly if I even tried. I mean, well, whatever. But that doesn't mean I can't recommend something else for him to read. There's a really great fantasy series that I just finished that he might like. It has a lot of suspense and was a fast-paced read. Maybe I'll suggest that."

Ridley nodded. "It's great that you're helping him. Bennett is such a sweetheart. He needs to learn to have fun. Jackson worries about him a lot, I can tell."

Katie could understand that. She envied how close the Alexander siblings were. Whenever she saw them together, it made her miss her own family.

They spent the next hour talking and laughing while the kids played upstairs and by the time she was ready to go home, Katie felt a lot better about her plan to help Bennett. The girls had given her some other great suggestions of places she could take Bennett to help him relax, everything from going to the movies to see the newest comedy in theaters to taking him to the beach for the day. But Katie was pretty sure that starting off simply was best. Reading a book after work was a great way to ease him into the idea of relaxing more.

On the way out, Ridley finally noticed that she was still carrying the racy book from earlier.

"Oh, I thought you weren't going to give that to Bennett?"

Katie lowered her voice so the kids wouldn't hear and ask any questions. "I'm not. That's for me!"

———

BENNETT LOOKED up at the sound of his cell phone ringing. Usually at this time in the evening he was working out, reading his case notes from the day's work or catching up on world events. But when Katie had left that day, she'd warned him to keep his phone close because she'd be calling with his first homework assignment.

Quite surprisingly, he'd been looking forward to it all afternoon.

"Hello?"

"Hey! Are you ready to have some fun?"

Bennett smiled. He hadn't expected her to be so into this project but her enthusiasm was definitely infectious. He usually only felt like this when he was working on a new project or reading about a new scientific breakthrough.

"I'm not sure. But you sound excited."

Katie laughed softly, the warm sound making him feel like he was part of an inside joke. When she laughed, it never felt like it was at his expense which was a nice change.

"I am excited. I had a lot of fun coming up with ideas for

you today. But you have to remember that you promised to keep an open mind."

Bennett squelched the first twinge of worry. In the past whenever people said that, it usually meant they were going to do something he wouldn't like but he'd resolved to trust Katie and give this a chance. Plus, it wasn't that hard to trust her. Working with her the past few days, he'd discovered that she was truly as kind as he'd thought. For the first time in a long time, he was comfortable trusting in someone else. He didn't think she'd ever do anything to intentionally hurt or embarrass him.

"I'm being open-minded. What's the assignment?"

Katie took a deep breath. "It's a book assignment."

Bennett cheered immediately. He'd always been light-years above his peers' reading level in school. If this was the assignment, then he would definitely ace it. He relaxed slightly. This wouldn't be difficult at all.

"Okay. That doesn't sound so bad."

"Were you worried?"

"Yes."

Katie laughed. "Your honesty is refreshing. But don't thank me yet. Part of the assignment is not to read the description of the book online. Just buy it and start reading. Can you do that?"

That seemed a little odd but certainly not out of the question. "I can do that. So am I supposed to do a book report or something?"

Katie was quiet for a moment. "Um, yes. But I think an oral book report will be fine. Your assignment is to read two chapters each night for the next week at least. If you don't like it at that point, then you can tell me why and we'll try another book. Okay?"

"Okay. That sounds easy enough." Bennett wasn't sure what to think. So far it didn't feel much like homework at all. Two chapters? Considering how fast he read, he could probably do that in fifteen minutes. And no written report? This was the easiest book assignment ever.

"So I'm going to text you the link to the book. Remember, don't read *anything* about it, just buy it and start reading."

"No problem."

"Oh yeah and Bennett? The point of this is to have fun. Try it, okay? It won't kill you."

After they hung up, his phone dinged immediately with a text. Bennett clicked the link she'd sent and it pulled up the product page for the book. He clicked the button to buy it, deliberately not enlarging the screen on his phone to read the description. He couldn't help noticing that the cover was a deep maroon with gold lettering and some kind of design embossed on the cover.

"Don't look, remember." Determined to follow the rules, Bennett walked into his bedroom to find his personal tablet. He opened the app he used to read and the book was at the top of the page. The title was *The Secret Life of Senator Drake.*

"A political tale? Interesting choice." Bennett wouldn't have thought Katie would choose anything political for him to read but maybe she thought it would appeal to his intellect.

He settled on his bed and propped a pillow behind his head. As he read, he wondered what made Katie choose this book. Then he flipped the page and had to read a few of the sentences more than once to be sure he was getting the meaning. One of the characters had just shed his skin and turned into a dragon.

"Huh?"

Bennett kept reading. Perhaps Senator Drake actually had a problem with illicit drugs or alcohol and this was simply a hallucination. It was a problem that plagued quite a few in positions of power.

But that didn't appear to be the case. The main character had continued on with his day as if nothing had happened. No longer able to keep his word, Bennett went back to the book's product page and read the description. The character wasn't having a hallucination. The book was a fantasy novel about a society of sentient dragons.

Bennett laughed aloud. No wonder Katie had told him he wasn't allowed to read the description. The entire thing sounded ridiculous. He went back to the book. His assignment was to read two chapters. How hard could it be?

After reading a few more pages, he put down his tablet in frustration. He just couldn't get past the fact that none of it was real.

"What's the point of reading an entire story when after I'm done, I haven't learned anything useful?"

Then he imagined having to go to work tomorrow and tell Katie that he couldn't even read two chapters. He'd promised to give it a try no matter how hard it was. He could almost hear Katie's voice telling him to try having a little fun.

"It won't kill me, she says. Well, that remains to be seen." He picked up his tablet again and started reading, determined to pretend that dragons were real and somehow able to live unnoticed among humans. At least the main character seemed to be a sensible type of man. Bennett actually liked him quite a bit. He was a lone spot of sanity in a crazy story.

The next time he glanced up, it was four hours later, his

eyes were burning and every one of his joints ached from sitting in the same position.

"What just happened?" He looked around in confusion.

He'd only meant to read the assigned two chapters so he could tell her that he'd given it a try. But then the main character had revealed that he was actually a shapeshifter also. Then when it had been revealed that he was there for the sole purpose of influencing human politics in ways that would benefit the hidden shapeshifting dragon population, well he hadn't been able to stop reading then. Especially since he'd identified with the main character's sense of isolation.

A smile tugged at the edges of his lips. He felt ridiculous getting worked up over something completely frivolous but at the same time he couldn't deny that he was actually reluctant to go to sleep. If his eyes weren't burning so badly after a long day, he'd probably read for a little longer.

It turned out that having a little fun wouldn't hurt him after all.

He put his tablet aside but he was thinking about the story the whole time as he took a shower and pulled on a loose pair of pajama pants.

His last thought as he climbed into bed and turned off the light was that he couldn't wait to tell Katie about it.

eight

THE NEXT DAY, Bennett barely managed to get downstairs before Katie was knocking on the door. He rolled his neck and grimaced at the tight pain between his shoulders. For someone who had always been a morning person, he wasn't used to feeling like roadkill in the morning.

His crankiness must have been obvious because Katie skirted around him gingerly once he opened the door and let her in.

"Rough night?" she asked as she hung her jacket in the front closet. She had to stretch up on her toes to hang it and it made her long tunic top ride up to show the curve of her bottom.

"You could say that," he muttered.

When she turned around, Bennett averted his gaze quickly. He rubbed his eyes. "I just haven't had coffee yet."

Katie hummed in agreement, the soft sound settling in his cranky, tired brain like a pornographic moan. Bennett stiffened and willed himself not to get hard. *Please not now.* This was almost as bad as the time he'd gotten an erection watching his math teacher write equations on the chalkboard. Luckily he'd been sitting down at the time but it was still mortifying, especially since that erection had persisted all through class. He was a big guy all over. It wasn't so easy to hide a massive boner while trying to carry an armful of books between classes. For the first time in his life, he'd actually considered just going home early and skipping the rest of his classes that day.

But just like then, he managed to get himself together. "Would you like some?"

Katie shrugged. "I could do with a cup. Is it weird that I don't drink anything in the morning? Everyone I know swears by either tea or coffee but I just drink whatever's in the fridge."

Bennett regarded her with mock horror. "Yes, that's weird. And I'm the authority on weird."

She laughed and the sound lifted his mood instantly.

"See? I guess we have something in common after all," Katie said.

He moved around his small kitchen, brewing two cups of coffee and arranging the sugar and creamer on the countertop for Katie. He didn't take anything in his coffee but watched with interest as Katie dumped several spoonfuls of sugar and a bunch of creamer in her cup before taking a big sip.

She glanced at him before taking another sip. Bennett smiled slightly before putting everything back. When he turned around again, she was still looking at him with that funny little smile.

"Is everything okay?" he asked.

"Oh, yeah. Fine. Totally fine. So what are we working on today?"

Bennett led her over to where a new aquarium had been set up and they ran through procedure for sifting the soil, adding the measured amounts of water for each sample and how to record it all in the shared folder. Katie asked a few questions and then he left her to it.

He sighed. There were plenty of things that he could work on today but he didn't feel like doing any of it. It was a completely unfamiliar feeling to not want to work. Bennett made a face.

"Are you okay?" Katie asked from across the room.

"No, I'm not okay. And it's entirely your fault," he grumbled.

Katie's face fell. "What? What did I do?"

Feeling ridiculous but already committed to the conversation, Bennett crossed his arms. "You made me read that damn book and now all I can think about is whether Senator Drake is going to be revealed or whether Natasha can keep his secret!"

Katie stared at him for a long moment, nothing moving on her entire body except her lashes as she blinked at him. Then she suddenly let out a startled peal of laughter. "You read the book!"

Her smile was so open and so beautiful that Bennett was momentarily thrown having it directed at him. "Yes, I stayed up half the night reading. I really enjoyed it."

She trotted over to him in excitement. "Was it hard to do something fun for a change?"

She was smiling so he knew she was teasing. Or at least he thought she was. But this didn't feel like the type of teasing he was used to. This made him feel kind of hot and breathless. He hadn't felt like this since he'd first tried to flirt back in high school.

"It was at first. I couldn't understand the point of reading about something that isn't real. Then I suddenly found that I didn't care. I just wanted to know what happened next."

Katie's clasped her hands in front of her, a pleased smile on her face. "That's usually how it happens. Welcome to the world of book hangovers!"

Bennett laughed. "Is that what they're called? Book hangovers? I guess it's better than the usual type."

"I agree. But now that you've admitted to liking the book, I have to confess that you almost got stuck reading something else. Your sister-in-law recommended a book for you that was extremely inappropriate."

Bennett really wanted to ask what kind of inappropriate book but before he could, she was already talking about something else.

"I can't wait until you get to the next part. Natasha is perfect for him but there're so many things about her you don't know yet. But no spoilers! I won't say anything else."

Her eyes danced with glee at the prospect. Bennett wouldn't have thought it was possible for anyone to be this excited about something as simple as a book. It was also fun to share the experience with someone else. Something he would have never thought would matter to him.

"I used to read for pleasure all the time when I was younger. I'm not sure when that changed. But I'm glad you gave me a little push."

"Me too. I can't imagine a world without make believe. When I was growing up, whether I was hungry or lonely or sad, I could get lost in a book and be somewhere else. I could travel a thousand miles in the blink of an eye and suddenly none of the bad stuff mattered. Books are the only place magic exists anymore."

For a moment, she looked so sad that Bennett actually felt a little pang in his own chest. Katie was unrelentingly optimistic so the sight of her looking so defeated seemed wrong. And made him feel helpless.

"Well, you really helped me, Katie. After years spent learning new things, it's humbling to realize that I could have forgotten something that used to make me so happy."

Just like that, her smile was back. She patted his arm. "I'm glad that I was able to help you remember. I'm sure it's not like the books you're used to reading. Don used to read those medical journals with the tiny print. I tried one once and I couldn't understand anything. It might as well have been a different language."

Bennett gritted his teeth at the mention of her ex. "You weren't missing anything. Why should you be up on technical jargon for a field that you have never studied?"

Katie shrugged. "Oh I know. I didn't expect that I would understand it all. But I was just trying to be supportive. Don always said that I couldn't understand how hard he worked and how much he was expected to know. So I was trying to show him that I was interested in his world. Not that he appreciated it. He laughed when he saw me reading it. Told me to stick to my gossip magazines."

She shrugged but the usual twinkle in her eye was gone and she had the hunched posture he remembered from her first day at work. Like she expected to be made fun of again.

"There will always be someone who knows more than you. I've met people who are vastly superior in their fields and have accomplished way more than I have in mine. I actually had a classmate in graduate school who made fun of my first patented invention. He said it looked like something that would be sold on TV for three easy payments of $9.99."

Katie's mouth fell open. "What a jerk! I bet he'd never invented anything."

Bennett laughed. "Actually he had. The guy was a prodigy. He probably had several patents under his belt before he even entered high school."

"Well, whatever. I bet all his inventions sucked donkey balls and so did he!"

Bennett burst out laughing. "Wow. I don't know about that but he was an asshole and everybody in that class hated him. All that intelligence couldn't win him any friends. I may not be Mr. Popular but I don't think I have any enemies either."

Katie looked shocked. "*Mr. Popular?* Bennett, no matter how you may feel, everybody likes you. All I used to hear before we met was how the oldest Alexander brother was some kind of super genius and the hottest one of them all."

Bennett almost choked. "Hot? Who said I was hot?"

"Um, every woman in New Haven with a pulse has probably said that at some point. But besides that, everyone respects you. You should hear the way Jackson used to talk about you. He's so crazy proud of you. They all are."

Bennett could feel the flush rising from beneath his collar. Not for the first time, he cursed being the palest one in his family. He'd never been able to hide his feelings.

He was also the only one in his family who'd ever had a sunburn. His brothers had loved teasing him about his perpetually red cheeks in the summer.

Katie covered her mouth. "Did I embarrass you? Sorry, I just meant that you're nothing like that guy, Bennett. You have a lot of friends. We're just working on making it easier for you to talk to them."

"Right. Talking to them." Bennett watched absently as Katie patted his arm and then went back to her workstation.

He tried to get some work done but after attempting to read the same lab results multiple times, he gave up and just watched Katie. It was surprisingly relaxing to watch her move around the lab. She was a generally cheerful person and often hummed or sang to herself. He wondered if she was even aware she did it.

She claimed that they were just working to get him comfortable talking to people but he hadn't had any trouble talking to her today. Something about Katie always made him feel good. Accepted. He really enjoyed talking to her.

He scowled remembering her story about the medical journal. Her asshole ex-husband had clearly done a number on her confidence. He hated to see her doubting herself due to that guy's put-downs. She was so kind and deserved better than a guy like that.

What, a guy like you?

Bennett sighed. He probably wouldn't do any better. Katie was a social butterfly and made friends easily. Sure, she didn't mind correcting his social missteps now because he was paying her. But what woman wanted to have a boyfriend that she constantly had to apologize for? At least her asshole ex had probably known how to behave in public.

Their conversation had shed quite a bit of light on things nonetheless. He'd always thought he was an embarrassment to his family. The strange one that they had to explain to others. It was nice to know that they'd been praising him behind his back all this time. But that wasn't the part of the conversation he most wanted to revisit. He really wanted to backtrack and talk about this "every woman thinks you're hot" business.

Did every woman include Katie?

KATIE MENTALLY KICKED herself as she made another notation on the tablet in front of her. They'd been having a perfectly great conversation and she'd just had to go and ruin it by telling Bennett that every red-blooded woman with a pulse thought he was hot.

Hot. She'd actually told her boss that he was sexy and women lusted after him. If he hadn't been watching her so closely she would've smacked herself in the forehead. Katie sighed. When was she going to learn to keep her big mouth shut? She just got so worked up sometimes and it had truly taken her off guard that Bennett didn't seem to know how women viewed him. Really, how could he not know? Did he not notice the way women looked at him? Because Katie was pretty sure that she'd stared at him with her tongue hanging out a time or two.

Or seven.

Finally, after a few minutes of awkward silence, Bennett got up and wandered into his office. Once his door closed behind him, Katie let out the breath she'd been holding. If she was going to work here, she had to learn how to keep her cool. Bennett was easily flustered and she was supposed to be helping him learn to be comfortable with people, not making him feel worse. Besides, there was no point to telling him those sorts of things anyway. What chance did she have with him even if he knew she thought he was attractive? Not that she knew anything about his preferences but she could only assume he was into women who were as smart as he was. Probably some female wunderkind with a million different college degrees who could flirt with him in Latin.

Ugh. Katie pushed the thoughts aside and focused on finishing up her work. That was what she was here for. *To do a good job and get paid. That's it.* It was worth taking the time to remind herself of what was at stake here because she couldn't afford to screw this up. Her bills were already piled so high that she could swim in them. This job was her chance to dig her way out of that hole. With renewed determination, she focused on her work.

After she was done making notations, she straightened up the tabletop. One of the water droppers she'd been using to add moisture to each sample fell off the table. When she bent to pick it up, she noticed something on the floor under the table Bennett usually worked on. She walked over and then stooped low to get it.

It was an invitation. Katie skimmed over it quickly. Bennett had been invited to a gala for a group called Mentor Science.

"That's an award ceremony that I've been invited to."

At the sound of his voice, Katie almost dropped the invitation. She wasn't sure why she felt guilty. It wasn't like she'd been snooping around. The invitation had been on the floor in plain sight.

"You're a mentor? That's awesome."

Bennett shrugged but she could see the compliment pleased him. "I'm receiving an award for mentoring my last assistant. I also did a few sessions where I stood in as a guest teacher for one of his classes."

Katie could just imagine what it was like for those young

college girls to have a teacher like Bennett. If he'd been teaching any of her classes in school, she wouldn't have learned a damn thing.

"I bet you did a great job. The kids were lucky to have a teacher with so much experience."

Bennett smiled. "I'm not sure they were so happy about it. One of the extra credit projects involved them coming out here to the farm. Not all of them were thrilled with stepping in manure."

"Hmm. I could see how that might be a problem."

He smiled at her. "But anyway, that Mentor Science award ceremony is what started this whole thing. My friend Olivia is going with me and I wanted to learn how to be a better companion."

It took Katie a few seconds to really understand what he was saying. She looked down at the heavily embossed invitation in her hand again. Bennett was getting an award at a fancy ceremony. His friend Olivia was going with him. No, correction, his friend Olivia was his date. She swallowed as her earlier embarrassment returned threefold. No wonder Bennett had run out of here like his ass was on fire. He definitely didn't want his assistant flirting with him.

He was doing all this to impress another woman!

Katie squared her shoulders. All of this was irrelevant. There had never been anything between her and Bennett other than a work relationship and a distant acquaintanceship. But over the past week, she'd come to think of him as a friend. He'd asked for her help and she'd promised to give it to him. Katie considered her word to be solid. So despite her silly daydreams, she was going to give him the best help she could.

"You know, if you're trying to be a good date, there's really only one way to make sure of that."

Bennett suddenly looked nervous. "There is?"

"A practice date. We should get dressed up and go out to eat somewhere."

"A practice date," Bennett echoed. He was quiet for a moment and then nodded firmly. "Yes, we should do that."

Katie thought about where she could take him. It was probably a little silly for him to go on a practice date with her. After all, what did she know about any of that? It had been ages since Don had taken her out anywhere and she'd been too chicken to date anyone since her divorce. "Okay, I'll get us a reservation somewhere. I can get Ridley to watch the kids. Then we can go this weekend."

"Maybe this is a bad idea." Bennett sat on one of the stools next to his worktable. "I haven't been on a date in a long time. Maybe I should just call the whole thing off. Dating has always been a mystery to me."

Katie knew all about feeling like a failure at dating. Despite what Mari thought, she *had* signed up for a few dating apps in the past year, thinking that it would be an easy way to get back into the dating pool. But once she'd started getting messages, an alarming number of them were men sending naked pictures. She still couldn't understand how modern dating worked. What woman wanted to see a picture of a random ... apparatus?

She covered her mouth so Bennett wouldn't see her smiling as she thought about it. Some things in life needed context. Penises definitely fell into that category.

"You're not the only one. But this is no big deal. Just two friends getting dinner. We'll have some great food and talk, just like we do here. You haven't had any trouble talking to me here, have you?"

Bennett shook his head. "No, in fact, you're very easy to talk to."

Katie ignored the tingle of pleasure she got at his words. But strangely enough, she felt the same way about him. Even though they had vastly different interests, Bennett was one of the least judgmental people she'd ever met. He never made her feel like he was looking down on her or didn't want to hear what she had to say. As a result, she'd found that she could just talk to him about anything. It was probably not a good thing, since she found herself just blurting out things without thinking about it first.

Like when you told him everyone thinks he's hot?

Yeah, like that. She probably needed to be a little less comfortable around Bennett. He might be easy to talk to but he was still her boss.

She handed him the Mentor Science invitation. "I find it easy to talk to you, too. That's how I know we'll have fun. Do you trust me?"

Bennett smiled. "Do I trust the woman who tricked me into reading a book about dragons? Absolutely."

Katie grinned at that. "Good. This might seem just as strange at first but then it'll be fun. We'll have you whipped into shape in no time. You'll be the perfect date by the time I'm done with you."

nine

BENNETT WASN'T sure what to do with the things he was feeling. So he did what he always did when he wasn't sure what to do. He called Olivia.

In retrospect, he could admit that his tendency to rely on Liv as his human translator probably wasn't the healthiest way to approach life. But for years, she'd been his go-to, the one person he knew wouldn't make fun of him because he didn't understand something. Well, the one person outside of his family.

He could always ask one of his brothers and they would drop everything to help him. They'd also worry about him and then discuss him when he wasn't around. Bennett smiled at the thought. His brothers would hate to be described that way but they truly were a gossipy bunch. Nothing was ever private for long in the Alexander household and the last thing he needed was to give his mother any reason to worry about him.

Olivia answered with a muffled voice.

"Hello? Liv?"

"Bennett?" She sounded surprised to hear his voice. Which

was strange since she never answered the phone unless she recognized the number.

"Yes, it's me. Are you okay? You don't sound like yourself."

Liv sighed. "Sorry. I thought you were someone else."

Bennett wasn't sure what to do. Did that mean she didn't want to talk to him because he wasn't the person she'd been expecting? Not to mention that she sounded like she'd been crying. Liv had only cried on the phone with him once before and it was after a particularly nasty exchange with her father. Normally in a situation like this, he'd just make an excuse to get off the phone instead of dealing with it. But this was as good a time as any to try out some of the things Katie had tried to teach him.

"Did you see your parents? Is that why you're upset?" Bennett figured that was an educated guess.

"Actually, yes. I did. But that's not why I'm upset. It's just ... hard to explain." Liv was quiet for a moment. "Have you ever been in love?"

Bennett's mouth fell open. Then he considered the question seriously. He believed in love. It would be almost impossible to be raised by Mark and Julia Alexander and not believe in love. His parents had been happily married for more than thirty years and he still caught them kissing in the kitchen on a regular basis. Unlike his brothers, he'd never been grossed out by how affectionate his parents were. It made him happy to think that you could make a choice of companion and still be content with that choice decades later. It gave him hope.

"I don't think so. Have you?"

He was suddenly very curious to hear her answer. Ever since it had occurred to him that Liv might be a perfect match for him, he had been so focused on the idea of making himself into the kind of guy that she'd consider and he hadn't even thought about whether she might already be in love with someone else. He really had gone about this whole thing backwards.

"There's this guy. His name is King." She sniffled and there was a rummaging sound.

Bennett waited patiently. Liv was an emotional person and did things on her own time. There was no rushing her when she was telling a story.

"He's a member of the club I manage. I knew I shouldn't get involved with him. He's exactly the type of guy I should avoid. Rich, arrogant ... just trouble. What the hell was I thinking?"

"It sounds like he's not very nice. Why are you dating a guy that you don't even like?" Bennett was sure there had to be more to the story or this was just one of those things he would never understand.

It made him angry to think of some guy making Olivia cry. She was perfectly capable of taking care of herself, he knew that. She'd gone through so much after her parents turned their back on her and had grown into an amazing woman. But that didn't mean she didn't get hurt sometimes, too. Maybe it was a holdover from taking care of her when she was first thrown out of her parents' house but Bennett felt a strong wave of protectiveness for her.

"It's not like that. Okay, maybe it is a little bit. But there's just something about him. When I'm around him, I feel alive. You know? Haven't you ever felt that around a certain person?"

Bennett's thoughts went back to Katie's passionate defense of him when saying his old classmate sucked donkey balls. He laughed out loud at the thought.

"What? Why are you laughing?"

"Sorry, I was just thinking of something ridiculous my assistant said earlier."

"Oh you hired someone else? Another grad student?"

"No, a friend of a friend. Katie is one of Jackson's neighbors."

Liv hummed. "Katie, huh? You've never had a female assistant before."

Bennett wasn't sure if she was expecting him to respond to that. It was a statement, not a question, but somehow it seemed to require a response.

"No, I haven't. But Katie has been very helpful so far." He didn't add that she was mainly helping him figure out how to appeal to Olivia.

Then Bennett realized that the entire time he'd been talking to Olivia, he hadn't felt even slightly jealous that she was talking about another guy. Shouldn't he feel jealous? Or at least a little upset? That was what he'd observed in others who were in romantic relationships. But the thought of Liv with this King guy didn't bother him at all.

Then he thought of all the times Katie had mentioned her ex and could practically feel his blood pressure rise. Even the idea of her asshole ex talking down to her was enough to make him want to punch something. Bennett smiled. Maybe he wasn't as abnormal as he'd thought.

"Liv, I'm sorry this guy has been a jerk to you. You deserve better than that."

"Thank you, Bennett. I'm sure I'll figure it out. But I want to talk about you. Something is going on with you."

He could have pretended he didn't know what she meant but found himself suddenly desperate for the female perspective. Olivia had been through a merry go round of bad relationships over the years and he'd had a sideline view to all of it. The drama, the tears, the breakups, the makeups. It had always seemed messy and unnecessary to him before but now he hoped that she could help him decode some of what he was feeling.

"Liv, when you care about someone, do you think about them at random moments throughout the day?"

"Yup. And you especially think about them when you're supposed to be doing other things." Liv chuckled softly.

"And they seem to understand you, even when no one else does?"

"Yup."

"And the thought of them with another man makes you have vivid fantasies of punching the other guy in the face?"

Liv paused. "Bennett? Do you want to protect this girl?"

"Yes," he answered immediately.

"Would you be willing to sacrifice something you wanted if it meant making her smile? Does her smile brighten up your entire day? Is it torture to imagine not seeing her for a long time?"

Baffled, Bennett nodded along with every one of her statements. "Yes to all of that. How did you know?"

Liv sighed dramatically. "Oh boy. Bennett, congratulations!"

"For what?" He made a face. "I haven't done anything yet."

"On the contrary, you've already done the most important thing. You've fallen for someone."

Bennett thought about it and objectively compared all the facts. The things he'd outlined to Olivia and the laundry list of scenarios she'd presented did seem to point to one conclusion.

For the first time in a long time, Bennett Alexander had a crush.

And a date.

———

ON SATURDAY, it wasn't until after lunch that Bennett remembered why the day was special. Katie was taking him on a practice date. *No*, he corrected himself. *You are taking her on a practice date. Or maybe even a real date.*

Ever since his talk with Olivia, he'd been thinking about the time he spent with Katie. They had fun together and she never seemed exasperated or annoyed by his quirks. There had been several occasions where he'd done his usual routine of drifting off into musings and instead of taking it as an offense, Katie always seemed mildly amused by him.

He liked her. And he wanted her to like him back.

Not that he had any idea of how to go about making that happen. After all, he'd hired her to teach him how to hit on a woman. How was he to know that he'd end up wanting to hit on his teacher? Now they were going on this practice date that suddenly felt more real than any real date he'd ever been on.

The entire thing was a tangled mess and he had half a mind to cancel the whole thing.

Just the thought of that made him scowl. He might be awkward but he was no coward. He was taking Katie on this date and he was going to make it the best damn date *ever*.

How, well, he hadn't worked that part out yet. But he had a good idea of who to call to get it all started. His younger brother Nick was a self-proclaimed "clothes-whore" and was married to a high fashion model. If anyone could handle this situation, it was Nick. And he wasn't as nosy as the others. Okay, he was but at least he wouldn't try to run a background check on Katie the way their brother Elliot would.

Nick answered after several rings. He sounded suspiciously out of breath when he did. "Hello? Bennett?"

"Yes, I'm here. Is this a bad time?" He sincerely hoped that it wasn't because he only had a few hours until it was time to pick up Katie.

"No, it's fine. I'm just ... Well, never mind that. Are you okay?"

"I'm fine. Well, actually no I'm not fine. I, um, well it seems I have a social commitment this evening and I'm not sure what to wear."

Nick didn't say anything for a moment. "What kind of social commitment? Meeting an old friend, business-related, what?"

"Not business. It's personal." More silence. "Okay, fine. I have a date. With a woman."

More silence then Nick said, "I'm coming over," and hung up.

Bennett sighed.

By the time Nick arrived, Bennett was convinced that he should have asked his brother to meet him at the mall. Everything he owned looked like it belonged at either a wedding or a funeral, not surprising since those were usually the only places he wore suits.

Without saying a word to him, Nick walked straight through the laboratory and up the stairs and into Bennett's bedroom. Bennett jogged to catch up. When he got there, Nick stood staring at the bed where his two choices were laid out.

"This is sad, big bro. Really sad. You're lucky I anticipated this and came prepared."

Curious, Bennett peered over Nick's shoulder as he started pulling clothes out of the garment bag Bennett hadn't even noticed. There was a shirt in a startlingly bright shade of blue, a thin sweater with an argyle design on the front and a more casual T-shirt.

"A T-shirt?"

Nick shrugged. "I wasn't sure where you were going. I came prepared for a multitude of options. Hell, I'm glad I was able to find anything I was so shocked that you had a date."

Bennett laughed. "It happens occasionally."

"I bet it does. We always figured you just kept your business to yourself. Nothing wrong with that. So ..." Nick took a seat on the edge of the bed and crossed his arms. "Who's the lucky lady? Anyone I know?"

Bennett debated whether he should mention that he was taking Katie out. It didn't seem right to make it out as a regular date when he knew Katie didn't see it that way but New Haven was a relatively small town. People were going to see them. Those same people would likely mention it to his family. Katie didn't seem concerned about being seen with him in public so it probably didn't matter who he told.

Nick held up his hands. "I don't mean to pry. Oh yeah, I heard you hired Katie. How is that going?"

"Great. She's picking things up quickly."

"Good, good. I'm glad you were able to help her out. She's a nice lady and the kids love her. She's also really pretty." Nick glanced over at him innocently.

"You think so?" Bennett picked up the sweater and examined the pattern. He could feel the heat of Nick's gaze on the back of his neck.

When there was no answer, he turned to find his brother regarding him knowingly.

"What?"

"Don't give me that. You want me to believe you're working in here with her all alone and you haven't noticed that she's pretty?"

"I didn't say that I didn't notice. Of course I noticed."

"And?"

"There's no 'and' involved. She's my employee. We're going out to dinner so I can learn how not to be such a weirdo." Frustrated, he threw the sweater back on the bed. "Fuck it. I'm not going."

Nick held out his hands. "Whoa. Slow down. I wasn't trying to piss you off."

"Then what are you trying to do, Nick? You have no idea what it's like. This all comes so easily to you. You know what to wear, what to say and I'm just ... "

All at once, the fight drained out of him. Bennett sat on the edge of the bed wearily and ran a hand over his hair. What the hell was he doing? He looked at the clothes strewn over the bed and the shoes he'd pulled out of the closet, the ones that always pinched his feet.

None of this was him. He felt like a fraud trying to pretend that he could ever be what a woman like Katie needed. Because in the end, no matter what outfit his brother dressed him up in, he was still the same tongue-tied nerd he'd always been.

"Ben, listen to me." Nick knelt on the floor next to him, his face grave. Since he was usually such a prankster, it was all the more striking when he got serious.

"I don't know what's going on between you and this girl but you don't need to be like anybody else. I'm pretty sure she's smart enough to like you exactly the way you are. So if you don't want to wear one of these outfits, don't. Hell, you could probably show up in jeans and she'd be just as excited to see you."

Bennett shook his head. "She deserves the kind of guy who knows how to show her a good time."

"And you will. You'll give her a great time. By being *yourself*. She wouldn't have agreed to this if she didn't like you as a person. Now you just have to show her that there's more to you than the lab coat."

A beat later, Nick grinned. "So, Katie is the one you're going out with. Knew I'd get it out of you."

Bennett shook his head at his brother's trickery. "Yes, I'm taking Katie out to dinner." He laughed when Nick pumped his fist in the air. "Don't celebrate yet. It's just dinner."

"Everything starts with *just* something, bro. If you're going to dinner, I think the blue button down works best. You're taller than me so it might be a little short but if you roll the sleeves up that won't matter."

Bennett took his shirt off and then shrugged into the blue one. It was a little short in the sleeves, but once he buttoned it up and rolled the sleeves, he had to admit that Nick was right. It looked pretty great. The color made his hazel eyes seem even lighter.

"Thank you, Nick. This was a big help."

"Anytime, man. You know we'd do anything for you. For what it's worth, Katie seems like one of the good ones. She's practically family already. Just remember, man: show her what's under the lab coat."

Bennett made a face. "That doesn't sound right."

Nick grinned. "I didn't exactly mean it like that but hell, you might want to show her that, too. I'm not judging. I came prepared for that, too." He was laughing as he left. That's when Bennett noticed the other thing Nick had brought him. A box of condoms. He laughed, caught between mortification and appreciation. His brothers were nosy as hell but at least they were practical. He seriously doubted if he'd need condoms tonight but Mark Alexander had drilled it into their heads that being prepared was always preferable to the alternative. So he slipped several packets into his wallet and then went to get ready.

Bennett showered, shaved, ran a comb through his curly hair while it was still wet and slapped on a small bit of cologne. Then he dressed carefully in the borrowed blue shirt and his own pair of gray trousers. The shoes pinched but that couldn't be helped. He took in his reflection in the mirror.

The guy staring back looked determined and excited.

"Remember what Nick said. Show her what's under the lab coat." It sounded ridiculous but Bennett wasn't averse to using every one of his talents. Science wasn't the only thing he'd studied over the years.

He was more than happy to show her just how accomplished he was in the bedroom, as well.

KATIE STOOD in front of the full-length mirror in her closet and threw yet another dress on the floor. This was useless!

How was it possible that she'd gained so much weight that none of her dresses fit properly? She didn't feel any bigger. Peering into the mirror she assessed herself from all sides. Considering that she'd had two kids, she didn't think she looked too bad. There was a maze of faint stretch marks on her stomach that stood out starkly against her deep skin tone, but other than that, it wasn't too bad.

Ugh, this was all Mari's fault. She'd been goading Katie to try dating. That must be why she'd suggested this. Fired up, she grabbed her phone and sent her sister a text.

> Took your advice. I'm going on a date.

It wasn't long before she could see the dancing bubbles indicating that her sister was typing a response.

MARI

Good. Hopefully he'll have a nice ass. And don't make those weird faces when you don't agree with something.

She stuck out her tongue at the screen.

What faces?

She sucked in her belly and then turned to the side. When she couldn't hold it anymore she let out her breath and returned to her usual state of looking vaguely pregnant. It was hard to see how much her body had changed over the years, especially after having her marriage crumble around her. What if she never got up the nerve to take her clothes off in front of anyone else? At least Don knew what battle scars she carried. Bennett had probably never seen what a woman looked like naked after childbirth.

Stop it, she thought. *It's not like Bennett is going to see your stomach. Or any other part of what's going on under your clothes. This is not a date. This is a teaching tool.*

"Mom! Miss Ridley's here!"

The screech from right outside the closet door startled her so badly she almost fell into the rack of clothes. Katie grasped wildly at the closest thing which turned out to be a dress. There was a loud ripping sound as it was torn from the hanger.

"Coming!"

Katie snatched a robe from one of the hangers and wrapped herself up in it, leaving the crumpled dress at her feet. She was being ridiculous. What difference did it make if she had stretch marks and a bit of a pooch belly? This was a practice date. P-R-

A-C-T-I-C-E. She repeated the word to herself as she went downstairs.

Ri was already on the bottom step making her way upstairs. "Hey, girl. I'm coming up. I'm just slow as usual."

Ridley leaned on the rail heavily as she made her way up the stairs. Once she reached the top, she followed Katie into her room.

"So, Jackson and I planned to make popcorn and s'mores for the kids so they can have a movie night."

"That sounds fun. They always have a good time when they're with Chris and Jase."

Ridley suddenly narrowed her eyes and took in the disheveled state of Katie's room. Her eyes slid over the makeup spread across her vanity table and then to the open closet door where heaps of clothes were visible on the floor.

"I thought you said you were just hanging out tonight. You're going on a date?"

"It's not ... it's not what you think." Katie winced. She should have known that her friend wouldn't buy her needing a night alone story. Ri was too much of a natural born detective not to notice all the clues.

"Uh huh. Who's the lucky guy?"

Katie didn't answer as Ridley pushed past her. She picked up the lipstick on the table. Katie almost laughed when Ri turned it over to see the color. There was no reasoning with her friend when she was on the scent of something juicy. She noticed things such as whether you were planning to wear red lipstick or not.

"You know how I'm supposed to be helping Bennett with his social skills?"

"Yeah. How's that going, by the way?"

"Good. Tonight we're going out to dinner so he can get more comfortable being around people and having a good time. I've never met anyone who finds relaxation so difficult. It's like his brain never stops working."

Ridley's eyes narrowed as she took in the destruction of the room and then swung back over to the makeup on the table.

"So, it's not a date?"

"No. It's a work thing. Maybe I went a little overboard but it's just because I'm excited to actually have somewhere to go for once. It's not like I get out much. It's really no big deal."

"Hmm. Are you sure about that?"

Katie gulped. "Of course I am. Besides, I'm pretty sure Bennett already has his eye on someone."

"Whoa, what? I've never heard that! Who is it?" Ri put one hand on her belly in surprise.

Katie turned away and started cleaning up the desk. *Oops.* Bennett obviously didn't want it to be common knowledge that he liked his friend Olivia or Ri would have heard about it from Jackson. He was such a private person and he would hate to be the subject of gossip.

"Never mind. I probably got it wrong. I just figured he had a girlfriend since ... Well, what Alexander guy isn't drowning in women, right?"

Ri hummed in agreement. "That's the truth."

Something about the face she made struck Katie as more than just general agreement. Ri chewed on her bottom lip the way she always did when she was upset.

"Not that you have to worry about that sort of thing. Jackson is so devoted to you." Katie watched her friend's face closely as she spoke.

There, what was that? Her friend flinched like she'd been

hit. What was that about? Jackson and Ridley were one of those couples that everyone else pointed to as an example of the perfect relationship.

Ri shrugged. "He's a man, too. We all have to worry about it."

"Hey, what's going on with you? I've never seen you like this." Katie led Ri over to the chair in front of her vanity since it had the sturdiest seat.

This was the kind of conversation she needed to be sitting down for.

"It's so stupid. I know it is. But I found this business card in Jackson's pocket with a woman's phone number on it and I can't stop thinking about it." Ridley rolled her eyes. "I knew it was a bad idea to look in his coat but it was sticking out of the pocket. What was I supposed to do?"

Katie swallowed against the sinking feeling she had listening to Ri blaming herself. It all felt so familiar, the excuses you made for the man you loved, the tendency to blame yourself for the whole situation, the despair. She'd spent years feeling like that before she had the courage to confront Don and she hadn't been heavily pregnant at the time.

"Ri, you don't have to justify anything to me. I would have looked, too."

All of sudden Ri gasped. "Oh Katie, I'm so sorry. I forget sometimes that you've gone through this."

"It's okay. I'm way over him. Plus, this doesn't mean that Jackson is doing the same thing that Don was. You guys are in a completely different situation. My ex-husband never looked at me the way Jackson looks at you. Maybe there's an explanation for this?"

Ridley forced a smile. "I'm sure there is. I'm not sure what's wrong with me lately. Hormones, I guess."

"Well, feel free to vent. I've certainly done it to you enough times."

Ri glanced over at the closet again. "Have you decided what to wear yet?"

Katie took that as a hint that she was done talking about this. Not that she didn't understand. When you were in the middle of a rough patch with your spouse, sometimes talking about it didn't help much. Sometimes what you needed was a distraction.

Katie walked into her closet and retrieved the two dresses she'd been debating before Ridley arrived. "It's a tie between this purple wrap dress and my standard little black dress. These are the only two dresses that still fit me."

Ri pursed her lips. "The purple looks great against your skin. And I bet you have a pink lipstick that would look amazing with that."

"I do, actually." Katie didn't usually wear a lot of makeup. Really, who had time for all that? But she'd always loved the simplicity of lipstick. You could slick it on in two seconds flat and suddenly feel completely glamorous.

She changed in the closet and when she walked into the room, Ridley whistled softly, making her blush.

Katie covered the wrap neck of the dress which revealed way more cleavage than she remembered.

"Wow. I know you said this isn't a date but you might have to check Bennett's pulse after he sees you in that. Girl, your tatas look amazing."

"Oh my god. Ri, you are such a trip." Katie looked down and had to admit that her friend was right. Ever since she'd had kids, her chest had gotten bigger. It looked like she was busting out of the top.

"Seriously though, if you want a chance with Bennett, you should take it. He's a really nice guy and I must admit, I love the idea of you being my sister-in-law."

Katie yanked the top of the dress together and searched through her dresser for a safety pin to keep it closed. "Like that's going to happen."

"You know, it's okay to like a guy. Even if he's your boss. Maybe this was meant to be."

"I don't think I'm that lucky, Ri."

"You never know. Sometimes the universe has a twisted sense of humor. I think you two would be great together."

Katie looked at herself in the mirror and imagined Bennett's face when he picked her up and saw this dress. Would he like it? Would he wonder what she looked like out of it? Or would he be eager to get this whole thing over with so he could go hit on Olivia?

"Maybe we would be great together. There's just one problem." At Ri's blank look, she continued. "Bennett already likes someone else. That's why we're going on this practice date in the first place."

Ri's face fell slightly. "Oh, well that doesn't mean you don't have a chance. He's not engaged or married or even committed. He's fair game as far as I'm concerned."

"I don't want another guy who considers me his second choice. I want to be first for once."

Katie ignored Ri's look of sympathy and walked back into the closet to find her heels. If she was going out wearing this clingy dress, she might as well go all the way and wear shoes that screamed sex, too.

She'd never liked to do things halfway.

———

A FEW HOURS LATER, Katie was just finishing up the last of her makeup when the doorbell rang. She took a deep breath and pressed her palm against the flock of birds that had just taken flight in her stomach. She'd taken a bubble bath to relax but her nerves suddenly returned full force. These feelings were so unexpected that it made her feel an uncharacteristic lightness. She wasn't used to feeling this kind of anticipation for anything.

She loved her life and adored her children but there was definitely a sense of monotony to her everyday life. She worked hard, made dinner, played with her boys and then fell into bed exhausted at the end of each long day. Only to wake the next morning and do the exact same things all over again. For years, she'd been on a schedule of rinse, cycle, and repeat, and today it felt like she'd stepped completely out of her orbit.

When she opened the door, she got an even bigger shock to see not only Bennett but Hunter. Her son was staring up at Bennett with wide eyes.

"Mommy, he's tall."

Even though the boys had seen him several times, she could imagine his height seemed even greater when standing right next to him, especially from a child's perspective. She found herself forgetting just how tall he was sometimes herself until he came over to show her something and she had to crane her neck.

Katie nodded. "Yes, he is. Hunter, did you say hello to Mr. Alexander?"

"Hi!" Hunter waved enthusiastically and then ran past Katie into the house.

Katie looked behind Bennett and saw Ridley standing on the sidewalk.

Her friend smiled smugly. "Hi, guys. Sorry, Hunter forgot his favorite pillow."

"Right. Sure he did," Katie teased.

"Uh, hello Ridley." Bennett looked between them uncertainly, probably wondering why Katie looked annoyed and Ri looked gleeful. He had no idea just how devious his sister-in-law could be.

Hunter came back then carrying his pillow. "Got it. Bye Mommy!"

"Bye baby. Be good for Miss Ri, okay?"

"Okay." Hunter looked up at Bennett again. "Are you going to kiss my mom?"

Katie's mouth fell open. She realized it was unexpected for the kids to see her with a man other than their father. That was why she hadn't dated. She hadn't wanted to confuse them, and okay, truthfully she hadn't really wanted to go out with anyone anyway. If she'd thought it would be an issue she'd have had a talk with the boys about dating. But apparently a talk was long overdue if Hunter thought that all men and women automatically kissed each other.

"Hunter, Mr. Alexander is my friend."

Bennett gave her a strange look before he knelt next to Hunter. "Buddy, I only wish I could be lucky enough to kiss an amazing lady like your mom. But first I need to show her that I'm a good guy. So tonight I'm taking her to dinner. Is that okay with you?"

Hunter nodded, like this made perfect sense. "Just don't chew with your mouth open. She *hates* that."

Bennett slanted a look in her direction. "Sounds like good advice to me. And by the way, my mom hates that, too."

Ridley waved as she led Hunter down the sidewalk toward her house. Katie picked up her purse from the front table and locked the door behind her. She followed Bennett down the driveway to the pickup truck she'd seen at the Alexanders. He held the door open for her and took her hand gently to assist her into the cab.

Once he closed the door behind her, Katie put a hand over her heart. She was trying so hard to pretend like she wasn't freaking out but wow, she hadn't dated anyone as well-mannered as he was. He did it so naturally, like it was second nature instead of begrudgingly like the so-called gentlemen she'd encountered in the past. Then there was the way he'd handled Hunter. Bennett might not have children of his own, but it was obvious that he was comfortable with them. He'd handled the situation directly and with a kindness and understanding that she hadn't been expecting.

If she'd been the blunt type with men, she might have just asked then and there if they could skip dinner and get right to dessert.

Practice date, remember? Katie blew out a breath, trying to cool down since her cheeks felt uncomfortably hot. It was harder than she'd thought to remember that this wasn't a real date. Bennett was just as smooth as his brothers when he wanted to be!

They were quiet on the way to the restaurant. Finally Bennett glanced over at her.

"You look beautiful."

Katie blushed. "Thank you."

"Sorry that took me so long but ever since you opened the door, I've been trying to think of something better than 'You look beautiful' and I honestly can't think of anything. Those words don't seem like enough."

Katie could have melted right there on the spot. How was it that this man thought he wasn't good with words?

"You clean up pretty nicely, too. I like your shirt."

For some reason, that amused him. "It's not mine. Nick loaned it to me. Apparently I've been too busy to go shopping for the past decade or so. My brother declared my wardrobe as tragic."

The image of the completely competent Bennett asking his little brother for fashion advice thoroughly charmed her. Not to mention that it was incredibly flattering that he'd cared enough to ask for help.

"He did a great job. I guess he would know about clothes, huh, considering that's Raina's thing."

Bennett nodded. "Exactly. That's what I thought, too. One of the perks of being an Alexander. There's always a brother or cousin who can help you with any situation."

They arrived at the restaurant and found a parking space in the back. After Bennett turned the engine off, they both sat, unmoving. His fingers clenched and unclenched against the steering wheel and Katie saw what she'd been too self-absorbed to notice earlier.

Bennett was nervous. Really nervous.

"Want to know a secret?" When he glanced over curiously, she took one of his hands off the steering wheel and gently uncurled his fingers. "I'm nervous, too."

Bennett let out a long breath. He didn't ask how she knew what he was feeling. "You are?"

"Absolutely. I changed clothes a bunch of times. You're not the only one who has trouble with dating. In fact, this is the first date I've been on in years."

Bennett leaned over. "I find that very hard to believe but that's probably a good thing. Maybe you won't laugh too hard when I inevitably embarrass myself. Wait here a second."

She watched as he got out of the truck and then came around to her side to open her door.

"You didn't have to do that. You opened it for me when I got in."

"And I'll open it for you when we come back out, too."

"There's no rule that says you have to open it all the time," Katie teased. She clutched her bag against her chest, trying to act like she was used to handsome men attending her like she was a princess.

"Well, somebody might want to tell my father that because he'd knock me upside the head if he found out that I didn't know how to treat a lady."

Katie smiled all through being seated at a quiet table, all the way through the perky waitress reciting the day's specials and into their appetizer. They were halfway through chicken nachos that were making Katie wish she'd ordered several plates, chatting about random things before Bennett looked at her suddenly.

"How am I doing so far?"

"Great. I'm having so much fun."

His shoulders lowered. "Oh good. It just occurred to me that I was having a good time. Usually when that happens it means I've gone off on some tangent talking about something that bores everyone around me."

Katie thought back to all the things they'd talked about. He'd told her a few random facts about where most restaurants sourced their jalapenos from but that could hardly be considered a tangent, right? They were in fact eating jalapenos, so that was actually relevant.

"You're not boring. Besides, what's wrong with being passionate about things? I think you've been too hard on yourself. You just have a lot of interests."

Bennett took another bite of nachos and then fixed her with an intense look. "I want to ask you something but I'm pretty sure I'm going to do it wrong. And I really don't want to hurt your feelings."

Katie winked at him. "Go ahead. I promise not to take offense. Even if it's pretty bad."

He looked down at the plate between them, dragging a chip through the cheese and salsa left on the plate. "It's about your ex-husband."

"Oh. I think I already know what you want to ask. Why did I stay with him so long?"

"Yeah. It doesn't sound like he was worthy of you."

"That's nice of you to say. Hmm, that's a difficult question though. I honestly don't know why I stayed as long as I did."

Bennett peered at her worriedly. "Sorry, I probably shouldn't have brought it up."

"No, it's okay. We're friends, right? Friends talk about real things. I've definitely vented for hours about this to Ridley."

Katie sighed. It wasn't that she didn't want to tell him about her marriage. It was natural that he'd be curious. It just wasn't so easy to admit to someone who was hyper focused and accomplished like Bennett that she'd floated through life for years without much ambition or direction of her own.

"When I was in school, I was just an average student. I didn't excel in any one subject so most of my teachers didn't pay too much attention to me. No one really encouraged me to go on to higher education. My sister and brother were the smart ones. I was the nice girl. I had lots of friends."

"I bet you did. You attract people like a flower attracts bees. If I didn't know better I'd think you were releasing some kind of special pheromone."

Katie laughed. "Like a secret weapon to snare people into my web. I like that. Anyway, after high school I was working in a clothing boutique and Don came in. He was on vacation with some friends. He was really flirty and complimentary at first. It felt good to get so much attention from a handsome, sophisticated American guy. My mom really liked him. She couldn't believe that I caught a doctor."

Bennett made a face. "Caught? It's too bad you didn't throw him back."

She smiled at that. "I'm glad I didn't. He's the real loser here. I have amazing kids, the best friends and neighbors you can ask for and now I have a great, new job where I'm learning tons. I'm happy to be exactly where I am."

Bennett picked up another chip. "I'm glad you're here, too."

eleven

BENNETT TOOK a sip of his water, watching Katie surreptitiously from behind the glass. They'd had a great conversation so far, after his stupid question about her ex. But her answer had made him feel better. She didn't seem to be carrying a torch for the guy which was good and she hadn't seemed like spending time with him was a hardship.

Now he just had to remember all the advice that Nick had given him. Bennett cut into his steak and tried to think of something he could say that would show her more of who he was. If he was supposed to show her that he was more than just a scientist, he was going to have to do better than small talk about their families and the restaurant.

"I can hear the gears moving in your mind." Katie smiled gently.

Bennett paused mid-chew. "Sorry. I guess that was kind of an awkward pause."

"Silence can be nice sometimes, too. I'm always a little suspicious of people who have to fill every moment with activity, you know? It's exhausting trying to keep up with that."

Katie twirled her pasta around her fork. She'd confessed that pasta was one of her weaknesses. Especially pasta with seafood in it. Another thing he filed in his mental notes about her.

"I'm used to being the quiet one in a crowd of noise," Bennett said. "Growing up with three younger brothers who never stopped moving taught me to find an oasis in the middle of pandemonium. Plus, my Aunt Maria and her two kids lived with us for a while also when I was really young. My cousins Langston and Laura are like additional siblings. It was a constant party."

Katie leaned forward. "Was it crazy? You seem like such a solitary person. I can't imagine you growing up in a big family."

"It was difficult at times. With so many people around, there's always someone asking you for something or making noise. Finding time alone was almost impossible. Luckily we have so much land that we were all outside a lot. I'll have to take you to some of my favorite spots one day."

"I would love that." Katie placed her fork by her plate and sat back with a satisfied sigh. "That was so good. I'm sure it's all going to my hips but that's okay. It was worth it."

Bennett took his last bite of his own food. His brother had recommended the restaurant and he'd described it as upscale without being pretentious. Sweeties was known for great food and a romantic atmosphere but of course it all came with an extremely high price tag. However, it was definitely worth the outrageous price. Bennett was feeling languid and satisfied after such a good meal.

The waitress appeared then and set a dessert menu on the table between them. Bennett wondered if she thought they were a real couple. He considered the idea. What did other people see when they looked over at their table? He was so used to being considered strange or an outsider that he found he liked the idea of being a part of a couple with Katie. She made him feel like he belonged, exactly the way he was.

The waitress took their plates. "Dessert? We have a seasonal berry crumble that is absolutely delicious."

Katie groaned. "Okay, you twisted my arm!" She made a face as the waitress disappeared. "I have no willpower at all."

Bennett chuckled at her pained look. "So you have a weakness for sweets? I'll have to remember that if I ever need to bribe you to do something."

"You wouldn't need to use pastry to get me to do something," Katie mumbled under her breath.

Bennett almost choked on the sip of water he'd just taken. He grabbed his napkin and blotted his chin. Had he heard that correctly? But Katie was checking her phone and didn't look as though she'd just said something inappropriate. His face heated. She might not have even realized she'd said it out loud.

He was trying to think of something to say but kept coming up blank. Should he pretend he hadn't heard that? Or was she secretly hoping he had and waiting for him to acknowledge it? The secret language of flirting was such a mystery to him and he couldn't exactly ask Katie to decode her own signals.

Bennett sighed. So much for being himself. Maybe he could excuse himself and call Nick for more advice. But he quickly nixed that idea. His brother had already made assumptions about his relationship with Katie and he definitely didn't want to embarrass her or reveal anything to people she had to socialize with regularly.

While he was contemplating this, Katie put her napkin aside. "It's been a while since I've been here. Aren't the bathrooms down that hallway?" When Bennett nodded, she stood. "Great. Excuse me."

He watched the sway of her hips as she walked away and then jerked his attention back to the table. The last thing he wanted was for her to turn around and see him ogling her. Although, considering what she'd said earlier, maybe she wouldn't mind?

Nick's words from earlier came back to him. *Show her what's under the lab coat.* He hadn't meant it in a dirty way but Bennett was starting to think that Katie wouldn't have a problem with that plan.

———

KATIE WASHED her hands in the sink, wishing she could splash the cool water over her face without ruining her makeup.

What the hell is wrong with you?

She'd been lucky that Bennett hadn't heard her dirty little comment earlier otherwise he'd probably have already asked for the check. Katie wasn't sure what had gotten into her lately. She'd never been this unpredictable before but there was something about Bennett that made it easy to let her guard down. She found herself doing and saying things that she would normally filter out.

It was telling that she felt this comfortable around him. Don had always been so critical of everything that she'd tried to morph herself into what he'd wanted. Nothing she did ever seemed like enough so over the years she'd started to assume that everyone felt the way he did. That all her friends were just tolerating her or that they all secretly pitied her.

Living with someone who was emotionally abusive was such an insidious thing. She'd even considered it constructive criticism at first. Don had always made it sound like he just wanted her to improve and reach her highest potential. But after seeing other people's relationships, she'd finally understood that the way he treated her wasn't normal and it wasn't healthy. There was nothing wrong with wanting to improve yourself as long as you were doing it for the right reasons.

Not because you had someone else's voice in your head telling you that you weren't good enough.

Well no more. She'd finally found the strength to take control of her own life. Yes it was scary and maybe she wasn't doing so well with her bills but at least she was doing it on her own. Katie was proud of herself for not giving up. She knew that if she really needed help, her siblings and her friends would help. But that wasn't what she wanted. There was something really satisfying about working to fix her problems herself.

"Okay just go out there and have fun. Don't take it so seriously."

The woman at the next sink glanced over at her curiously. "Honey, are you on a date too?"

Katie dried her hands with a paper towel. "Yeah. Sorry about talking to myself. I'm just trying to remind myself not to get my hopes up."

The other woman flipped her long blond hair over her shoulder. She held her hands over her stomach that was completely flat in her super tight dress. "I know what you mean. I met my guy on that new MeetNChill app. I'm not expecting much other than to get some. These men out here aren't shit." Then with a little wave she walked out of the bathroom.

"Well, okay then." Katie chuckled all the way back to the table. At least she wasn't the only one frustrated with the whole dating thing.

By the time she got there, her berry crumble was waiting for her. Katie slid into her seat and immediately picked up her fork. If she wasn't "getting any" like her friend in the bathroom, at least she would have a great dessert. She'd take her pleasure where she could get it.

"I can't believe you didn't get anything," she told Bennett. It made her feel a little weird to scarf down this whole berry pie while he just sat there.

"No, I rarely eat processed sugar. It's easier to maintain my ideal muscle-to-fat ratio if I only eat sweets on special occasions."

Katie gaped at him. "That sounds awful. I'm supposed to be teaching you to have fun so I cannot let you continue to live a pie-less existence. No one should only get to have sweets on holidays or whatever. Here." She held out her fork.

Bennett leaned forward hesitantly but took the bite of pie she offered. His eyes closed as he chewed and swallowed.

"Damn that's good."

Katie grinned. "See? Don't worry. I'm sure your perfect body fat percentage won't be ruined because you had a bite of something yummy."

His lips pulled up at the corners like he was fighting a smile. "I'll be sure to think of you tomorrow when I'm running an extra mile on the treadmill."

Katie's stomach sank until she noticed his shoulders shaking with laughter. "Oh that was just mean. I actually felt bad for a second there. I was trying to share because I felt guilty enjoying this decadent dessert while you didn't have anything."

"Don't feel guilty. I'm enjoying myself watching you."

A warm rush of heat spread through her as she took another bite of pie. She wasn't sure if Bennett really knew what he was doing when he said things like that. He probably thought it was just a nice thing to say and she didn't want to be the brazen hussy who told him those things were sexually suggestive.

Or that her panties were uncomfortably damp every time he said something like that in his deep voice.

Katie managed to finish the rest of her dessert without embarrassing herself. In the car as Bennett drove her home, she mentally prepared herself for what would happen. She'd tell him that he did a great job and he'd probably give her a friendly hug to say good night.

Then she'd go upstairs, change into her nightgown and probably pull out the vibrator that she rarely even used anymore.

When they parked in her driveway, Katie realized she'd forgotten to leave the porch light on. Without it, the interior of the car was so dark that she could barely see anything more than Bennett's shadow.

"Hold on. I'm coming around."

Goose bumps sprang up on her arms at the soft hush of his voice in the darkness. She waited patiently as he circled the car to open her door, and then walked her up to her porch. The lights she'd left on inside spilled through the front windows, casting a warm glow over them both.

Katie pulled out her keys and opened the door. Neither of them said anything. It suddenly struck her as funny. Normally this was when she'd be worried about whether the guy would kiss her or whether she wanted to rush in and slam the door in his face.

"This is usually make it or break it time," she joked.

"What does that mean?"

"Oh, you know. It's the end of the night and usually you're a little tipsy at this point. So in high school you'd park the car somewhere and make out but as an adult, normally you just kiss goodnight before going inside."

"Well, that doesn't sound that difficult."

"Oh, you'd think it would be easy. Just lean in and smooch but you have to be smooth with it. You have to read the signals."

Bennett sighed. "And you lost me again. Why can't the signal be when she says *I'd really like it if you'd kiss me now?* That would be so much easier."

Katie put her hand over her mouth to smother her laughter. Looking at things from his perspective, it was kind of odd that there were all these unspoken rules about something that should be instinctive but it was impossible to ignore that the rules existed, whether they were official or not.

She remembered the first time Don had kissed her. It was bittersweet to remember it now, being so young and naive that she'd required so little to feel cherished. But all she'd wanted was to feel like someone saw her as special.

"The rules seem annoying, I know, but it all comes back to one thing. You want to make sure that she's as into it as you are. And everyone isn't good at articulating what they're feeling. So you have to be able to read the signs. Body language."

"So, if I can learn to read body language then I'll know what to do?"

"Most of the time, yes."

"Well, if I could learn German then I should be able to learn this."

Katie laughed softly. "I still can't believe you know all those languages. Is there anything you can't do?"

His face fell. "I think we've established that there are quite a few things that I can't do."

In that moment, Katie suddenly understood what a monumental mistake she'd made. This whole thing was so wrong and she was swamped with shame for her part in it.

"I made a mistake agreeing to this."

"To what? This date? Why?"

Bennett looked slightly hurt so she grabbed his hand before he could pull away.

"Because by agreeing to teach you, I'm participating in the idea that you need to change somehow. That you need to be different for a woman to like you. And that's not true. Bennett, you have *everything* you need already. You have the most important thing. This, right here."

She pressed her hand into the center of his chest, relishing the strong, steady beat thumping beneath her palm.

"You have the biggest heart. The way you love your family and care about everyone around you, even your former employees, proves that. You don't need to change a thing. I think you're perfect the way you are."

Without her knowledge, her hand had roamed over his chest, feeling the hard muscles beneath.

"I think you're perfect, too." Bennett's eyes were intense on hers before he looked down. He seemed mesmerized by the motion of her hand. Katie knew she should stop; she was practically pawing him but he felt so good.

"This is the most fun I've had in a really long time. I think you are beautiful and fun and I wake up every day excited now because I know you'll be there."

"Bennett," she whispered, completely stunned by his heartfelt words.

"I'm trying really hard to be a gentleman but since you don't seem to mind honesty, it's been hard to concentrate on anything tonight when all I wanted to do was peel this dress off and show you just how much I've learned about multiple orgasms over the years."

Katie's mouth fell open. Of all the things she'd expected him to say, that didn't even rate. Now she had the image of Bennett studying the Kama Sutra in order to learn the best way to please a woman. Considering how seriously he took education, she had no doubt that he'd been as diligent studying the mystery of the female body as he was with anything else.

And she wanted nothing more than to experience everything he'd learned firsthand.

The hand she'd placed on his chest stopped moving. She clenched his shirt between her fingers, feeling his muscles flex beneath her touch. Then she took a deep breath and made her decision.

"Bennett, I'd really like it if you'd kiss me now."

twelve

BENNETT COULDN'T BELIEVE what was happening.

One minute they were talking about how confusing signals could be and the next, Katie was rubbing his chest and kissing all over his face. She'd grabbed him by the shirt and pulled him over the threshold into the house. He barely registered the distant slam of the door behind them as her hands continued their frantic exploration of his chest and shoulders. Bennett bent slightly so she didn't have to strain so hard to reach his lips. Then he realized that bending wasn't going to cut it. She wasn't that petite but everyone was short next to him. He picked her up and then froze.

"Are you sure?" he whispered.

Katie hooked her arm behind his head and brought his lips back to hers. Bennett growled in satisfaction. Even he could read that signal.

All at once, the uncertainty he usually felt fled and his confidence returned full force. Bennett grinned. He was only uncertain about what led up to the bedroom.

He was completely confident about what to do once he was there.

"Where's your room?" he whispered between kisses.

She pointed and he followed her directions until he found the right room. The door was already open and he stumbled until they fell onto a huge bed. Katie slid up the bed and then crooked her finger to indicate that he should join her. Bennett crawled over her until he settled right between her legs. When he rested his full body weight on top of her, she let out a deep satisfied sigh.

She enjoyed feeling his weight. Good to know.

Bennett couldn't keep away from her lips for long. She had the softest lips and he already found himself longing for more of her taste. It wasn't long before they were writhing on the bed as their tongues tangled. Katie sucked in a desperate breath when they finally separated. They hadn't turned on any lights in the room yet so he couldn't see well. That wouldn't work. He'd been thinking about this moment for too long. He needed to see everything.

He reached over to her nightstand and felt around until he found the switch on the lamp. Soft light flooded the room.

Katie sat up and squinted at him slightly. "You want the light on?"

Bennett paused while unbuttoning his shirt. Who wouldn't want the light on so they could see what they were doing? He shook his head. Her ex-husband really was a dumbass if he had someone as beautiful as Katie and didn't even want to see her when they made love.

Without answering, he took his shirt off and threw it to the side. Bennett wasn't arrogant. He was well aware of his faults but he was also aware that his daily workouts had given him the kind of body that most women considered ideal. Hell, he was determined to use any advantages he had.

Sure enough, Katie's mouth fell open slightly when she saw his bare chest. Her eyes got soft and slumberous as she looked over his whole chest down to the sharply defined V-shaped muscles that led from his abs down into his trousers.

"Oh we can definitely leave the lights on," she said.

He laughed. "Good, because I want to see you, too."

That seemed to bring her out of her stunned state. She shook her head frantically. "I don't know about that. I mean … I don't look like that," she stammered, pointing at his abs.

"I hope not," Bennett replied as he unbuttoned his slacks and kicked them off.

Katie sighed as she watched his pants land near his shirt. "You know what I mean. I've had two kids. Things aren't as perky as they used to be. While you look like you don't have an ounce of fat on you anywhere. You weren't kidding about only eating dessert on holidays, huh?"

Bennett climbed back on the bed. She was making jokes but he could tell she was truly uncomfortable which was the opposite of what he wanted. It was crazy to him that she could be worried about this when she had him on the verge of coming like a teenager just from a few kisses. Katie was gorgeous and he liked everything about her looks. Not just the pillowy mouth that had fueled quite a few fantasies but her large, brown eyes always had a mischievous twinkle that made her look like she was up to something. Her dark skin contrasted beautifully against his and she was curvy in all the right places. He hated that she was worried about not being perfect in some way.

"You are beautiful. And I plan on showing you that. But if it makes you more comfortable right now, you should know that

I'm blind as a bat without my glasses. So all the things you're worried about, I won't be able to see them anyway."

Katie chuckled and the motion made her chest jiggle which of course sent a shaft of desire downstairs that made him even harder.

"I like how you always get right to the point of things." She reached up and carefully removed his glasses and set them on the nightstand.

He leaned over and kissed her neck, enjoying her soft moan. "Of course without my glasses that means I need to stay very close."

"I like the sound of that, too."

Bennett lifted the hem of her sexy dress and placed his palm on the inside of her thigh. Her head fell back at the touch and she pulled her legs even wider. His hand shook slightly as he traced soft, smooth thighs up until his fingers encountered silk at her core.

Incredibly damp silk.

He shuddered at the evidence that she was just as into this as he was.

"I should take this off." Katie sat back slightly and then untied the sash that wrapped around her waist. Then she took a safety pin out of the top. Immediately the cloth pulled open revealing her black bra.

Bennett's mouth went dry at the sight of the plump mounds pushing over the cups of her bra. Then he nudged the dress all the way open to see that the damp silk panties he'd just felt were black also. She looked like a wet dream, an erotic present that was his to unwrap.

He kissed the tops of her breasts before reaching behind her to unhook her bra. She shrugged out of it and deposited the dress and the bra on the floor next to the bed. Bennett continued his exploration of her sexy breasts, cataloguing every one of her sighs, moans and deep breaths as he played with her nipples. He took it all in, learning what she liked and getting her ready for what came next. Katie was skittish and a little shy about being naked. He needed her completely relaxed.

Especially since Bennett had no shame about enjoying sex. It was completely natural and he didn't think anything should be off-limits as long as both parties were enjoying themselves. He got the sense that Katie was definitely more buttoned up and not as comfortable with nudity as he was. He wanted her too dazed with pleasure to think too hard about anything, especially the silly things she probably imagined were "wrong" with her figure.

He moved up her body, biting and kissing the whole way until he reached her mouth again. Katie moaned as he kissed her deeply, his fingers inching down her stomach until he reached her panties. He hooked his fingers in the side and pulled them down. She lifted her hips to allow them to come off. Then let out a cry when his fingers curled into her, pressing right against her G-spot.

"Bennett!"

He smiled against her neck. That was the spot. He stroked the soft area firmly, reveling in her soft cries and the tightening muscles that told him how close she was to coming.

"You feel so good." He'd never been much for talking during sex, too many opportunities for him to say the wrong thing, but with Katie it was different.

He could feel the difference already. She accepted him and liked him the way he was. Bennett didn't feel the need to be constantly on guard, worried that he'd screw up. She liked him.

For the first time, he could be himself and just be in the moment.

Bennett, I think ... " She gasped and her eyes flew open, her arms almost strangling him as she tightened around his fingers.

"*Damn*, that's it beautiful. Just let go."

Katie looked into his eyes the whole time, making the sexiest little noises in the back of her throat as she came. It took every bit of self-control he had not to hook her legs over his shoulders and get inside her right then and there. He took a deep breath and petted her gently, bringing her down from her climax slowly.

"Wow," she whispered a minute later. "What the hell was that?"

He laughed softly and kissed her neck. She smelled amazing and he wanted that scent all over him before they were done. His dick throbbed angrily in his boxers as if to remind him that he'd been very patient so far.

He moved around awkwardly to get his boxers off but Katie still stiffened when she saw what he was working with.

"Wow," she said again.

He shouldn't have been so complimented but it made him feel good to know that her asshole ex obviously couldn't compare. Then he realized what he'd forgotten.

He stood and got his wallet from his pants. Thank God for Nick being so pushy otherwise he might not have been prepared. He took out one of the condoms he'd brought along. Katie watched with avid interest as he rolled it on. Her eyes on him only made him even harder.

When he climbed on the bed again, his eyes almost rolled to the back of his head when she reached out and gripped him. She guided him between her legs. Bennett paused her with a gentle hand on her stomach then put one hand under her to adjust her hips. Katie looked up at him in confusion but the expression on her face changed to pure pleasure when he slid in at an angle that allowed him to stimulate her G spot with every thrust.

"Oh my god," she cried out and squeezed her eyes shut.

"Look at me," he whispered. "I want to see your eyes."

With a cry, Katie opened her eyes. Seeing the lost expression on her face only amped his arousal even higher. Damn if it wasn't the hottest thing ever to watch her lose all control as she unraveled. Then she curled her leg around his waist, hooking her feet right under his ass, using them as leverage to urge him to go faster.

"Fuck, you want more?" he growled, unable to resist giving her everything when she nodded frantically.

Bennett had always prided himself on having excellent stamina but he had to take deep breaths to keep his response under control. She was warm and so damn wet and her fingers wandering all over his back like they couldn't decide what to touch next were driving him crazy.

He drew in a deep breath, trying to hold back his own pleasure as Katie's cries got louder. She deserved to feel special and wanted. Bennett wanted to be the man who showed her that. For her, he wanted to be Superman.

But as her nails dug into his back and she cried out in release, he let go of his control and shuddered with her. As they both fought to catch their breath, Bennett was already mentally planning how he could torment her with more pleasure.

This was an unexpected end to the evening but Bennett wasn't one to waste an opportunity. He planned to show Katie that he was worth taking a chance on.

KATIE WOKE to Bennett's tongue sliding between her folds and screamed as an orgasm ripped through her with no warning. She panted, completely disoriented as the last vestiges of sleep cleared. Bennett raised his head and sent her a naughty grin before folding one of her legs behind his waist and taking her with one deep thrust.

After passing out after another orgasm, she was awakened again by him sliding into her from behind.

"Oh my ... What?" She could barely understand what was going on but the intense pressure between her legs clued her in.

Bennett's arm slid under her breasts, holding her in place as he edged inside her gently. In this position he felt huge and Katie panted helplessly at how small and delicate she felt in his arms. His hand roamed downward to where they were joined and rubbed small circles that had her moaning in time with his slow thrusts. When they came this time, it was together.

She'd never felt anything as satisfying as hearing Bennett's deep groan in her ear as he clutched her to him.

When she woke next, it was to faint streams of light coming through the sheer curtains. She blinked sleepily. It was that bluish light that indicated early morning. She shifted and every muscle in her body screamed. That's when it came back to her at once.

She'd gone on a date with Bennett Alexander.

She'd gone to bed with Bennett Alexander.

Katie blushed from head to toe at the thought of what bedtime with Bennett was really like. *Holy cow.* Perhaps it shouldn't be a surprise that his hyper-focus and single-minded concentration carried over but she would have never guessed that he'd be so intense. So demanding. After being woken up the second time, she'd wondered if he was planning to let her get any sleep at all.

She looked over to the other side of the bed where Bennett slept on his stomach, one arm thrown over his head. Katie withheld a sigh of appreciation. The muscles in his back were a truly fine sight to wake up to. It had been a long time since she'd shared her bed and she'd never had this kind of eye candy to look at before. It was tempting to take this opportunity to run her hands over that insanely sculpted body but she didn't want to wake him up. He was clearly exhausted and no wonder. The man had put in quite a performance last night.

She swung her legs over the side of the bed and got up, hoping she could brush her teeth and fix her hair before he saw her looking so awful. First she had to deal with the fact that she was stark naked. Katie blushed and immediately went to her dresser to find a long T-shirt. She wasn't the type who could walk around naked without being self-conscious. She hadn't been comfortable with that even when she'd actually had a flat stomach and perky boobs.

Once she got to the bathroom, she closed the door as quietly as she could and then turned the light on. Then she made the mistake of looking in the mirror.

"Oh my god!"

Katie clapped a hand over her mouth, hoping she hadn't woken Bennett. Because she definitely didn't want him to see her looking like this.

The image staring back at her from the mirror looked like the victim of a natural disaster. She hadn't washed her makeup off the night before so she had black smudges around both eyes and her skin looked blotchy and chapped, the dried makeup having settled into every one of the fine lines on her face.

She went to work, scrubbing her face several times with cleanser and then brushing her teeth. Once she slathered her face with moisturizer, she felt slightly more human. She rubbed her hands over her hair and tried to tame the wayward curls that stuck out in every direction. Katie sighed. Nothing short of hopping in the shower was going to fix her hair, so she would just have to make do with extreme bedhead.

When she left the bathroom, Bennett was sitting up against the headboard. She skidded to a halt outside the door.

"Hi. You're awake."

He looked rumpled and sexy and completely focused on her.

"Good morning," he rumbled in the sexiest, deepest morning voice she'd ever heard.

Suddenly she felt awkward as hell. Was he regretting what they'd done last night? The man was an absolute Adonis and seeing him all naked and growly only drove the point home. All her parts warmed at the sight of him like they were hoping for more attention.

Not that she could handle more attention. She tried not to wince as she walked but it was becoming more obvious just how sore she was. It probably hadn't been great to jump into a sex marathon after being celibate for so long. She walked back over and got in bed, pulling the covers up over her bare legs.

It was weird waking up and not having to worry about the kids. Ridley would be calling in a few hours so she could go pick them up. But what if she didn't call and just brought them over instead? They would see Bennett or at least see his car out front.

If Hunter was confused by the idea of her kissing another man, how strange would it be for him to find a man in the house in the early hours? On one level, Katie knew she was being ridiculous. Even Ridley wouldn't be so devious as to show up in the early morning without calling first, but she still couldn't stop the full-scale panic attack that had come over her. She put a hand over her chest trying to calm her racing heart.

"Are you okay? You're breathing so fast." Bennett rubbed her back in gentle circles. Under any other circumstances it would have been comforting but it only made her feel worse.

He was being so nice and what if he wanted to have sex again? She was sore and freaking out and all she wanted was to pull the covers over her head and go back to her boring routine.

"I think you should go," she blurted.

His hand stopped moving on her back. Katie immediately felt awful.

"Um, not because I didn't have a great time. I did. I really did. It's just the kids will be home soon and they've never seen me with another man, you know?"

Bennett nodded slowly. "I understand. Let me just get dressed."

Katie averted her eyes as he climbed out of bed but it was impossible to ignore six feet four inches of pure male hotness. Her core clenched as his abs flexed when he stepped into his pants. Certain parts of her wouldn't mind going for a second round despite being sore, clearly.

Once he was dressed, he hesitated next to the bed. Finally, he knelt and kissed her cheek.

"I had fun. I'll let myself out so you can get a little more sleep before the kids get home."

Katie sighed. He was always so considerate. It made her feel even worse.

"Thank you, Bennett. I had fun, too."

She bit her lip as he walked out of the room. His footsteps faded as he went downstairs and then a few seconds later, she heard the front door close behind him as he left.

thirteen

BENNETT READ the same line in his book easily five times before he gave up. There was no point pretending to relax. He'd spent the entire drive home from Katie's house going over every aspect of their date in his mind, looking for where he'd gone wrong.

She'd been friendly and flirtatious at the restaurant. Obviously his conversational skills hadn't been that bad. Then at her house, he'd tried to slow things down. She'd pulled him down to her and wrapped her legs around him. Clearly she'd been on board with the plan to get naked. And there was no way she had an issue with his actual performance between the sheets.

Bennett took a deep breath as he was slammed with images from their night together. He ran a hand over his hair. It had been so damn good and he knew it had been good for Katie, too. Despite what a lot of people thought, orgasms actually weren't that easy to fake if a guy knew what a real one looked like.

He chuckled, remembering something Nick had told him in high school when he'd been known for having quite a few girlfriends. *If it doesn't look like a demon is being exorcised through her face, it's not the real thing.*

He'd later learned that as crudely put as it was, Nick's advice was spot on. Katie definitely hadn't been faking it. She'd screamed loud enough to shatter the windows several times and a woman couldn't fake getting that wet. She'd nearly burned him alive with how responsive she was.

So why did she kick you out this morning?

Frustrated, Bennett decided he could go around and around the issue all day and not get anywhere. Something had gone wrong unless he was imagining how eager she'd seemed to get him out of her house that morning. Maybe it was as simple as she'd said and she was worried about her kids finding him there. He'd never dated anyone with children before so he couldn't say if that was a common concern but it seemed reasonable to him.

He went about running his errands, going to the grocery store, jogging five miles on the treadmill and working on lesson plans for a community college course he'd committed to teach over the summer. There was no point stressing over something he couldn't change and Katie was the straightforward type. If he'd done something wrong, he had no doubt that she'd tell him when he saw her at work the next day.

It wasn't until he woke up Monday morning to a voicemail from Katie explaining that she wasn't coming in that he got the sense that he had well and truly fucked things up.

All morning, he went through his usual routine but couldn't concentrate. Finally he gave up and went to his office to see if there was anything administrative he needed to do. Unable to stop himself, he picked up his cell phone and listened to Katie's message again.

How pathetic was he? He was so desperate for the sound of her voice that he was sitting here alone listening to the only recording he had of her voice. Bennett scowled. It was better than sitting in the lab and pretending to get work done. He'd been completely useless all morning.

Halfway through the message he sat up straight. He'd been so focused on the part about her not coming in that he'd completely ignored the reason she'd said she had to miss work. He skipped to the beginning of the message and played it again.

I got a call from the guidance counselor at Hunter's school. They requested a conference for today at two o'clock. I'm not sure what's going on. I hope he's not in trouble. Anyway, sorry for the late notice but I'm not coming in today.

Bennett hung up and glanced at his watch. He had just enough time to get over to New Haven Elementary if he hurried. He shrugged out of his lab coat. He wasn't sure what was going on between him and Katie just yet but none of that mattered when she sounded worried. Not that having him there was going to do much but at least he could offer support if she was about to get bad news.

Maybe this thing between them wasn't meant to be and maybe he was reading too much into this and she wouldn't be happy to see him at all. But if he'd learned anything growing up as an Alexander, it was that being there for the people that mattered to you was important. So he'd be there until Katie told him she didn't want him around.

He only hoped his heart and his ego could take it if she did.

———

KATIE LOOKED up when she heard the sound of her name. She'd been sitting outside the guidance counselor's office for the last ten minutes, wringing her hands. She still had no idea what this meeting was about and could only hope that Hunter wasn't in some kind of trouble.

She didn't think he was. He'd always been such a good kid. He'd been a little more sullen since the divorce but that was to be expected, right? Even though Don had been gone a lot, he'd still spent time with the boys in the evening whenever he wasn't working and she knew both of the boys missed that. He'd been a terrible husband and a mostly absent father but he loved his children. That was part of what made it so hard to see their relationship deteriorate completely.

"Yes? I'm Katie Mason, Hunter's mom."

"Hello, I'm Miss Meadows. Come in, please. Have a seat."

The guidance counselor looked like she'd just graduated from high school herself. Geez. Katie wondered when had she gotten so old? Everyone looked like an infant to her lately.

She took the seat in front of the counselor's desk and placed her handbag on her lap. The other woman rifled through some papers on her desk and then put a pair of glasses on.

Finally when Katie couldn't take it anymore, she asked, "Hunter isn't in any trouble, is he?"

The other woman looked up then. "Oh no. I'm sorry if I gave you that impression. Hunter has always been a model student."

"Oh good. I've been a little worried about him since the divorce." Katie swallowed hard at the admission. It was hard not to feel guilty, as if she was to blame for her family falling apart. Even when she knew people weren't judging her, it still felt like it sometimes.

"Actually that's why I called you in today. The students had an assignment last week to write about their family. This is Hunter's work." She held out a piece of construction paper.

Katie took it with trembling fingers.

It was a picture of a woman and two kids. A man was in the corner of the picture with a white mask over his face. She gasped. Hunter had drawn Don wearing blue scrubs and a white mask but he'd drawn Katie with tears on her cheeks. Both of the little boys in the picture had sad faces.

The counselor spoke softly. "When I asked him about it, Hunter said that his mom is always sad and he misses his dad. I just thought you should see this."

Katie looked up, sure she wasn't hiding the devastation she was feeling. "Yes, I did need to see this. Thank you for letting me know."

The counselor nodded. "There are quite a few programs in New Haven that provide free counseling and I'll be working with Hunter one on one also. We just wanted to let you know that there are services available that can help."

Katie hoped she nodded in the right places and said the right things. By the time they were done, she was on the verge of tears. She needed to get the hell out of there before she broke down in front of this girl who looked like she still wore a training bra.

"Thank you again. Just ... thank you."

Katie didn't look back as she left the counselor's office, just kept her head down and walked as fast as she could. She wasn't even sure where she was going but she needed to be alone. That was the thing about small communities. Everyone knew everyone and if she was seen crying in public, all of her friends and neighbors would know about it within an hour.

Strong arms grabbed her and Katie gasped. Then she looked up into Bennett's worried eyes. It was a strange thing to notice in the moment but they seemed darker today, the green flecks surrounded by more brown.

"Bennett! What are you doing here?"

His gaze took in her damp eyes and the death grip she had on her handbag.

"When I heard that you had a meeting about Hunter this afternoon, I thought you might need a friend."

Katie didn't think twice or question her instincts. She just walked straight into his arms and hugged him.

His arms wrapped around her with no hesitation. Nothing had changed in the past few minutes but there was no question that she felt ten times better about the situation than she had before.

It took her a few moments to gain her composure before she pulled back reluctantly. Bennett seemed just as hesitant to let go. In light of how they'd left things, okay, with how she'd kicked him out on Sunday morning, Katie wasn't even sure what to say. He certainly didn't owe her anything and if the tables were turned, she doubted she would be so nice to someone who'd treated her like a booty call.

But that was Bennett. He didn't hold grudges and when the chips were down, you could always count on him to come through. It was just who he was.

"Thank you for coming. You really didn't have to."

He smiled. "I know. I take it that you got bad news?"

Katie sighed. "Sort of. It's kind of hard to explain."

Bennett hummed a non-committal sound. He glanced

behind her at the closed door to the guidance counselor's office. Then he held out his arm.

"Let's get out of here."

Katie accepted his arm and the unspoken offer of support. "Where are we going?"

"Remember when I told you I wanted to show you some of my favorite spots on the Alexander homestead? Now is as good of a time as any."

Katie wasn't sure what she was going to do about Hunter or even what she was going to do about the situation between her and Bennett. However, if he was willing to put the weirdness aside for a while, then so was she.

***

WHEN BENNETT MADE the suggestion to Katie, he wasn't sure exactly where he was going to take her. But as she followed his truck back to the Alexander farm, he suddenly knew exactly where they should go.

By the time she parked behind him, he was waiting next to her door to help her out of the car. She smiled at him gratefully.

"Thank you again for coming to the school. I'm sorry for getting so emotional back there."

"I told you it's no big deal. Come on. I know exactly what I want to show you first."

Bennett tucked her hand into the crook of his arm and started walking. Although Katie wore a nice blouse, she had luckily worn low-heeled shoes and a pair of jeans with it. If she'd been wearing high heels or a skirt, his plan probably wouldn't have worked.

When they reached the barn behind his, he went inside

and took the key for one of the small tractors off its peg on the wall. When he emerged from the barn riding it, Katie burst into laughter.

"Seriously?"

Bennett grinned. "Unless you want to end up walking about two miles or so in total. I'm game if you are."

Katie climbed on the back of the tractor eagerly and he laughed. When he drove off, she squealed in excitement and her arms tightened around his waist.

There wasn't as much to see at this time of year— mid-April was still too early for the corn to be planted but it was a clear spring day and the air was refreshingly cool against the skin. There were few things Bennett loved more than exploring the rolling terrain of his family's property and knowing that he was part of preserving it for future generations.

He rolled to a stop after about five minutes and turned off the engine. Katie climbed down carefully and looked around.

"It's just this way," Bennett said, gesturing ahead of where he'd parked.

Katie took his hand as they walked and he tried not to read too much into it. Maybe she just wanted help to keep her footing. As they walked, the earth under their feet changed and became rockier.

"Wow, this is beautiful." Katie shaded her eyes from the sun as she got her first glimpse of the river. "How did I not know this was here?"

"This river serves as an unofficial boundary between New Haven and the next county, West Haven. That land over there," he pointed to the other side of the river, "belongs to my father's brother."

Katie smiled. "So all of this is Alexander land? How cool."

"There's an interesting story behind it, too. Because there was a time when the land wasn't divided. But all of that changed with my grandparents' generation."

He walked back about fifty feet from the river's edge until they came to a tree. Bennett placed his hand on the trunk and traced his fingers over the initials carved into the bark. A heart with initials inside was clearly visible. His father came around periodically and kept it fresh.

Katie leaned closer to examine the mark. "MA + JB. Is that your parents?" Her eyes sparkled in wonder.

Bennett nodded. "This tree is called The Alexander Oak. It was planted on The Alexander homestead in the late eighteen hundreds. Our family was descended from freed slaves and the story goes that the first Alexanders in this county, John and Sarah, carved their initials into this tree to mark their territory. Every family that has lived here afterward has done the same. They fade over time of course but my father keeps his carving and the one his father did fresh by touching them up from time to time."

He stopped suddenly. "Sorry, you probably didn't want a mini-history lesson."

Katie touched his arm gently. "No, I love hearing about your ancestors. I've always been fascinated by history. By the idea that something we do can last for generations. Sometimes I wonder what my legacy will be or if I'll even have one. I don't feel like I'm contributing much to the world."

"Of course you are."

She rolled her eyes teasingly. "That's easy for you to say *Mr. Ten Patents*. Your name is being inscribed in history books even as we speak. You're making a real difference in the world, Bennett. Whereas I'm just trying to keep it together. Since my kid is drawing pictures at school of our fractured family, clearly I'm not doing such a great job."

Katie sat at the base of the tree and glanced around. Not wanting to push her, Bennett lowered himself to the ground next to her. There was something comforting about sitting here where so many of his ancestors had stood and worked to overcome obstacles far greater than any he'd ever see in his lifetime. It made him think that no matter what happened, if you had family, you could get through it.

Bennett looked over at Katie. His father had once told him that families aren't just born, they're created. He'd thought he understood at the time. After all no one was born married with children. But in that moment, he understood with greater clarity. No family was ever created without someone taking a chance. Someone reaching out and taking that leap, to love another with their whole heart.

"Katie, you are a great mother. I've seen you with your children and they are bright, curious and well-loved little boys. Your name will be remembered for generations to come by your children and their children. You don't realize how instrumental you are in their lives. Just like I'm telling the story of John and Sarah Alexander, your children will tell stories about their brave mother who traveled here from Barbados to a new life."

When she looked over at him, she wore her insecurity on her face like a mask. "You really think so? Because I feel like I'm trying to juggle so many things and failing at all of them."

Shock had Bennett sitting up straight. Katie thought she was failing at everything? He could understand she had concerns about her children, but how could she not know how much she'd helped him?

"How can you think you're failing at everything? Look at

how much you've helped me. I successfully participated in an inane conversation about the weather at the grocery store this morning. With a stranger!"

As he'd hoped, she laughed. "I hope you didn't have to interrupt anything important to come here today."

Bennett thought about the meeting he'd rescheduled with his architect. For the fourth time. He winced. It would be a miracle if the guy didn't quit.

"Nothing important."

Katie didn't look like she believed him but luckily she didn't call him out on it. "Thank you for talking me off the ledge. I just saw that picture that Hunter drew and it hit me really hard. He's never had any kind of problem in school before. I'd hate to think that all this stuff with the divorce is ruining his life."

Bennett reached over tentatively and took her hand. Her fingers flexed in his but she didn't pull back.

"I had some problems in school when I was his age. If I'm this awkward now, I'm sure you can imagine what I was like at seven. My parents were worried about me, too. That I wasn't fitting in and that I would struggle in life as a result. They had no idea what to do either so they just loved me harder and despite my issues, I'm doing all right. I have my doctorate. Plenty of money. Financial freedom. Hunter will be just fine, too. How could he not be with a mom who'd do anything for him?"

Katie leaned her head against his shoulder. He couldn't resist pressing a gentle kiss to her forehead. All at once, she sat up ramrod straight as if just suddenly realizing how intimate their position was.

Bennett cleared his throat. "So I should probably apologize for this weekend."

She glanced at him from the corner of her eye. "You should?"

"Well, probably. Although I have no idea what I'm apologizing for exactly. I had a great time and then an out of body experience in your bed afterward."

Katie made a choking sound.

"But I'm probably not supposed to talk about that either, I guess. So I'm sorry for whatever I did that made you uncomfortable. And I really hope you aren't going to quit."

She still hadn't said anything and Bennett was really starting to get nervous.

"And I also feel like I should point out that I warned you ahead of time that I was really bad at all of this dating stuff and was probably going to offend you," he added.

Katie finally turned to look at him directly. "You didn't offend me. You were amazing. And that scared the hell out of me."

Bennett knew he was bad at decoding all these flirting signals but he truly was lost if being amazing in bed led to getting kicked out the next morning. "So you asked me to leave because things were too ... good?"

"I handled that so badly. But I wasn't sure what to think. A guy like you probably wouldn't want to be with me long term. You're this super genius and you have those abs," she sighed. "It just hit me all at once that you were probably just having a fun, one-night stand and I was getting in too deep and probably going to be hurt."

"Katie, that wasn't a one-night stand. Not for me. I respect you. I admire you. The fact that I fantasize about your lips all the time doesn't negate those facts."

Her brow crinkled slightly before her head dropped to her hands. "Bennett Alexander. You have dirty fantasies about me?"

"On a constant basis. It's actually a good thing my lab coat is so long and covers everything."

She snickered and he joined in. Before she could think too hard about things and possibly come up with more reasons to be afraid of this, he figured he'd better state his case.

"I meant what I told your son on Saturday. Any man would be lucky to spend time with you. And that's all I'm asking for. I know you've been hurt before by an asshole who didn't deserve you. But I'm asking you to take a chance on me."

Katie scooted closer and rested her head on his shoulder. And said the sweetest word he'd ever heard.

"Okay."

fourteen

BENNETT SHIFTED the wrench he held from his left hand to his right and walked outside to get a breath of fresh air. His hands were sweating already inside the heavy work gloves he sported and his back was aching from bending over the broken tractor for so long but he barely even noticed. All of his attention was drawn back to the woman watching him from across the field.

"You think we need a new axle?"

The voice of Grady, one of the ranch hands who'd worked for his family the longest, came from behind him. Bennett didn't fool himself into thinking that the other man actually needed his opinion on what was wrong. Just looking at the machine, it was obvious what the problem was. However, a broken axle meant the machine was out of commission and that it would probably be cheaper to buy a new one. Since his mother was the one who approved new machinery purchases on the farm, it was likely Grady just didn't want the responsibility of telling Julia Alexander that they needed to spend around twenty grand on a new one.

"Unfortunately, I think we need a new tractor. Fuck."

Grady chuckled. "Don't let your mama hear you. You'll get both our mouths washed out with soap."

That made Bennett smile, too. It was one of his mother's favorite warnings when she heard foul language.

"That'll be the least of our worries when she finds out we need a new tractor already."

Grady winced. "Good point. Well, you seem to have this in hand. I'll let you handle it while I check the rest of the equipment."

If he hadn't been so agitated, Bennett would have laughed at the other man's obvious relief. His mother could never be called a tyrant (she was much too sweet for that). However, she had a stare that could make a grown man feel like he was about two feet tall. She was also very frugal. His grandfather used to say she'd squeeze a penny so tight it would squeal. Considering how economical his grandparents were, this was the highest compliment his grandpa could give.

And now he was the one who'd have to tell her they were officially over budget for equipment and they hadn't even gotten through planting season yet.

He sighed and wiped at his forehead absently before going back inside the barn. The temperature had soared over the last few days and it was even higher inside the old structure. The air was thick around him and Bennett had to concede that he'd spent way too much time inside lately. His body wasn't used to this much physical labor anymore.

Glancing around, he reached over his head and yanked his shirt off. He wrinkled his nose at the sight of the sweat stains on it. Taking the shirt off wasn't helping that much as far as temperature but at least he didn't have the clammy material clinging to his skin anymore. He turned his attention back to the machine in front of him and concentrated on removing the broken axle. It would likely cost a pretty penny to try to get it repaired, but it was worth a try.

Something made him look up just then and his eyes met Katie's again. The heat that overtook him was altogether foreign and unfamiliar. The past two weeks, by unspoken agreement, they'd decided to enjoy whatever this thing was developing between them.

He wasn't sure what to call it and she hadn't offered any suggestions for defining it either. Truthfully he was a little scared to push her for anything more than what she'd already granted. He knew it was a huge step for her to trust another man with her body and her heart but she'd managed to worm her way into every area of his life until he couldn't imagine her not being there.

The one thing she wouldn't budge on was spending the night. Bennett scowled as he yanked at the wrench, trying to pull the mangled axle away from the body of the machine. He channeled his frustration into the metal. He understood that she couldn't just blow off her responsibilities, he truly did. She had children and they were her first priority, rightly so. But there was definitely a part of him that wondered if it said something that she seemed to have no interest in putting him anywhere other than last on her list.

Something ugly and twisted sprang up in his mind as he remembered the horror show of dating in college. The girls who were more than happy to take advantage of his sexual prowess under cover of night but didn't want any of their friends to know they were together. Good enough to fuck but not enough to be seen in public.

Katie wasn't like that, though. She'd never acted like she was embarrassed by him and they'd been out in public plenty of times.

Not as a couple, though. That was a practice date and it wasn't like we were kissing in public. Be honest: how do you think she'd react if you tried that move?

Bennett flinched, the mental image of Katie recoiling from him in public so vivid that he dropped the wrench. On reflex, he tried to grab it before it fell into the body of the machine and his arm made contact with the ripped metal.

"Fuck!" His anguished shout carried throughout the barn but he was in too much pain to care. Blood streamed from the long gash on his arm and he took several deep breaths before carefully maneuvering his arm back out of the machine.

When he turned around, he stopped short. Katie stood right behind him.

"Bennett, what's wrong?" When her eyes landed on his bloody arm, she swayed slightly. "Oh my god, what happened?"

He grabbed his shirt from the ground and pressed it against the long gash, hoping the dirt on it wasn't going to give him an infection. "I need you to call someone for me. Take my phone out of my back pocket."

She did so, her fingers shaking slightly and then input the passcode he dictated for her. Bennett had hurt himself plenty of times around the farm; it was an inevitability when there were machines, and tons of work to do. However, he knew that Katie wasn't used to this sort of thing.

"Find the contact information for Grant."

She scrolled the list and when she found the right one, she glanced up at him. "Grant Alexander?"

He nodded. "Yeah, he's my cousin. I need you to tell him I got hurt and ask him to come."

She hit the contact and waited patiently as it rang. And rang. He could see the panic rising until she finally hung up.

"He's not answering. Let me take you to the emergency room."

Bennett froze. There was no way in hell. He hated hospitals. They were filled with everything he tended to avoid in one place: people, germs and lots of questions.

"No, I'm fine. It's just a scratch. We can just wait until Grant can come out. He's patched me up plenty of times before."

Katie swallowed and then motioned toward his arm. "Um, Bennett. That's way more than just a scratch."

He looked down at his arm. The shirt he was holding against the cut was soaked with bright red blood.

———

KATIE FOCUSED on the action at hand instead of the blood-soaked fabric on the table. It had gotten her through plenty of unpleasant situations before.

Hold steady.

Wrap the gauze.

Tuck the ends under.

She followed Bennett's soft verbal instructions until his entire arm looked like it had been mummified. It made him look even worse which was hard to do after he'd almost keeled over at the sight of his bloody arm.

Damn men and their egos. Even after almost face planting into the ground, he'd still been dead set against going to the hospital. He'd just started walking toward his lab and she'd had no choice but to follow. She didn't want to push too hard. For all she knew he'd had some traumatic experience in the hospital as a child, but if they hadn't been able to get the bleeding under control she was prepared to take drastic measures such as knocking him out and dragging him to the hospital against his will. Or doing the one thing he'd begged her not to do.

Tell his mother.

"See now it's fine. It'll probably be scabbed over by the time Grant even gets here."

Katie rolled her eyes. After calling several times, she'd finally gotten the elusive Grant on the phone and his annoyed voice had changed immediately when he heard Bennett was hurt. She was glad someone seemed to be taking this seriously. Her eyes slid over to Bennett sitting up at the stainless steel worktable, looking for all the world like he was actually impatient that he couldn't immediately go back to work.

"Does it hurt a lot?"

He shrugged. "It's not as bad as the time I fell out of the old hayloft. I fractured my arm that time."

Katie shook her head. "You'd think I'd be used to this by now after having two boys. But you just scared the hell out of me."

That got his attention. "I'm sorry I scared you."

Although she'd wanted his attention, it was more than a little overwhelming now that she had it. The past few weeks she'd tried to do the modern, casual thing and just live in the moment. But every day that got harder and harder. How did you pretend that you weren't getting attached to someone? There were times when he'd look over at her in the lab and the next moment, they were wrapped around each other. They could go from screwing each other's brains out to working in complete silence easily. Well, it was easy for Bennett anyway. She'd observed the way he worked and he was a master at compartmentalizing. Katie couldn't do that though. She didn't know how to love him just a little or only at the appropriate times.

She feared that she was quickly becoming addicted to him and these stolen moments in the middle of the day weren't going to be enough.

"Knock, knock," a deep voice called out.

Katie jumped at the unfamiliar voice but Bennett just raised his uninjured arm in a half-hearted greeting.

"Hey Grant."

His voice sounded slightly slurred and Katie suspected the effort of fighting off the pain was taking its toll. Not to mention the strain of appearing calm so he didn't freak her out. Damn it, she couldn't help that she got a little frantic at the sight of blood! Wasn't that some sort of biological emergency instinct? You were supposed to freak out at the sight of blood.

"What's this I hear about my cousin almost losing an arm?"

Bennett looked at Katie. "This is my cousin, Grant. Grant, this is Katherine Mason. Mrs. Katherine Mason."

Katie furrowed her brow. Katherine? He'd never called her that before. Why was Bennett suddenly acting so formal?

She held out her hand in greeting. "Hi, Dr. Alexander. I'm Bennett's assistant, Katie."

Grant was tall with honey colored skin and curly dark hair. He also looked a little like Bennett except his eyes were as dark as his hair. Then he smiled and Katie could have sworn she heard angels singing in the heavens above.

"*Jesus.* Aren't there any ugly Alexanders?"

At Grant's snort of laughter and Bennett's scowl, Katie realized what she'd just said. "Oh god, I'm sorry. That was rude."

Grant set a black bag on the stool next to Bennett. "You're fine. And yes, there are definitely a few of us who got the short end of the stick aesthetically. Poor Bennett here must not have been around the day the gods were giving out looks."

Katie's mouth fell open at the mean comment. What the hell was this guy's problem? Then she saw that both of the guys were chuckling and figured it must be an old joke between the two of them.

"I mean, really. Ole' green eyes here is a hideous sight."

"My eyes are hazel," Bennett interrupted.

Grant held out his hands in surrender. "My apologies." Then he turned back to Katie. "As I was saying, Hazel-eyes here has always been the ugly duckling. I don't know how Aunt Julia does it. This is truly a face that only a mother could love."

Katie crossed her arms. "Okay I'm not getting in the middle of whatever this is," she said, gesturing between the two of them.

"You sure?" Grant's brown eyes held a naughty twinkle. "Because according to my ex-girlfriend, being between two Alexanders is a common fantasy around these parts."

Embarrassment made her stutter. "You don't ... I can't even talk to you right now."

"Leave her alone, Grant." Bennett looked murderous and like he was a second away from slugging his cousin, hurt arm be damned.

Grant had been busy unraveling the gauze covering Bennett's arm and when he finally got all the layers off, the sight of the ragged bloody skin had him hissing in dismay.

"Hmm. This doesn't look good. Are you sure you don't want to go–"

"Just stitch me up, Grant."

Katie put a hand against her stomach. The gash looked even worse on second glance. "I have to go. The kids will be home soon."

Bennett nodded. "Of course. Sorry to keep you late."

She hesitated but before she thought it through, she leaned over and kissed him lightly on the cheek. "Listen to what the doctor tells you. Even if he is kind of a jerk."

Then she left before she couldn't get the strength to do it.

———

AFTER THE DOOR shut behind Katie, there was complete silence. Bennett figured it probably wasn't a good idea to rip into the guy who was about to shove a needle through your skin so he mentally recited the periodic table. Then he made the mistake of looking up and into his cousin's smug face.

"If my arm wasn't throbbing like a bitch right now you'd be missing some teeth."

Grant continued setting out his supplies on the sterile pad he'd unfolded on the table. He didn't say anything just raised one elegant eyebrow. Somehow that damn eyebrow just ticked Bennett off even more.

"And what the hell was that 'every woman fantasizes about being between two guys' thing? Do you even hear yourself sometimes?"

Grant shrugged and the fact that he couldn't be bothered to defend himself only made it worse. Bennett could feel himself getting more and more worked up and it annoyed him that his cousin could get under his skin so easily. Especially since he knew that annoying people was the reason Grant acted the way he did. He'd always been a troublemaker, even when they were kids.

"You don't have to try to seduce every woman you come across, you know?" Bennett huffed, finally running out of steam.

"Now where's the fun in that?" Grant drawled, right before he injected Bennett with something.

"Oh shit."

All his anger drained out at the sharp prick. Luckily the sharp pain was followed by a blissful numbness. He let out a sigh of relief.

He hadn't been lying to Katie when he told her that he'd had worse. But having your arm throbbing angrily for an hour wasn't an experience he was keen to repeat any time soon.

"You enjoy torturing people. That's the real reason you went to med school. Don't pretend. You can't fool me."

"Oh no. You've found me out," Grant deadpanned.

Bennett looked in the other direction but he could still see the up and down motion of his cousin's arm as he stitched the wound, along with feeling the slight tug and pull on the numbed area.

"You're going to need help for a few days. It's better if you don't move this arm too much in the beginning or you'll pull the stitches out. This is a bad cut. You really should have gone to the hospital right away."

Bennett ignored his cousin's stern stare. "Your serious doctor face doesn't work on me. I've seen you pee on yourself, remember."

Grant grunted. "Treating family is the fucking worst. I'm

serious, Ben. I know you wanted to look tough for your girl-friend but the next time you open a vein on a piece of rusty metal, get your ass to the hospital."

Too shocked to even address his cousin's bossy directive, Bennett just shook his head. "I wasn't trying to be tough for Katie. You know I hate hospitals."

"I know that. But even you usually aren't this stubborn about it. Plus, you're in control now. It's not like when you were little and having all those tests."

Bennett grunted. As a child, he was non-verbal for quite a while which of course had concerned his parents. He'd been subjected to so many different medical tests and had blood drawn so many times that just the sight of a hospital made him nervous, even now. It hadn't even been worth it. After all those tests, the doctors never found anything abnormal. He was just different.

Grant tied off the last stitch and swabbed the stitches with something wet and cold. "I don't blame you for wanting to stab my eyes out earlier. She's beautiful and obviously cares about you. I'd be jealous if my better looking cousin was hitting on my girl, too."

Bennett scowled. "I wasn't jealous. And you *wish* you were better looking."

Grant grinned. "You would have punched me if your arm wasn't all fucked up." When Bennett still didn't concede, he continued. "So, it wouldn't bother you if I asked her out? Since you two aren't anything serious?"

Bennett gritted his teeth. "Stay away from her. She's not your type. She's too smart for your bullshit."

Grant smiled knowingly. "Okay. I'll leave it alone for now.

But I hope you're at least going to use this turn of events productively."

He wasn't going to ask. He was not going to ask his man whore cousin for advice.

"What do you mean productively?" his lips asked against his will.

Grant waggled his eyebrows and then sauntered into the kitchen to wash his hands. Bennett had to wait not so patiently for him to finish. When he came back, Grant picked up his bag of supplies and patted Bennett on the shoulder.

"Milk this injury for all its worth, my man. If you play your cards right, your pretty girlfriend will come back and take care of you."

fifteen

WHEN KATIE FIRST GOT HOME, she didn't notice anything unusual. She dropped her bag on the floor in the entryway and then put her keys on the small hook next to the coat rack. It was almost time for the kids to get home and she was relieved she'd managed to get there before the bus. She didn't like cutting it this close but it had been so hard to leave without knowing if Bennett was okay.

She snorted thinking of Bennett and his cousin Grant. He might be a bit of a jerk but at least he seemed to know what he was doing. Katie shuddered thinking of the cut on Bennett's arm. Actually, they'd both been freakishly calm about it. Clearly this wasn't the first time something like this had happened.

Well, at least she'd been confident that Grant had things under control. Bennett didn't joke around with just anyone so it was obvious the two were fond of each other, in the slightly antagonistic way that a lot of men were.

As she slipped her shoes off, there was a loud clanking sound from the kitchen. Katie's head shot up at the unexpected sound in what should have been an empty house. A soft rustling a moment later was followed by the sound of ... voices? Her mouth fell open. There was someone in her house!

Holy shit, had someone broken in while she was at work?

She backed up slowly. It was strange that they hadn't heard her come in, she hadn't exactly been quiet, but whatever the case she wasn't going to wait around for them to discover her. She grabbed her keys again. She'd drive down the street and then call the police from a safe distance.

Before she could get to the front door, there was a sound right behind her and a dark shadow moved at the corner of her eye. Instinctively she grabbed the small bowl off the front table and held it out like a weapon.

"Whoa, calm down! It's just me."

Once her heart left her throat, she realized it was Don. He glanced worriedly at the bowl in her hand so she lowered it. Slightly. Then raised it again when she noticed that he was standing in the hallway wearing nothing but his underwear.

"What are you doing here?"

The danger past, Don shrugged and then walked back toward the kitchen. Annoyed, Katie had no choice but to follow. Then she was annoyed all over again when he went back to the island and the sandwich he'd been making.

He was eating her food?

She pressed her fingers to her temples. "What are you doing here?"

"I came to see the kids. It's my weekend." He took a bite of his sandwich, like it was completely normal that he was standing in *her* kitchen, eating *her* food, while wearing nothing more than a pair of raggedy boxers.

"I know it's your weekend. That still doesn't explain why you're standing in my kitchen in your underwear."

He looked at her like she was stupid. "I spilled mustard on my clothes at lunch. I put my clothes in the washing machine earlier." His eyes narrowed and then focused on her.

When they'd been married, he'd gotten used to seeing her in nothing but jeans and T-shirts, casual clothing appropriate for wiping noses and playing outside. Now that she worked for Bennett, she tried to step it up a little. Not that he'd asked her to do that but she wanted to. It was nice to feel professional and in control.

"Where were you?"

Katie rolled her eyes. "Out. Not that it concerns you."

His face darkened. "Let me guess, over at Ridley's house. You're still chummy with them, I see."

"They've been very good to me. But no, that's not where I was."

"So why are you all dressed up?" he asked snidely.

Katie rolled her eyes. "I have a job."

His jaw worked as he tried to formulate an answer. "I heard you've been working for one of them. The weird one that still lives at home with his parents." He chuckled. "I guess you figured if Ridley could marry up, why not you, huh?"

She crossed her arms. "What do you want, Don? Really?"

"Nothing. Just making sure my kids are still being taken care of properly. All I'm hearing is how much time you're spending cozying up to the Alexanders and it makes me wonder who's taking care of my boys."

In that moment, Katie learned that it was possible for your blood to literally boil. She wouldn't have been surprised to look in the mirror and see steam coming out of her ears.

"How *dare* you insinuate that I would ever neglect my children? I've done nothing but take care of them every day since they were born. Which is more than you can say. If you hadn't stopped paying child support I wouldn't have to work so much to afford to take care of them, did you think of that?"

He opened his mouth to say something but Katie was too livid to even listen. She marched into the laundry room and opened the door to the still running dryer. She knelt and grabbed his damp clothes from the machine. His shoes were sitting on top of the washing machine, so she grabbed those, too. When she came back into the kitchen, she threw his clothes at him.

"Get your crap and get out. You told me when you left that you had better things to do, so go back to your barely legal girlfriend and stay out of my business."

When he didn't move, she threw one of his shoes at his head. He apparently hadn't been expecting that because he didn't even try to duck. The shoe struck him square in the middle of the forehead. He dropped his sandwich.

"Ow! Shit! What the hell is wrong with you?"

"What's wrong with *me*?" Katie held the other shoe over her head.

That seemed to communicate her sincerity because Don grabbed the pants she'd thrown at him and hurriedly stepped into them.

"You can get dressed outside. I'm not on your timetable anymore."

He stared at her in disbelief but rushed to grab the rest of his clothes while backing out of the kitchen.

"I don't know what the hell is going on with you. I'm just trying to see the kids."

"That's fine. I've never tried to keep you away from them. But you won't just show up whenever you feel like it and let yourself in."

Katie followed him out of the kitchen and watched as he hurriedly redressed. By the time he finished, his shirt was on backward and he was only wearing one shoe.

"So what am I supposed to do?" he whined.

"You need to show up on time and ring the doorbell. Not early. *On time*. And if I'm not here, you can wait in your car. Things are different now. Get used to it."

He stepped out onto the front porch. When he turned around, he opened his mouth, probably to make some sort of smartass comment. Katie threw the shoe she was still holding out the door after him and then slammed it shut.

A half an hour later, after a whirlwind of packing clothes for the weekend and making sure that Hunter had his favorite pillow this time, Katie watched from the window as the kids drove off with Don. It was always hard to see them go, even though she really wanted them to have time with their father.

No matter how bad things were between her and Don, he was still their dad. She thought back to how much she'd missed her own father after his death. She'd never want to take their father away from them. But it didn't make it any easier to watch them leave.

Especially since now that she was faced with the prospect of a long weekend without the kids, there was nothing to distract her from her earlier thoughts about Bennett.

What the hell were they doing?

Katie picked up her phone. Should she call him? Seeing him covered in blood had jarred her today. But they didn't have that kind of relationship. They had fun together and he did things to her with his tongue that were practically inhuman but was that all it was? He seemed happy with the way things were and she wasn't sure how she felt. Did she really want to get in deeper with another man after being hurt so badly?

What you have with Bennett is a dream. A handsome man that rocks your world and doesn't expect you to pick up his dirty laundry. What more do you want?

Katie thought of Bennett alone in his loft, trying to maneuver alone with a bandaged arm. Before she could talk herself out of it, she quickly typed out a text to him.

Katie: Are you okay? Do you need anything?

Bennett: I'm okay.

Nothing else. Katie sighed. Bennett wasn't great at volunteering information. That just wasn't how his mind worked. If she wanted to know more, then it would be because she was brave enough to put herself out there first.

Katie: I wish I was there.

Bennett: I wish you were here, too.

She smiled. Bennett wasn't one to volunteer information but when asked directly, he always told the truth. Just that easily, she knew what she needed to do.

Thirty minutes later, she parked behind Bennett's pickup truck and grabbed her overnight bag off the passenger seat. The door to the laboratory wasn't locked, so she let herself in, making sure to lock it behind her so she wouldn't have to come back down.

If he lets you stay.

Katie ignored the negative voice ringing in the back of her mind that reminded her that she was taking a very big chance. It was entirely possible that Bennett liked their relationship or arrangement or whatever you wanted to call it, the way it was. Maybe he liked having hot sex during the day without the chore of having to make conversation at night.

But there was a bigger part of her that remembered the way he'd looked at her that afternoon. He didn't seem as though he found spending time with her a chore. Maybe, just maybe, he cherished their time together the same way she did.

"Bennett? Are you here?"

All at once it hit her how silly it was that she'd come over without warning him first. What if he wasn't even here? Maybe he'd gone to stay with his parents so Julia could take care of him. He had a great family that lived on the same property, so that was hardly out of the question. Just when she was about to turn and leave, Bennett appeared at the railing that separated the loft.

"Katie? You came back."

She shuffled her feet. "Yeah, I thought you might need some help tonight. And also, I just ... missed you."

He stared at her for a long moment and then he smiled. And just like that Katie Mason lost what was left of her heart.

————

BENNETT THOUGHT he was hallucinating when he first heard Katie's voice. He'd just gotten back into bed after taking a shower. The effort of trying to wash while holding his bandaged arm out of the water had exhausted him but once in bed, he'd just stared at the ceiling dispiritedly.

He was used to being alone. Save holidays and other family functions, he spent the majority of his time on his own. So why did the loft suddenly seem so quiet? Just when he'd been contemplating turning on the television, something he rarely did, he heard the voice he'd been longing for floating up from the lab below.

Now he stood at the railing watching as Katie ascended the stairs. They'd made good use of the fact that his bed was up here over the past few weeks but it was entirely different having her here at night.

"Hi." Katie set her bag down on the floor at the foot of the bed and shrugged out of her jacket. She folded it over her arm awkwardly. Her eyes roamed over his bare chest and the loose pair of plaid pajama pants he wore. "Didn't think you'd be a pajama pants only kind of guy."

The observation amused Bennett. "I'm not. But having your mom walk in on you when you're buck naked will convince almost anyone of the merits of wearing pants to bed."

She covered her mouth with her hand but it couldn't hide her smile. "Traumatized for life, huh?"

"Pretty much."

She twisted the edge of her shirt in her hands. "So, I probably should have called first."

Bennett sat on the edge of the bed, the burst of energy he'd gotten when he first heard her voice now lagging. Katie took one look at his face and then rushed to his side.

"You're not okay, are you?" She clucked softly under her breath and then gently pushed him to recline.

He allowed her to fuss over him, enjoying the scolding more than he would have thought possible. Mainly he enjoyed watching her, the curve of her lips as she smiled down at him, the exasperated look on her face when she saw the bottom of his bandage was wet. Just her. He wished he could bottle this moment because despite being exhausted and in pain, he never wanted to forget what it felt like to be the one Katie took care of.

"Why are you looking at me like that?" she asked, tucking the sheets around his body.

"Like what?" He could hear that his voice was slurring slightly and wished he hadn't given in and taken one of the pain pills Grant had left with him.

He usually never took any kind of pain medication because he hated how groggy they made him feel, but Grant had insisted on leaving a few samples in case he changed his mind. He'd given in to the temptation after the torture of holding his arm out of the shower.

"You're staring," Katie clarified, before tucking a stray curl behind her ear.

"I'm just watching you. I like having you here."

Katie stilled and her eyes met his. "Really? I felt a little pushy coming over without asking first but ... I was worried about you."

She seemed embarrassed by the admission and immediately went to the end of the bed to rummage in her overnight bag. He watched as she pulled out a pile of clothes and a small toiletry bag.

"Okay, I'm going to get ready for bed. Do you need anything right now? Medication? Water?"

He shook his head and she went into the bathroom and closed the door behind her.

Bennett dozed in and out while listening to the sounds of water running and the soft hum of Katie's voice as she talked to herself. He smiled. He was willing to bet she had no idea she did that but it was incredibly endearing. Comforting also. It was a strange feeling to be so content while resting in bed listening to the sound of her talking to herself.

Then it hit him why he was so happy despite being hurt. Over the years, he had always been on the outside looking in. With his family, with his classmates, just everywhere. All around he watched people pairing off into happy couples and never thought he could be a part of something like that. He'd never met anyone that made him feel like he could be a part of a unit.

But here, resting quietly and listening to Katie's off-key rendition of some random Christmas song, he felt like he belonged. He might not be able to read in-between the lines or take a hint, but with Katie he didn't have to. She was the only woman he'd ever met who didn't play games or expect him to read her mind. She was honest and open and entirely genuine.

And he was incredibly happy she was there.

When she emerged from the bathroom, she was wearing a long nightshirt. Her skin was scrubbed clean and she had her hair pulled back into a ponytail. She made her way around the bed and got in on the other side. Earlier she'd set her tablet on the nightstand on that side and she picked it up before arranging the covers over her legs.

"Do you mind if I read for a little while? Will the light keep you up?" she asked.

He shook his head. "I'm a pretty sound sleeper but I'm not ready to go to sleep anyway. Would you ... would you read some to me?"

Her eyes betrayed her surprise before a soft smile touched her lips. "It's probably not your genre. It's a romantic suspense."

He moved closer and rested his head on her shoulder,

keeping his hurt arm propped up on a pillow. "I don't care. I just want to hear your voice. Just the sound of it makes me feel like all is right in the world. Hearing that when you come to work every morning is the highlight of my day."

Katie's fingers tightened around the edge of the tablet. "One minute I think we're just dating and having fun, but then you say stuff like that. Bennett, what are we doing here?"

He tilted his head and kissed her bare shoulder. "I don't know what you're doing but I'm pretty sure I'm falling in love."

Katie's gasped softly and her dark eyes searched his. He wasn't sure what she was looking for but he hoped she could see his sincerity.

"You are? But it's so soon. We've only been on one date."

"And I knew before we left your driveway."

Her eyes welled slightly before she gave her head a slight shake. In the blink of an eye an entire conversation passed between them. Bennett liked that he knew her well enough now that he could intuit what she was thinking. But if she thought he was going to let her go another minute without telling her how he felt, well she hadn't been paying attention. He may not be socially adept but he'd never been accused of lacking initiative. When he wanted something, he went after it.

And he wanted Katie. Every sweet, no-nonsense, bubbly bit of her. From the moment she'd entered his life, he'd experienced what it was like to feel not only accepted but appreciated. She made him feel that all of the odd things about him were fascinating and special. Being around her made him stand just a little bit taller and it wasn't an exaggeration to say that Bennett suspected he was getting addicted to the way she made him feel.

He'd drink her up like champagne if she let him.

"The things you say sometimes. You're so unbelievably sweet, Bennett."

Although it was a compliment, Bennett found that he didn't want them from Katie. Those were the kinds of words you said to someone when you didn't feel the same way but didn't want to hurt their feelings. He didn't want platitudes. Hell, he'd rather her hate him than to think of him as just a *sweet* guy. At least hatred was a strong emotion. He wanted to invoke that kind of emotion in her. He wanted to affect her in the same way that she affected him. Overwhelmingly.

"I'm not sweet," he grumbled.

Katie's laughter soothed some of his wounded pride. She was happy and that was really all that mattered. Even if the time they'd spent together didn't mean as much to her as it had to him, as long as he could see a smile on her face, Bennett would count it as a success.

"Yes, you are. You're such a contradiction. Brilliant but unsure. Serious but funny. Composed but so ... lovable."

When her words registered, Bennett peeked up at her. "Lovable?"

"Very lovable," she whispered. "Just today, I was worried that I was getting too attached to you because it seemed so foolish to fall for someone else after being hurt so badly."

Bennett held her eyes as he spoke. "Katie? Do me a favor."

"What's that?"

With his good arm, he curled his hand around her neck, bringing her mouth closer. His lips brushed against hers when he spoke.

"Be a little foolish tonight."

———

KATIE STILLED, her lips pressed to Bennett's. Was he … trying to start something?

"I'm not sure about this. Aren't you hurting?"

He smiled, his lips moving against hers. "I already feel better."

She laughed at his blatant lie. "I think you might be a little high on those pain pills."

He buried his face in the crook of her neck. The tender gesture made her smile. He was so sweet sometimes and it was a thrill to discover all the hidden facets of his personality. He even had a tattoo on his lower back, something she'd only noticed because they'd showered together the other day. When she'd asked about it, he'd just shrugged and said he'd gotten it in college. But he'd looked so smug that she *knew* there was more to the story.

She leaned back. "So, if you're a little drugged up, now will you tell me about your tattoo?"

"It's the chemical formula for my first soil additive." There was an element of pride in his voice.

All at once Katie understood. "You love it because you managed to get the formula right even while you were three sheets to the wind, huh?"

"Yeah." His deep chuckle vibrated against her skin.

"You're just full of surprises, aren't you?"

Bennett leaned back slightly. "My parents still don't know I have a tattoo, if you can believe it. Although considering how many Jackson has, I doubt they'd even care at this point."

She kissed his forehead gently. "No matter how old we get, we still want our parents' approval. My mom is still disappointed that I'm divorced."

His eyes stayed on hers. "She should be proud that she raised such an amazing daughter. The time I've spent with you...you've made me so happy."

Katie was stunned at the heartfelt words. He'd told her how much he appreciated her help around the lab before. He'd even told her that he enjoyed their time together. But there was something about the way he was looking at her right now that made Katie feel cherished.

"You've made me really happy, too."

He pulled her down again but this time there was no smile on his face. His expression was completely serious and when their lips met, desire exploded between them. Careful not to jar his arm, Katie kissed him back, pouring all the love, trust and hope she felt into that one embrace.

He groaned and then shifted slightly. "Sorry, this angle is bad."

She carefully climbed on top of him avoiding his bandaged arm. Bennett watched her from beneath hooded eyes. The way he looked at her sent a sensual thrill through her blood. He watched her like he could never get enough of her.

"The way you look at me is magic. No one has ever made me feel like this before. Like I'm perfect."

Bennett squeezed her thigh with his good hand. "That's because you are. To me, you are nothing short of perfect."

Emboldened by the words, Katie pulled her nightgown over her head and let it drift to the floor beside the bed. It was amazing how much easier it was to take your clothes off when you had a man who looked at you like a goddess.

With a little creative maneuvering, they were able to slide Bennett's pajama pants off. Luckily they'd already had the birth control conversation and since Katie was on the pill, he wouldn't have to deal with trying to put on a condom with one hand. Although that would have been an interesting sight, Katie thought.

"I'm still not sure I should be doing this. I feel like I'm taking advantage of you instead of nursing you back to health."

Bennett's gaze trailed over her nude body, coming back to rest on her full breasts. "*Please* take advantage of me." His words trailed off on a groan when she grasped his hard length firmly.

She raised up so she could take him inside. Bennett groaned long and low as her muscles squeezed and massaged him all the way down.

"That's the best medicine in the world right there. You were made for me, Katie."

He lifted his hips and she cried out. His eyes glittered with triumph before he did it again. She caught his rhythm and soon, they were rocking against each other in rolling waves of pleasure and Katie thought she'd die from it.

His hand clenched on her hip. "I love you, Katie. I know you think it's too soon but I need you to know how I feel."

His eyes searched hers and Katie couldn't deny him. Despite knowing that it *was* too soon and that this whole thing was probably crazy, she could never deny him anything. So she gave him the words.

"I love you, too."

LATE MONDAY AFTERNOON, Katie went about her work watering the soil samples all while trying to keep the huge, cheesy grin off her face. She glanced over her shoulder at Bennett, who was nose deep in his tablet. When he looked up and caught her eyes, he smiled. A private, intimate smile that made her blush from her head to her toes.

Oh, the things that man could make her feel.

This weekend had been perfect. After making love Friday night, they'd fallen into an exhausted sleep. She'd fussed over him the next morning, making breakfast they could share in bed. Then they'd wasted the day away watching Netflix and cuddling. Bennett was a fan of British comedies and Katie loved murder mysteries so they'd alternated shows. It had been fun to see what kind of television he enjoyed. That night, Katie read to him until he fell asleep with his head pillowed in her lap.

Katie sighed. She'd looked down at him in that moment and wished that could be her real life. Going to sleep with him each night, sharing their stories about what happened when they weren't together, venting when they had a bad day. It had been hard to go home on Sunday, even though she'd missed her boys. He said he loved her and she believed he meant it. But Bennett didn't have a lot of experience with how fickle and strange love could be. It burned so bright in the beginning and if you'd never been that close to the flame before, you couldn't imagine that it would ever go out. But Katie knew from experience that no flame could burn forever.

Eventually, their intense passion would cool and all the things he found cute about her now would become annoyances. He didn't mind the differences in their education when things were shiny and new but what would happen a year from now? Would he get frustrated if she couldn't understand his new research or if he couldn't get her input on some scientific break-through? There was no way to know for sure but Bennett seemed determined that it wouldn't matter.

She was surely going to get her heart broken but she couldn't help loving him back.

The rest of the day sped by until it was time for her to go pick up the kids. The butterflies she'd been ignoring all after-noon flared brightly. They'd decided that it was time for Bennett to spend a little time with them so she was going to pick them up and bring them back here for the rest of the after-noon. Katie was unreasonably nervous about it.

"So you're going to go get them and then come right back?" Bennett looked just as nervous as she felt.

"Yes. Grady mentioned that one of the barn cats had kittens so I figured we could show them."

Bennett nodded. "Also when my mother heard the kids were coming over, she said she would bring us dinner." He smiled sheepishly. "I think she's afraid that I was going to attempt to cook for you."

Katie tried to suppress a smile. As talented as Bennett was at keeping chemical formulations in his mind, he couldn't seem to focus on a recipe long enough not to burn everything he tried to make. She'd seen that for herself this weekend when he tried to "help" her make breakfast. It was actually kind of reassuring to see that he wasn't great at everything he attempted.

"That was really nice of her. She's always been so sweet to us."

"You know my mother is going to start dropping the marriage hints pretty heavily now that she knows we're seeing each other. You should prepare yourself."

Bennett turned back to his work as if he hadn't just dropped a huge conversational bomb on her. Marriage talk? What?

Katie put a hand to her throat. She seriously doubted if Julia was enthused that Bennett was dating a divorcée who already had two kids, let alone with the idea of marriage.

"I doubt we need to worry about that," she muttered. "I didn't even know you told her that we were dating. I figured she was just being nice since I'm an employee."

Bennett looked up from his work. "Are you kidding? This is the happiest my mom has been with me in ages. She's practically salivating at the idea of gaining two new grandkids at once."

Longing rose up in Katie so swiftly she almost choked on it. What was it like to be a part of a family that accepted you so completely that they'd welcome two new step-grandkids with the same excitement as their own flesh and blood?

Don's parents were nice enough but distant. It was something that Don had complained about when they were first married. His father was a surgeon also and he'd always said he wanted to be a more present father than his own had been. She'd truly thought he would be but after the divorce, the time between his calls and visits to the kids got longer and longer. She hated having to see their disappointment every time he didn't show up for something at school or forgot to visit.

Not that she would tell Bennett any of that. If their relationship was going to have a chance, his interest in the kids would have to develop naturally. She didn't want him to feel obligated to spend time with them before he was ready just because they were so hungry for a male role model.

"Your family is the best," she said finally. "Well, I'll be back."

Katie didn't look at him again as she grabbed her purse and jacket and left. The whole way home she thought about what he'd said. He hadn't seemed at all alarmed at the idea of Julia's marriage agenda. She smiled softly.

No, you aren't going there!

She mentally shut down all thoughts of getting married again. Likely Bennett wasn't worried about his mother's agenda because he knew it wasn't going to happen. There was nothing to be gained from allowing her imagination to go wild with thoughts of being Mrs. Alexander. She pulled into her driveway and waited until the school bus pulled up on the corner. Hunter and Matthew were the first ones off the bus. They raced down the sidewalk to her car.

"Mom! Are we going to see the kittens now?" Hunter was almost vibrating with excitement.

Matthew looked back and forth between them in confusion. Katie hadn't told him about the kittens that morning. If she had, he wouldn't have paid attention all day in school.

"Yes, we're going to the Alexanders' right now. Come on."

They piled into the car excitedly, Matthew wiggling as she hooked him into his booster seat. When they pulled up in front of Bennett's barn, Hunter put his face right to the window.

"Why are we back here? Isn't Ms. Julia waiting for us?"

Katie twisted her hands but kept her voice upbeat as she said, "We're not here to see Ms. Julia this time. Do you remember my friend, Bennett?"

Hunter nodded slowly. "Yeah. He's really tall."

"Well, we're here to hang out with him today. And he's going to take us to see the kittens, okay?"

Hunter watched her with strangely knowing eyes before he nodded. Matthew didn't seem to pick up on any of the strange undercurrents thankfully. They walked up to the barn where Bennett was waiting in the doorway. He must have heard the car pull up.

"Hi guys. Are you ready to have some fun?"

Matthew was so excited he couldn't hold still and started dancing in place. Bennett laughed and motioned for them to follow him.

"This way. Grady has picked a few of the more social ones for you to play with."

Hunter trailed behind as they all walked toward the barn directly behind Bennett's. Katie watched him worriedly. Unlike his brother, Hunter seemed to have picked up on the fact that this visit was more about spending time with Bennett than the kittens.

And he didn't seem too happy about it.

"Ooh look! They're so little!" Matthew raced ahead with his arms outstretched.

"Let's be very gentle, okay?" Bennett scooped up Matthew easily and then placed him right next to the table where Grady was waiting with a basket. Once they were closer, Katie could see three kittens, two tabbies and one black, inside.

Katie's heart melted a little when she saw how Matthew clung to Bennett. Hunter still hung back, peeking around her to see but not approaching the table directly.

"These little guys are about six weeks old, too young to go to new homes yet. But soon, we'll find new families for them."

Matthew stretched out a hand when Bennett placed a kitten right in front of him. Katie moved to the other side of the table, giving Grady a smile. He was slightly less grumpy now that he'd gotten used to seeing her around the farm but he still wasn't overly warm. But he chuckled at Matthew's shriek of delight when the kitten licked his fingers.

"This one is going to stay with me," Grady said gruffly. "Black cats are a little hard to place. And he's a playful one. He'll be a good barn cat."

Hunter finally moved around Katie and approached the table. "How come they're different colors?"

Bennett picked up one of the tabbies. "Well, their mom has white fur with brown spots and we suspect their father is a black cat from the next farm over. There were two other kittens in this litter that are with the mom right now. Both of those have the same fur as the momma cat."

Hunter moved closer and closer as Bennett talked, until he was leaning on his arm. "They're so small. What if you can't find a home for them?"

Bennett continued petting the kitten in his hand, holding it out so that Hunter could touch it. His voice was soft and soothing as he continued. "Grady is the one who brought us the momma cat when he found her and she's been a barn cat here ever since. She's had one litter before and we found them all homes really fast. Don't worry."

Hunter glanced up at Bennett, his eyes sparking with interest. "You have a cat that lives in your barn? Cool."

Bennett chuckled. "Well, I don't have one in my barn but Miss Pepper lives in the barn where we store the hay. Grady says she does a great job keeping the rats under control."

Katie chuckled at Hunter's startled face. "I think he was on board until the rats part."

Bennett grinned. "I guess a tour of that barn is not on the agenda then, huh?"

Grady had some soft fuzzy toys that he produced so the boys could watch the kittens play. While they were occupied, Bennett turned to her with a smug expression.

"What?" she finally asked.

"Nothing. Just that things are going well. And you were nervous."

She laughed. "I was, a little bit. But I shouldn't have been. You're great with them, really patient."

"Having three annoying younger brothers has finally paid off."

Katie smiled since his statement was obviously teasing. It was obvious to anyone that the Alexander brothers were a tight bunch. He pulled her into his arms and she wrapped her arms around his waist.

When she pulled back she noticed Hunter watching them closely. He hadn't exactly been bowled over by the idea of her dating, she could tell. Maybe she should say something to him.

But Bennett took the decision out of her hands when he suddenly announced, "Dinnertime. Let's go eat!"

WATCHING Katie with her children warmed his heart. The warmth stayed with him even as they herded the boys to his loft to eat the dinner his mom had brought over. The boys scarfed down the fried chicken and mashed potatoes like they'd never had food before.

Afterward, he showed the kids some of the soil samples their mom helped to care for and gave them a tour. They thought sleeping in a loft was the coolest thing ever. Normally it would have felt strange to have people in his private space but Bennett found he didn't mind this time.

His cold lab had never felt more like home.

While Katie was showing Matthew the soil samples that contained the worms, Bennett noticed Hunter getting closer and closer. Quiet and introspective, the little boy had been the hardest of the two children to win over but also the one who reminded Bennett the most of himself.

"So you live here all by yourself?" Hunter asked.

Bennett looked around. He guessed from a child's perspective, it was a strange place to live. There were no couches or comfortable furniture. The only television was the one upstairs in the loft. It probably looked awful to a kid.

"I do. I've lived here for almost ten years now."

Hunter's eyes rounded. "Whoa. That's a long time."

Bennett chuckled. Ten years to a child probably sounded like forever. Just then there was a knock on the door and Mark stuck his head inside. By the gleeful smile on his face, he'd heard from Julia that Katie and the kids were there.

"Does anyone here want ice cream?" Mark came in and placed a plastic carton of ice cream down on one of the tables.

While Matthew immediately raced forward, Hunter hung back hesitantly. Katie noticed and glanced at Bennett worriedly. He motioned for her to go ahead. Then he knelt down so Hunter wouldn't have to strain to see him.

"You don't feel like ice cream right now? It's okay. We can save it for later."

Hunter kicked at the ground before glancing over at Bennett. "My dad is supposed to take us for ice cream soon. But he might forget. He does that a lot."

Katie had talked about her frustrations with her ex-husband's work schedule before. He wasn't going to pretend he understood how hard it was to balance work and family since he hadn't had that privilege yet. However, he sincerely hoped his family would always know that he valued his time with them more than anything else.

"I'm sorry about that, buddy. Sometimes adults mess up things, too. But that's not your fault. Your mom told me you're a great kid."

Hunter glanced over at his mother. "She did?"

Bennett was suddenly filled with empathy. He may not know what it was like to deal with divorce but he definitely understood wondering if your parents were proud of you. He took a chance and placed a hand on Hunter's shoulder.

"Your mom is very proud of you, Hunter. And even though your dad forgets things sometimes, I'm sure he's proud of you, too."

The smile on the little boy's face was better than any prize.

Just then Katie walked up. "The ice cream is really good. It's homemade."

Bennett stood and pulled her into his embrace. Katie stiffened and pushed away slightly. Bennett followed her eyes to where Hunter watched them curiously. He'd hugged her instinctively and hadn't realized that she might be hesitant about showing affection in front of the kids yet.

Hunter looked between them. "Are you my mom's boyfriend?"

Katie's little gasp of breath betrayed her surprise, but Bennett grinned. "Yes, I am," he answered decisively.

Hunter pursed his lips. "Did you remember not to chew with your mouth open?"

Bennett glanced at Katie in amusement. "I did. Thanks for the tip, buddy. I'm pretty sure that was a major point in my favor."

———

THE REST of the week passed uneventfully. Now that they'd gotten the initial awkward, boyfriend conversation over with the kids, Bennett had started to spend some evenings with Katie at her house.

Katie had been worried that he'd find the kids' noise and disruptions annoying. Bennett had to remind her that noise was what he'd grown up with. He laughed just thinking about it. His parents would get a kick out of that when he told them. Although just a few weeks ago he would have said that he preferred his solitude, now that he had someone to spend the evenings with, he could admit how lonely he'd been before.

Bennett was quickly getting used to having people who were happy to see him when he arrived.

The kids had been understandably shy around him in the beginning but they'd quickly grown accustomed to his presence. Now they greeted him with the same effusive joy they showed toward their mother the times he waited with Katie to meet their bus. She told him that Matthew had decided he was "sick" because he wasn't scared to pick up a bug with his bare hands.

Sick, he was told, meant that he was cool. Bennett held the compliment with the kind of esteem usually given to prestigious awards. He scored even further cool points when he showed them the rainwater collection device that was his first patented invention. It was the simplest of his patented designs, and the object of his old classmate's derision, but it would always be his favorite.

Hunter had asked if he could help invent something. Bennett wasn't sure how but he'd find something they could work on together. The surge of affection he'd felt explaining his design process to the little boy had taken him off guard. Children had always been something Bennett had hoped for one day but while talking with Hunter, it had hit him that he was looking at an image of what his own child might look like one day. If he was lucky, it wouldn't be too long.

It had taken a lot of effort for him not to mention it to Katie. He didn't want to scare her away talking about children too soon. What woman wouldn't run away if she knew her boyfriend was excited to get her pregnant as soon as possible? But maybe after she'd had more time with him, time to trust him, they could discuss it. It was enough just to know the possibility was there. Everything he'd ever dreamed of was within reach.

By the time Friday afternoon arrived, Bennett figured he was ready to bring it up. He'd wait until she had the kids in bed and then he'd pour her a glass of wine. That was the right environment to have a rational discussion about their future, right?

Suddenly, the alarm on Katie's phone went off. Bennett looked up from his notes at the grating noise. Katie sent him an apologetic glance.

"Sorry. I could have sworn I turned the sound off on my phone."

Bennett smiled so she'd know he wasn't upset. He had few rules in the lab but the ones he had revolved around technology. For some reason, he'd always found sudden sounds to be very distracting. He couldn't even work to music.

Katie pulled her phone out of her pocket and then smiled. "Oh, I almost forgot. It's Girls' Night tonight. I'm supposed to bring the tequila."

Bennett wrinkled his brow, his plans for a relaxing evening disappearing like smoke. "Girls' Night?"

"You know, it's when we all get together and complain about our men and drink margaritas." She laughed but her smile fell when he didn't laugh with her. "What's the matter?"

Bennett swallowed hard, his mouth suddenly as dry as sawdust. "So you're going to tell the others things about me?"

Katie looked confused. She probably had no clue why the possibility of her discussing their relationship would make him break out into a cold sweat. She was a social butterfly. Bennett's experience with large groups was usually being the butt of the jokes.

Then suddenly her face softened.

"Bennett, anything I tell them would be good things. You know that, right?"

He looked up hesitantly. "It would be?"

"Well, yeah. I mean, I can't tell them too much or I'd just be bragging." She lowered her voice to a whisper. "No one wants to hear about my brilliant boyfriend who gives me multiple orgasms over and over again."

Bennett grinned. "You can definitely tell them that part."

Katie's dirty laugh wrapped around him like a hug. She comforted him, he realized as Katie went into the office to do any last minute organizing before the weekend.

He guessed he wouldn't get to see her until tomorrow since she had plans with her girlfriends. The thought that he wouldn't get to see her tonight bothered him.

Bennett finally understood why people would do such ridiculous things for love. It was addictive, this feeling. It was actually a bit of a miracle, carrying around the constant knowledge that someone out there in the world loved you, not because they were obligated to by familial connection or proximity, but just because they couldn't help themselves.

Which was why he was so shocked when Katie came out of his office with a guarded look on her face.

"Is everything okay?"

He wasn't sure what could be wrong. She'd only gone into his office to check his messages since she'd forgotten to do it earlier. Since Katie had come, Bennett rarely even looked at his phone or listened to his messages anymore.

"Sure. You just had a message from Olivia."

"Oh. Well, I can call her back later."

That was clearly the wrong thing to say because Katie's eyes flashed fire.

"Bennett, she was asking about where you wanted to go for dinner before the award ceremony next weekend. Why does she still think you're taking her?"

He could feel the warning sound in the back of his mind but wasn't sure how to interpret it.

"Because I am. I usually visit Olivia a few times a year and it just so happens that our visit this time will be at the awards ceremony."

Katie's eyes practically bugged out of her head. "Wait, so you're perfectly fine with taking another woman on a date?"

The warnings sounds now came with flashing lights and barricades.

"No. It's not a date. It's just me hanging out with Olivia."

Katie's eyes narrowed. "The same woman that you hired me to teach you how to impress?"

Bennett opened his mouth to respond but Katie had already turned away.

"I have to go. Mrs. Hillard is bringing over her grandson to play with the kids tonight. She'll be arriving soon."

All Bennett could do was watch helplessly as Katie gathered her things. He tried to catch her eye but she wouldn't meet his gaze. Panic rose as he wondered what he should do. She didn't want to talk, that much was clear, but he couldn't just let her leave.

"Katie, wait. Please don't leave angry. Tell me what to do."

She tugged on her hand and hitched her bag up higher on her shoulder. "I can't tell you how to fix this one, Bennett. I need you to figure it out on your own. Because I'm not interested in sharing my boyfriend with someone else."

"I know it looks bad but Olivia and I are just friends. I can't cancel on her this close to the event. That would be rude."

Katie gave a sharp nod. "Right. *Pardon* me. Because you've always been so keen on following the rules of etiquette. Have fun at the award ceremony."

Bennett's mouth fell open as she pushed past him and closed the door behind her. He had to stop himself from chasing after her. If she was angry now, making a scene definitely wouldn't help his case.

But he didn't think he was being unreasonable. Was he really supposed to ditch a longtime friend just because he had a girlfriend now? Was that really the way things worked? He contemplated calling one of his brothers to ask but Katie's sharp words came back to haunt him.

I need you to figure it out on your own.

That burned. Her angry words had hit him right in the gut. Bennett sighed. If figuring it out on his own was the solution, then he might as well give up hope now.

seventeen

KATIE STIRRED her margarita and wished she liked the taste of tequila straight. Because these cutesy drinks weren't getting the job done tonight.

Girls' Night had gotten off to a roaring start when Raina had walked in and announced that she'd just been booked for her first major modeling campaign since having her daughter. Everyone was in a celebratory mood after that and the alcohol flowed freely. In addition to Raina and Ridley, Penny, Kaylee and her best friend, Sasha, rounded out the group. They were at Ridley's house, so she wouldn't have to go far, and they all felt comfortable letting their hair down.

Everyone except Katie, that is.

She took another sip of her drink, determined not to bring everyone down with her disgruntled mood. Katie hated to be the lone buzzkill, especially since she knew if the other girls found out she was upset, the entire night would become about helping her with her man trouble. It wasn't fair to put everyone in a bad mood just because Bennett was impossible.

Heat rushed to her cheeks as she recalled their tense

conversation. She wasn't even sure where things had gone so wrong. He'd been so sweet, worrying about what she would tell her friends. When she'd told him that she'd only be bragging about him, the smile that crossed his face had made Katie feel like she'd just won the lottery.

For a man as sensitive as Bennett was, it was a wonder he could be so clueless about why going on a date with another woman was a bad idea.

Katie sighed.

"You're not drinking. Is it too strong? I had to guess at how much tequila to add. Jackson tasted it before he left and said it was okay, though." Ridley smiled at the thought of her husband.

Katie had been worried about them but if the satisfied smile on her friend's face was any indication, they had worked things out. Just as Katie had known they would.

"No, the drink is good. I'm just daydreaming."

"Are the kids okay?" Ridley pressed.

"Oh yeah. They're fine. Mrs. Hillard is babysitting tonight and she brought her grandson Carter along again. They always have a good time when she babysits so it's not that."

"But it is something," Ridley argued, her eyes narrowing.

Kaylee plopped down on the couch beside Katie. "You might as well just tell her. You know how she gets."

The whole group laughed at Ridley's disgruntled face. Raina patted her twin's hand consolingly. "You know it's true, Ri. You're not happy unless you're meddling."

Kaylee covered her mouth with her hand she was laughing so hard. "You'd better watch out. If she thinks you're not moving fast enough, you'll end up booked into a hotel with Bennett."

"That was an accident. I swear," Ridley said.

Kay didn't look convinced. "I think your brain does matchmaking subconsciously."

Ridley sniffed. "I'm just concerned for my friends. I want you all to be happy, that's all." Her voice was small and Katie instantly felt bad about the teasing.

"I know you do, Ri. I'm happy. I'm just ... confused. Okay, here's the thing."

Katie took a deep breath. If she was going to tell them what happened, she had to choose her words carefully. No matter how angry she was, Bennett was still their brother-in-law.

"You know how Bennett and I have been dating, right?"

"Uh huh. Things seem to be going well. Julia's thrilled about it, you know."

Katie winced. "I'd hate for her to get her hopes up. Especially since it's probably already over."

Ridley's eyes widened. "Whoa. What does that mean?"

"You know how Bennett originally wanted me to help him so he could impress his friend Olivia?"

There was a chorus of nods and hummed agreement. Katie figured they'd all heard the story through the grapevine by now.

"Well, apparently even though we're together, Bennett is still going on a date with Olivia."

Ridley's mouth fell open. "Wait, what? Bennett wouldn't do that!"

"Oh, I didn't think so either. So I asked him point blank and he said he couldn't cancel on her so close to the event. That it was rude. The man who would barely say hello to his neighbors is worried about being rude."

"That's crazy. I can't believe Bennett said that. I'm going to give him a piece of my mind the next time I see him." Ridley looked outraged on her behalf.

"No, I don't want that. He should be with me because he wants to be. Not because he's afraid of his sister-in-law."

"He's not afraid of me," Ridley protested.

Raina looked at her twin from the corner of her eye. "Um, you haven't seen you when you're on a tear. You're pretty scary."

Kaylee got up and came back with the pitcher of margaritas. Without asking she refilled Katie's cup. "This sucks. I still think we should go kick his ass. Why do men have to be such idiots?"

Soon the room was a chorus of voices, all talking about the dumb things their men had done. It was supposed to make her feel better, but all the chatter only made her feel worse. The other girls were complaining about their men while secure in the knowledge that their guys loved them. They would complain for an hour but then they'd go home to that man's welcoming embrace.

While Katie would be climbing into her cold, empty bed. Alone.

All at once, Katie was tired of talking about Bennett. No amount of talking was going to fix this. He simply didn't want her enough if the idea of going out with another woman didn't bother him.

Maybe he really does see her as just a friend, a desperate part of her brain protested.

But Katie realized that it didn't really matter. Because if they were really just friends, Bennett would have invited her to come along as well. Wouldn't he want to introduce her to Olivia if they were such close friends?

Face it, Katie. You were his second choice all along.

The one thing she'd promised she'd never be again.

———

BY THE TIME Katie arrived at home a little after midnight, she was exhausted from too much alcohol and too many hours dissecting her relationship with Bennett.

The other girls had been happy to take her mind off things by discussing what was going on in their lives but truthfully, Katie had only been half listening. All she kept seeing in her mind was Bennett's face when she walked out.

Worse, he hadn't even called her. Was he really not even going to try to explain this?

There was a light on in the living room. Mrs. Hillard usually spent the night in the guestroom when she babysat so she wasn't shocked to see the light. However, when she stepped in the room to cut it off, she *was* shocked to discover Don asleep on the couch.

"What the hell?" she whispered.

Katie dropped her handbag on the floor and bounded up the stairs. The guest room door was open and the bed was made. Her heart racing, she pushed open the door to the room her sons shared. Hunter was in the top bunk as usual and Matthew was fast asleep on the bottom. Carter was asleep on the attached pull out trundle bed.

Katie closed the door gently on her way out. Where was Mrs. Hillard? She'd met the older woman at church and she'd become almost a surrogate grandmother to her kids. She wouldn't have left without a good reason. Not to mention that none of it explained why Don was asleep on her couch.

Downstairs, she shook Don's arm until he woke up. He grunted and turned his head toward the wall. At this angle, she noticed that he had a lot more gray hair than before. Apparently living the single life wasn't as much fun as he'd thought it would be. She shook her head.

After several more attempts to wake him, she finally turned on the overhead light.

"What? What time is it?" He blinked blearily into the light.

"It's the middle of the night. What are you doing here? And where is Mrs. Hillard?"

Don grunted again. "When I got here she said something about forgetting her medication. So I told her to go home since I would be here. She said she'd come get Carter tomorrow."

Katie relaxed. Slightly. "That explains why she's gone but it doesn't explain why you're here in the first place."

"I have a medical conference in Newport News tomorrow."

"Okay? I still don't understand what that has to do with you sleeping on my couch. Aren't those conferences usually held at a hotel? Why didn't you book a room there?"

"I shouldn't have to book a hotel room for a local conference." His words slurred slightly as he struggled to his feet.

What the hell? Katie shook her head in disbelief. "Are you drunk?"

"A couple of us were out at the bar before this. So what?"

He took a closer step and Katie held her hand over her nose. If he'd been closer before she wouldn't have had to ask if he'd been drinking. The smell of alcohol clung to him and the whiff of *eau de roadside bar* that washed over her was almost enough to make her tipsy, too.

"I wanted to come see you. I missed you. I miss the boys," he whined.

If anything, he probably missed having someone to clean up after him and make sure his dress shirts were starched the way he liked. But she swallowed her annoyance. As much as he'd hurt her, she'd vowed not to allow her personal feelings to keep him from their children. Hunter and Matthew pretended not to notice but it was obvious how much they missed their dad.

"Okay, I'm glad you're here to see the kids but I'm not going to wake them in the middle of the night. You should have gotten a hotel and come in the morning."

"I should be able to sleep in my own damn house!" Don's belligerent shout startled her and she took a step back, stumbling over the edge of the couch.

"It's not your house anymore."

"I paid for it", he grumbled.

Katie rolled her eyes at the predictable reply. He'd loved to rub her nose in the fact that he brought home all the money.

"Yeah, well so did I. With blood, sweat and tears as I took care of our kids and took care of you, too. Not that it matters anymore. You did me a favor when you left."

"What is that supposed to mean?"

"Just that I would have never known what I was missing if you hadn't left. Dating is actually fun and there are men out there who know way more about how to please a woman. I'm having fun for the first time in years."

Don looked livid and for the first time, Katie was actually afraid of him. She swallowed over the lump that grew in her throat as he advanced on her but she refused to back down. He wasn't getting that from her.

"Now I want you to leave. Our children are asleep upstairs and I don't want them to wake up and see you like this."

A touch of vulnerability entered Don's expression. "I can't afford a hotel right now." He fidgeted with the edge of his wrinkled shirt. "I'm having a little trouble at work."

Katie didn't say anything. Experience with Don told her that he'd spill the truth if she just let him keep talking. Sure enough, the silence was too much for him.

A few seconds later, he continued. "Some asshole said I was drunk at work. I *wasn't*, by the way."

Katie waved away the explanation. "Is this why you haven't been paying child support?"

He wouldn't meet her eyes. "I'll pay it. I just need a little time."

"Why didn't you just stay with your girlfriend?"

When he didn't answer, Katie suddenly understood why he was there. Not only was he having trouble at work but he was also struggling to pay off the costs of their divorce and his child support. Now that he didn't have as much money to spend on her, his girlfriend had probably left him. She almost laughed. Karma had a twisted sense of humor.

When he moved toward the door, Katie bit her tongue. She couldn't let him leave and possibly drive drunk and hurt someone. He was a mess right now but maybe if he had a little support, he could get it together. For her children's benefit, she could deal with having him around temporarily.

"Don't go out there. You've been drinking and it's not safe. You can stay in the guest room."

He nodded and for the first time in years, she saw a little glimpse of the man she'd married. The one who'd cared about more than himself.

"Thank you. I'll make it up to you, I promise."

Katie followed him up the stairs and waited until he was in

the guest room before she went to her own room. As she went through her usual nighttime routine, washing her face, brushing her teeth and moisturizing, she decided that tomorrow she was calling Don's parents. He might not want to admit it but he needed help from someone. She wasn't relying on his promises to get it together anymore.

She was tired of empty promises.

———

NOT CALLING Katie was one of the hardest things Bennett had ever done.

He'd cleaned up some project notes, sterilized the entire lab and then gone online to play a game of virtual chess against Grant. Which he lost.

That alone was proof that he was emotionally disturbed.

Bennett woke up on Saturday morning with a slight headache but a plan. He would go to Katie's house and surprise her with breakfast. He wouldn't cook (he wanted her to forgive him not get food poisoning), and then he would ask her to come with him to the awards ceremony. Olivia would understand and she'd be thrilled to meet his girlfriend afterward.

Bennett wasn't sure why he'd reacted so badly to the idea of calling off his evening with Olivia at first. Probably just leftover worry that having a girlfriend would mean leaving everything he cared about behind.

But he was a grown man and secure in who he was. This was an entirely different scenario than his failed past relationships. He trusted that Katie really liked him as he was and wasn't going to try to change him. Actually Katie had been resistant to the idea of changing him even when he'd asked her to do it.

As he got dressed, Bennett smiled at himself in the mirror. He should have trusted in her from the beginning. When it came down to it, he had very good taste in women.

He stopped by the grocery store and purchased breakfast sandwiches, croissants, fruit and a sad looking bouquet of flowers. Bennett wrinkled his nose at the faded blooms. He could only hope that it was the thought that counted since it was too early for the florist to be open. When he finally parked in Katie's driveway, his brow furrowed when he noted the unfamiliar vehicle parked in the driveway.

The babysitter. Of course.

Katie had mentioned that she had a babysitter staying with the boys while she was hanging out with her friends. He was glad he'd purchased additional food so there would be enough for everyone. He got out of the car and decided to come back for the food. It would ruin the effect if she opened the door to Bennett laden down with packages and couldn't even see his face.

He grabbed the flowers off the passenger seat and walked up to the door. Before he could knock, it opened and a man stepped out onto the porch.

When the guy finally noticed him, he stopped. "Oh hello. It's a little early for deliveries, isn't it?"

Bennett was so shocked at the sight of a man leaving Katie's house in the early morning that he didn't bother to correct him. Who was this? Katie had clearly said that her babysitter was an older woman with a grandson. The man before him was probably only a few years older than he was, so mid-thirties, but he wasn't carrying it well. His hair was liberally threaded with gray and the large bags under his eyes made him look bloated and tired.

It should have been consolation that the guy leaving her house wasn't some young stud but Bennett couldn't shake the sense of foreboding. Especially since he had a pretty decent idea who this guy was.

"I'm here for Katie."

The guy reached out for the flowers. "Yeah, I'll give them to her for you. Like I said, it's a little early for deliveries."

"I'm not a delivery man. I'm a friend of Katie's."

His words made the other man take a closer look at him. His beady dark eyes narrowed as he took in Bennett's tailored shirt and slacks. "Well, she's not awake yet. She's a little tired after last night. I'm just going to get breakfast for us now. We worked up an appetite last night, ya know? I'm Donald Mason. Her husband."

Bennett gritted his teeth at the implication. "Aren't you her *ex-husband?* Katie said you're divorced."

Don drew himself up to his full height, which was still half a foot shorter than Bennett.

"That was a mistake. Katie wants to keep our family together as much as I do."

Bennett's fingers tightened around the stem of the flowers. "Interesting how so many men discover they care about family after they've destroyed theirs."

Don looked annoyed and then suddenly chuckled. "You must be the guy Katie is working for. The weirdo. Yeah she told me about you."

Ice flashed through Bennett's veins at the word. One he hadn't heard in so long. "*Excuse me?*"

"Yeah, she told me she was working for some guy who was

really strange. Anything for a paycheck, she said. But she won't be doing that much longer. I'm back now so she can focus on taking care of the kids. That's what she's always wanted, you know?"

Bennett was squeezing the flowers so hard that the stems cut into his skin. Had Katie talked about him with her ex? He thought about all the time they'd spent together and how much fun they'd had over the past few weeks. Could that really have all been just to get paid? He didn't believe it. Or at least he didn't want to. But then he thought about everything that had happened between them and how utterly unlikely it was that a woman like Katie would truly enjoy spending time with someone like him. What was more likely, that Katie was the one woman in the world who could appreciate him or that she was just smiling to keep her job?

He flexed his fingers.

"Yeah, I know. I hope she gets everything she's always wanted."

Bennett left, wondering how it was possible that he was walking upright when it felt like he'd been shattered from the inside out.

eighteen

One week later ...

BENNETT LAUGHED at something the man sitting on his left said. Truthfully, he had no idea what he was talking about. He was sitting at a large circular table filled with strangers, their only connection that they all volunteered their time mentoring youth in their field.

As usual, Olivia could tell when he needed a rescue. She placed a hand over his arm in a comforting gesture before turning to the man. "Congratulations on your tenure, Dr. Marks. That's quite an accomplishment. And so young!"

The man next to him blushed and stuttered under Olivia's praise. "I'm not the youngest to achieve tenure at the university. Second youngest, but not bad, I suppose."

Bennett tuned out the rest of the conversation, wishing they could leave. He'd already received his award and mercifully, hadn't been asked to make a speech. Now he really just wanted to go but he wouldn't do that to Olivia. She'd been so excited to see him when he'd arrived at her apartment earlier that day.

They'd decided against going out to eat first, choosing to suffer through whatever chicken surprise was offered as dinner during the award ceremony. Olivia had barely touched her chicken and asparagus so they'd probably be going for burgers afterward.

Honestly, maybe if he suggested it now, they could leave early. He hated to do that when she'd gone out of her way to accompany him to the event but knowing Liv, she'd be more excited about the burgers than anything going on here.

He turned to ask her and that's when he noticed it. Her hand was on his arm. *She's touching me voluntarily.*

He grinned, imagining Katie's reaction. If she were here, she'd be pointing and saying, "That's the signal. She likes you!"

Then he remembered that Katie wouldn't be grinning at him at all. She thought he was a weirdo. Bennett's heart clenched at the thought even after days of turning that hurtful phrase over and over in his mind. He'd left her a message telling her that he was going out of town and that she didn't need to come to work that week so he'd have time to figure out what he wanted to do. It would be difficult to see her every day now that he knew what she really thought of him. She was probably thrilled that he'd been out of town all week so she could spend time with her ex-husband. The guy she'd married.

The one who treated her like garbage.

"Yikes, this chicken is even worse than it looks," Liv whispered. "Maybe we can pick up some pizza on the way home."

"Excellent idea. Let's do that." He stood and placed his napkin on the seat.

A startled Olivia followed suit. She made their excuses and

then followed him through the crowd. The director of the Mentor Science program stopped him to congratulate him on his award and Bennett mustered all his patience not to blow the guy off. Apparently there was someone there he wanted Bennett to meet. He should have known that making a quick getaway was not in the cards.

Once the director walked away, he turned and noticed Olivia staring at him. If he hadn't been so caught up in his own problems he would have noticed how tired and drawn she looked earlier. All at once, he was ashamed. Olivia had been dealing with relationship problems also and he hadn't even thought to ask how things were going. Some friend he was.

"Are you okay, Boo?"

For once she didn't protest at the nickname. "I'm going to be fine. Tell me about what's new with your family. I haven't seen everyone since Nick's wedding."

Over the next hour, he showed her pictures of Jackson's two boys, Chris and Jase, and a picture of Nick's daughter, Jada. Olivia cooed over the baby and promised to come visit soon so she could see them all in person. Somehow, he even found himself on the dance floor. Seeing Olivia laugh at his attempt to emulate the newest dance craze made the discomfort worth it.

Maybe everyone else thought he was weird but with Olivia he'd always fit in.

After the song ended, Olivia motioned toward the French doors on the other side of the ballroom. "Let's take a walk. It's nice outside this evening."

Bennett looked around but didn't see any sign of the program director. He didn't want to be rude and leave without meeting whoever it was the director had mentioned, so they might as well enjoy themselves in the meantime. He accepted the hand Olivia held out.

"Sure. The director mentioned that the gardens in this hotel are exceptional. I'd love to see what kind of plants they used."

He'd heard all night that the gardens were a must see. So he followed Olivia through the crowd until they reached the French doors he'd seen people coming and going from all night. As soon as they stepped outside, Bennett was glad they'd come.

Even Olivia appreciated the artistry because her eyes sparkled in delight as she looked at the life-sized maze of hedges. He could have done without the artificial lights woven through the foliage but she seemed to love it.

"This is beautiful."

Bennett walked up to the hedges. "Interesting. I was expecting Boxwoods but it appears they've gone with American Arborvitae."

Normally he would have wanted a closer look but tonight, it felt like he was just going through the motions. If Katie were here, she would love the romanticism of walking through a garden at night. The thought made him sad that he'd never get to show her this. That he'd never get to show her anything ever again.

He turned from his study of the hedges when Olivia grabbed his hand.

"Bennett. I wanted to say thank you for bringing me with you tonight. This has been a lot of fun. I've missed just hanging out with you."

"I've missed hanging out with you, too."

It was true. He'd always loved spending time with her. Olivia was his oldest and dearest friend. Bennett was incredibly glad that he hadn't canceled on her. He would have done it if he'd thought it would make Katie happy. That was the most pathetic part. He would have done anything and meanwhile she was laughing at him with her ex-husband.

Olivia didn't laugh at him. Olivia was currently perfectly happy to allow him to examine the greenery and marvel over the soil conditions even though she probably couldn't care less about those things. Olivia liked him.

Then she grabbed him by his collar and kissed him. Olivia kissed him. On the lips.

And Bennett could only think, *This is completely wrong.*

Maybe it had just taken the shock of feeling how utterly wrong being in another woman's arms felt but in that moment, Bennett's entire relationship with Katie flashed through his mind. He saw her shy and uncertain whenever she talked about her prior relationship. Most importantly, he saw the sincere joy in her eyes when she'd laughed at one of his jokes or when they were just sitting quietly and soaking up each other's warmth.

After a lifetime of being around people who were just tolerating his presence, Bennett would like to think that he could tell a genuine reaction from a fake one. Katie had not been faking it around him and she definitely hadn't been faking it in the bedroom.

Bennett's thoughts raced as the pieces all fell together. He'd reacted on instinct and allowed his past hurts to dictate his actions but looking back with a clear head, he couldn't believe that Katie would have said those things behind his back. Or at least not after she'd gotten to know him. Her ex-husband had obviously just been looking to get a reaction from him and Bennett was ashamed that he'd fallen for it so easily.

Thinking back, he remembered that he'd been carrying

flowers when he showed up that day. If he was Donald Mason and he'd lost an amazing woman like Katie, he'd probably lash out and be a jerk, also. He didn't like that the man had been leaving her house so early in the morning but he trusted there was a good explanation. Even if Katie didn't like him as much as he'd thought, there was no way she'd just go back to the guy who'd cheated on her and told her lies.

Bennett had made a grave mistake. And he needed to fix it. Immediately.

Olivia's arms loosened around his neck. "Bennett? Take a breath."

He coughed. His mind had been moving so quickly that he hadn't even been breathing. Everything inside of him was focused on one goal.

I have to get home.

I have to find Katie.

"You didn't feel anything either, did you?" Olivia sighed.

Bennett couldn't even lie to spare her feelings. He'd experienced what it was like to have a kiss completely rearrange your world. As convenient as it would be if he had that kind of chemistry with Olivia, it just wasn't happening. He wanted that for her, even if he'd lost his own chance at it.

"No, I didn't. I'm sorry. I would never want to hurt your feelings, Boo."

"You didn't. I'm in love with someone else. But I wanted it to be you. Stupid, huh?"

"No, it's not stupid. You're one of the smartest people I know."

"There's no way that's true. You're surrounded by literal geniuses all the time."

"Understanding science isn't the only way to be intelligent.

For years, you've been the one person I could count on to accept me as I am. You're that person for a lot of people, Livvy. Somehow you know how to be a great friend to everyone in your life, which seems pretty smart to me."

"God, I love you so much, you know that?"

It was a bitter pill to hear those words coming from the wrong woman. But love was love and Bennett was grateful for it, no matter where it came from. Even if Olivia wasn't *The One*, she would always be the woman who'd loved him before any other.

"I love you, too. I always will." Bennett pulled her closer and kissed her gently on the forehead. They stayed like that for a long time before Olivia smiled up at him gently.

"Go. I can take a cab home."

Relief swept through him followed immediately by guilt. He didn't want to just leave her here on her own.

Olivia smiled. "I'll be fine. And someday soon, I want to meet her."

He blushed. "I just hope she hasn't changed her mind about me."

Bennett took one last look at the sparkling hedges. It wasn't a shooting star but he decided to make a wish anyway.

If he was going to have even a chance of getting Katie back, he could use all the help he could get.

———

SUNDAY AFTERNOON, Katie rearranged the throw blanket covering Ridley's legs. They were downstairs in the living room relaxing in front of the window that overlooked the backyard. It was a beautiful day, sunny and bright, but Katie didn't mind staying indoors with Ridley who was on voluntary bed rest.

If she was at home, she'd only be puttering around the house trying to find things to take her mind off where she really wanted to be. Katie picked at a loose thread on the knitted blanket. Maybe she should take up knitting. Isn't that what perpetually single women did, knit things and play with their cats?

"You're going to pull a hole in that blanket," Ridley said.

Katie dropped it and sheepishly tried to push the loop she'd snagged back into the blanket. "Sorry. I guess I'm a little distracted. Is this warm enough?"

Her friend gave her a wan smile before waving her away. "No need to fuss. I'll just get hot in ten minutes and throw it off again anyway."

Katie didn't take offense at her friend's grumpy mood. As Ridley described it, she was about thirteen months pregnant at this point and very over it. She was bloated and achy and tired of waiting for her due date which was still three weeks away.

"I'm exhausted," Ri moaned. "I just want this baby to come out already so I can sleep with no one kicking my ribs and without getting up for the bathroom every five minutes."

Katie didn't point out that in a few weeks, Ri was still going to be exhausted because she'd have a newborn to deal with. Her friend would discover the joy of taking care of a newborn soon enough. Although considering that Ri had the most supportive husband in the world, she'd likely be able to sleep. Katie had mainly been on her own after the birth of each of her sons since her mother had only been able to come stay for a week afterward each time.

"Maybe we should watch a movie?" Katie suggested. "Or I can read to you so you can close your eyes for a while."

She was on Ri-watch for the next few days until Raina got back. Raina had a business meeting scheduled in DC and Ridley had encouraged her not to miss it. She'd argued that Katie and her mother-in-law would watch her like a hawk anyway so it wasn't as if she'd be alone. Katie could tell that Raina hadn't wanted to leave so she'd promised to stick extra close to Ridley today. Jackson had taken all the kids out for ice cream so they could have a little quiet time.

Secretly, Katie thought he'd just wanted to get them out of the house and away from Ri's cranky mood.

"No. I don't want to watch a movie. I want to know if you've made up with Bennett yet?" Ridley glowered at her.

Katie sighed. "He's out of town, remember?"

"Both of you have phones. You haven't called him?"

"I'm not going to call him. He made his feelings very clear when he fired me."

"He didn't fire you. He gave you a week of paid vacation."

When she raised her eyebrow, Ridley huffed. They both knew that getting a paid vacation was simply Bennett's way of avoiding her. No doubt as soon as he got back from the award ceremony, she'd get another voicemail message offering her severance pay. He was probably just trying to figure out how to let her go. Bennett hadn't done any paperwork since she'd been hired.

"It's just so odd that he would do that without even talking to you again. It isn't like Bennett to be petty. Why would he fire you just because of one argument?"

Katie sighed. "He probably thought it would be easier than having to see each other every day. He's a good person and he wouldn't want us to be uncomfortable working together."

"He is a good person." Ridley smacked her fist into her

palm. "Which is why this doesn't make any sense. Bennett is not the two-timing sort."

"I don't think he thinks of it that way. In his mind, Olivia is just a friend and he thinks he's being loyal. But the reality is that he's in love with her. We have fun together but they have history I can't compete with. I'm tired of competing. If a guy is meant for you then you shouldn't have to compete for him at all."

Ridley visibly deflated. "I'm sorry, Katie. Now I feel bad for encouraging this. But I saw the way he looked at you that day at dinner. I've never seen him look at a woman that way before."

"Well, I guess that's because Olivia isn't here. Although I'm sure you'll be seeing her around soon since they're spending the weekend together."

"I'm still not giving up on you two. Sometimes things aren't what they seem. Look at me and Jackson. I was worried about him cheating for nothing. Once I talked to him, I realized it was a misunderstanding and we worked it out. Two people who love each other can work through anything," Ridley insisted.

"He doesn't love me, Ri."

"Are you sure? Because I know what an Alexander man in love looks like."

Ridley struggled to her feet. Katie jumped up and helped support her back until she was upright.

"Now I'm going to take a nap in the office. My back has been hurting all day."

Katie watched her friend walk down the hall to Jackson's office. They'd put a daybed in there once Ridley got tired of walking up and down the stairs so much. Once she was out of sight, Katie pulled out her phone. Something about Ri's crankiness and the amount of swelling in her ankles didn't feel right to her. She sent a text to Jackson to see how far away he was. When he didn't respond, she called. After four rings it went to voicemail.

Katie clutched the phone against her chest, the vague unease she'd been feeling all day getting stronger. Maybe she was just being paranoid. Having swollen ankles didn't necessarily mean something was wrong with Ri. But she knew she wouldn't be comfortable unless she double-checked so she sent a text to Penny, who was a physical therapist. When she didn't get a response right away, she finally decided to text Don. He was a doctor and she had no problem swallowing her pride if it would help her friend.

Katie: Ridley has a lot of swelling in her ankles today. Is that dangerous?

Her phone rang immediately. She answered, shocked that Don would call her back so quickly. He'd never answered her calls so promptly when they were married.

"Hey, thanks for calling me. I'm kind of worried."

"I'm not sure how much help I'll be. My obstetrics rotation was a long time ago. Did the swelling develop suddenly?"

"Yes. They didn't look that bad yesterday. And she's been really tired today. I'm worried." She lowered her voice to a near whisper.

"Any blurred vision or headaches? Those can be warning signs of preeclampsia."

Katie bit her lip. "I'll have to ask her to be sure. Thanks for the help."

"Sure. I meant what I said about making things up to you. I'm going to do better this time, Katie. I really think we can make things work this time."

"Whoa, wait a minute. Don, we aren't getting back

together. I have a boyfriend." Even though that wasn't technically true, she was sure that even Bennett wouldn't begrudge her using him to get out of this situation.

"Yeah, I met him. The weird guy you work for."

Katie's breath turned to dust in her chest. "You met him? When did you meet him?"

Don didn't answer at first. Katie could feel her anger rising. He probably hadn't meant to tell her that. Now she was starting to wonder if Bennett's sudden and unexplained disappearance from her life wasn't so unexplainable at all.

"When, Don?"

"Last week. The day I spent the night. He came to the house early that morning with some tired-looking flowers. I told him that I was back now so you didn't need to spend your days working for the weird Alexander anymore." He chuckled at his own joke.

Katie closed her eyes, trying to rein in the desire to reach through the phone and choke her ex-husband. Of course Bennett wasn't talking to her. Her sweet, sensitive Bennett was a superhero in so many ways but even superheroes had their fatal flaws. His was feeling like an outsider. Someone like Don sneering at him and calling him weird was exactly the kind of thing that would hurt him. Especially if he thought that she was back together with her ex-husband and about to leave him.

Katie wanted to cry but also to drop everything and go find Bennett to explain. But first she had to go and check on Ridley.

"Thank you for the information, Don. I'll let you know if I have any other questions."

"Wait. You aren't mad?"

Katie sighed. "Why would I be mad? You were just doing what you always do. It would be like being angry with a snake for biting someone. That's what snakes do. But if you thought that little stunt accomplished anything, all it did was make me love him more. Because he could have told me what you said to turn me against you and he didn't. Even when he's upset, Bennett Alexander is a hell of a man."

She hung up while Don was still spluttering over his response and immediately went to look for Ridley. Hopefully her friend wouldn't be annoyed with her for waking her up but if she was, Ri would be mollified with hearing some gossip. The story of the jealous ex-husband who sabotaged her love life was exactly the kind of drama Ridley loved.

Katie pushed open the door to Jackson's office slowly. The blinds were closed so it was dim in the room. She tiptoed over to where Ridley was sleeping on the daybed. When Katie touched her hand, the skin was startlingly cool to the touch.

"Ridley. Ridley, wake up."

As her voice got louder and louder and Ri still didn't respond, Katie's fear only increased. She pulled out her phone again and dialed 911, wishing with every part of her soul that she hadn't wasted so much time talking to Don and had checked on Ri earlier.

nineteen

BENNETT WOKE up late on Sunday, exhausted but determined. It wasn't like him to sleep in but after the events of the prior night, he felt like he'd been hit by a bus. He rushed through a shower and then downstairs to the main level. Once he had coffee brewing, he mentally evaluated his options.

He didn't have a plan yet although he'd spent the drive home from DC the prior night brainstorming ways to approach Katie. The drive hadn't been particularly productive since he hadn't come up with much more than, *"I miss you."*

Although it was simple, perhaps simple was best. Bennett still wasn't entirely sure whether Katie was really getting back together with her ex-husband but either way, he wanted her to know how he felt. Even if it required swallowing his pride and putting himself out there.

Has that ever worked for you in the past?

Bennett ignored the niggling voice of doubt. He'd had bad experiences trusting women in the past, that was true. But he couldn't believe that what he'd had with Katie wasn't genuine. Ever since she'd come into his life, everything around him seemed brighter. Better. He had to believe that was based on something real.

But he couldn't deny that if he found out it wasn't, the knowledge was likely to break him in half.

A knock at the door interrupted his swirling thoughts. With a longing glance for the still brewing coffee, Bennett walked through the lab to open the door.

"Dad? What are you doing out here? You know you can use your key." Bennett stood back to let his father come inside. His parents both had keys and his mother certainly didn't hesitate to use hers.

Mark chuckled. "You're a grown man, son. And grown men need their privacy. Don't want to interrupt anything."

Bennett flushed. His father had said that to him before and he'd dismissed it then. After all, he rarely dated so what was the likelihood of his father walking in on anything inappropriate? However, he knew his father was referring to the fact that he was dating Katie now.

Considering how they sometimes were all over each other in the middle of the day, his father's comments were actually wiser than he knew.

"Well, I was just about to have coffee if you'd like some."

Bennett went back to the kitchen, aware of his father trailing behind him. He busied himself pouring the coffee into two mugs. When he turned around, his father stood on the other side of the kitchen counter watching him closely.

Bennett sighed. "What is it? You might as well just say what you came here to say."

Mark accepted the mug with a little smile. "Just wanted to check on my boy. You haven't been yourself this past week."

He should have expected this. His parents liked to pretend

that they gave him privacy, but they paid close attention to everything that happened. Katie's absence the past week would not have gone unnoticed.

"Katie is back together with her ex. At least I think she is. I'm ... well, I'm dealing with it." Bennett figured there was no point in keeping it a secret. In a town this small, everyone always knew your business anyway.

"I thought it might be something like that. But what do you mean you *think* she's back together with her ex? You don't know for sure?"

Bennett squirmed slightly under his father's pointed stare. The man hadn't raised four boys into men without the ability to make them feel like he could see straight through to all their sins.

"Well, I went to her house one morning and he was there. He told me they were back together and she didn't need to work for the town weirdo anymore. So I left."

Repeating the scenario out loud was even more embarrassing than it had been when it happened. But unlike last time, Bennett also felt himself get angry. Angry at Donald Mason for being a complete tool, yes, but also angry at himself for listening to someone who had a history of being untrustworthy.

When he looked up, he knew without even a word being spoken that his father felt the same way.

"You took his word without even talking to Katie? That's not like you, son." He sighed and there was a world of disappointment in the sound.

It settled over Bennett like a blanket, covering him in regret. There was nothing worse than feeling like he'd let down his father in some way. Well, maybe there was. Because spending the last week alone, without Katie around to lighten up the day, had been pretty miserable. The research he loved before seemed stifling without her cheerful interjections.

Maybe it would have been better to stay in the dark about how it felt to be a part of a couple. He was happier before he knew.

"I'm sorry to disappoint you, Dad."

Mark frowned. "You've never disappointed me. But I worry about you."

"Why? I'm doing so well. That's what everyone tells me." Bennett could hear the bitterness in his own voice.

Apparently Mark could hear it too because he put his coffee mug down and clapped a hand on Bennett's shoulder. "I'm not concerned about your brain. I'm concerned about your heart. The greatest fear of every parent is their child not being happy. I can't teach you that."

"You taught me everything that matters."

Mark nodded and clapped Bennett on the shoulder again, noticeably moved by the words. "I hope so. I'm certainly not perfect."

Being the oldest, Bennett had always felt that he'd been the most in tune with his father over the years. He'd watched as his dad had grown and changed into the man his brothers knew but he remembered a time when his father had been a little more hot-tempered than he was now. He'd like to think that his father could confide in him also if he needed a shoulder to lean on.

"Is everything okay, Dad?"

Mark coughed. "I worry that you haven't always seen a

good example in me. I've made so many mistakes with my family. Your mother and I have worked so hard to correct them but there are so many things I'd do differently if I had it to do all over again."

This was news to Bennett, who'd expected to hear about some health concerns or about some problem with the farm.

"Such as?"

His father let out a heavy sigh. "This feud with your Uncle Stewart for starters."

Bennett didn't speak, hoping his father would continue. Over the years, they'd all had their own theories as to why the brothers no longer spoke to each other. But he'd never heard it from his father's perspective.

Mark glanced at him sheepishly before continuing. "We've always been competitive. When you're young, you do things impulsively that hurt others. All the guys wanted Julia and she chose me. I didn't care that Stew had carried a torch for her for years. Didn't think about how that made him feel."

Bennett had never heard any of this before. All the theories he'd heard floated around before never mentioned a possible romance between his mother and his ... uncle? He grimaced a little at the thought. It was childish but he couldn't imagine his mother with anyone else.

"So what happened? They didn't ..." Bennett couldn't even finish the sentence.

Mark shook his head. "No but he tried to kiss your mother years later and she had to slap him. Your brother Eli walked in on that and it messed him up something terrible. But part of the situation was fueled by how badly I handled it in the beginning."

Bennett could relate. If he could go back, he'd change how

he'd handled a lot of things. "It's not too late, Dad. You can still fix it."

Mark's eyes swung to his. "So can you. Don't make the mistake that I did by waiting years to fix it, either. Family is more important than pride. Family is everything."

A burst of determination fired through Bennett's blood. He would go find Katie and talk to her. She'd been upset the last they spoke. He'd hurt her by refusing to cancel his evening with Olivia, he saw that now. So he'd start with an apology. Hopefully she'd be willing to listen. If she still chose her ex, it would hurt like hell but at least he'd know he gave it everything he had.

Alexanders weren't quitters.

"You're right. I shouldn't have just taken his word for it. I was hurt by what he said but that's probably why he said it. I have to talk to her."

Mark smiled. "Now that's the man I raised. The fearless one who has always lived life on his own terms."

It was strange to see himself through his father's eyes when he'd never seen himself as a trailblazer.

"And what about you?" he asked his father. "What are you going to do?"

Mark's eyes softened and he looked up to the ceiling for a moment. "I suppose it's time I take my own advice. I'm going to do what I should have done years ago. I'm going to call my brother."

Just then Mark jumped before he pulled his phone out of his pocket. "This dang thing. I'm still not used to something buzzing in my britches."

Bennett smothered a laugh at the disgruntled look on his

father's face. He hated the sound of all the ringtones so his mother had put his phone on vibrate.

After listening to whoever was on the other end, Mark's frown deepened.

"I'm on my way, honey. Bennett's with me; we'll be there right away. Hang in there."

Bennett moved closer as he hung up. "Who was that? What's happened?"

Mark motioned for him to follow. "That was your mother. We have to get to the hospital. Ridley's been admitted."

Bennett's feet started moving even as he did some quick mental calculations. "But wait? Isn't it too early?"

Mark's face was grave as they walked out. "Yes. It is."

————

WHEN KATIE EMERGED into the waiting room of New Haven General Hospital, she was instantly surrounded by a crowd of Alexanders.

"How is she?"

"What's going on?

"Is the baby okay?"

The questions flew fast and furious and Katie tried to answer them all. *Yes, Ridley is fine, just exhausted. Her blood pressure was dangerously high and the doctors had to induce labor. The baby is fine so far.*

By the time she was done giving her update, Jackson came out of the room and his family surrounded him with hugs. She was glad to allow him the opportunity to tell the family more.

"It's a boy!" Jackson exclaimed to a chorus of cheers. "His

name is Zane Michael Alexander. We let the boys help choose his name."

Katie moved to the side, happy to be out of the limelight. She leaned against the wall, trying to get her emotions under control. It had been difficult to keep a brave face while her friend had been in labor.

The ambulance had arrived about eight minutes after her call. She'd ridden alongside Ridley, trying desperately not to cry while answering all the EMT's questions as best as she could. She knew most of the answers but not Ri's blood type or what medications she was on. Luckily, Ridley woke up right before they got to the hospital so she'd been able to give them the information they needed.

Then once they'd arrived, she'd spent what felt like ages calling Nick, Julia and anyone else she could to let them know what was going on, since Jackson wasn't answering his phone. Jackson arrived at the hospital about fifteen minutes after they did. He hadn't heard his phone ringing over the noise in the ice cream parlor. He'd taken her place at Ridley's side while Katie supervised the kids who fortunately hadn't realized that something was wrong.

Julia had arrived not long after that. After checking on Ridley, Julia had taken the children home with her, promising to be back as soon as the babysitter she'd contacted arrived at her house. She'd also thanked Katie profusely for being there for Ri, which had only made her feel worse.

Why hadn't she listened to her instincts? She'd thought something was off with Ridley but she'd just chalked it up to her friend being cranky, not sick. All she could do was send up a thankful prayer that it had all turned out well.

"Katie?"

She whirled around at the sound of Bennett's voice. Katie tried to squelch the irrational surge of excitement at the sight of him. His brother had just become a father again. Of course he was here.

"Hey. Congratulations on being an uncle again."

"Thank you. And thank you for being here for Ridley. Jackson says you coached her like a champ."

Katie slumped against the wall, the hours of exhaustion catching up with her all at once. Going through childbirth for the first time was a scary thing and Katie knew from firsthand experience how hard it was to do it alone. Don had been in surgery when she'd gone into labor and she had asked them not to tell him. She'd known even then that he would be annoyed at the interruption instead of happy to be by her side.

Katie had been determined not to let Ridley feel alone. With no mother to support her and her sister out of town, Ri had been terrified. But her friend had hung in there despite things not going according to plan. Katie felt honored to have been there to hold her hand through it. They'd done the Lamaze breathing Ridley had learned in her birthing class together.

She *had* coached her like a champ, Katie realized. It had been scary and intense but she'd kept it together. It was a good feeling. An accomplished feeling.

Over the years, she'd allowed others to get inside her head and make her feel that she wasn't as accomplished just because she didn't have a university degree or high salary. But she was a nurturer and always had been. She had spent her time cultivating the most important things in the world—her relationships with her friends and family—and in return, they viewed her as someone they could count on.

That might not come with a diploma on the wall but it was an achievement all the same.

Katie was proud of herself.

"I'm glad I was there. She looked so gray when I found her. It scared me."

Bennett grabbed her hand and Katie soaked up all the warmth and acceptance that she'd missed so much. Then all at once she remembered how she'd wanted to find him before everything happened.

"Don told me that he met you. Whatever he said to you was bullshit. He's such a jerk sometimes."

Bennett squeezed her hand. "I shouldn't have listened to him anyway. And I definitely shouldn't have avoided talking to you. I was just hurt. I thought you'd gone back to him."

Katie grimaced at the thought. "Not a chance. There were so many times I wanted to call you but I figured you were prob-ably getting ready for your date with Olivia."

"It wasn't—"

She held up a hand. "I know it wasn't a date. I was just being jealous before. You've never given me any reason not to trust you and I know you'd never jump from one woman to the next like that, anyway."

"No, I wouldn't. I'm awkward but I've never been stupid. I'm smart enough to know that our relationship is special. I don't want anyone else."

Katie couldn't stop smiling. Maybe under any other circumstances she could play it cool but all her emotions were at the surface after watching her friend just bring new life into the world. Suddenly it felt like anything was possible.

"I don't want anyone else, either. I should have just trusted you more. You're perfectly capable of spending an evening with a female friend without anything happening."

Bennett bit his lip. His fingers tightened around hers.

After working so closely with Bennett for more than a month, she could read his facial expressions like a map. His face often telegraphed his thoughts even when he didn't realize it. Which was why his expression was so alarming.

Katie narrowed her eyes. "Bennett? Nothing happened with Olivia, right?"

"Um ... It was nothing. But she did kiss me. Once." Seeing her expression, he quickly stammered, "but it's okay! Olivia is in love with someone else. She doesn't even want me."

The door opened behind her and Jackson stuck his head out. "Oh hey, Bennett. I didn't know you were still here."

"Yeah. I'm still here." Bennett tried to keep hold on her hand but Katie yanked it away.

Jackson looked between them awkwardly. "Okay so ... Ridley's asking for you, Katie."

"I'm coming right now."

Bennett reached out for her. "Katie, wait. It's not what you think. I swear."

Katie felt a flush of embarrassment that Jackson was overhearing all of this. "This really isn't the best time to talk. Ri needs me right now."

He looked frustrated but let her go. "Okay."

Jackson stepped back so Katie could get in the room.

"Hey bro, why don't you come with me? I'm heading down to the NICU to check on Zane."

Bennett glanced over at her again and she could read the longing on his face. She was upset at the thought of him kissing another woman but they'd already lost time due to misunderstanding and not trusting each other enough. She wasn't going to make the same mistake again.

"We'll talk later, I promise. Okay?"

He gave her a quick nod and then held out an arm to his brother. "Come on, little brother. I can't wait to meet the newest Alexander troublemaker."

twenty

BENNETT LOOKED DOWN at the tiny baby in the incubator on the other side of the glass. Zane Michael Alexander might have been born a little early but he'd still weighed in at a little over six pounds and had a smattering of dark hair on his head already. Jackson stood next to him radiating pride.

"Look at him, Ben. Even though he's early, they said he's doing great. We can probably take him home after a few days of observation. My boys are fighters, huh?"

"That they are. Kind of like you were."

Bennett remembered vividly the day his youngest brother had been born. He'd been five years old and more than a little tired of being presented with a new brother every year or so. But Jackson had been such a funny looking baby that Bennett had decided one more was okay after all. Now he couldn't imagine life without the baby of the family.

"I was scared in there, Bennett. Really scared. I don't know what I'd do if anything happened to her." Jackson didn't take his eyes off the baby as he spoke. But the tension in his shoulders told the story of just how harrowing the last few hours had been for him.

"You're never going to have to find out. Because she seems pretty determined to be here with you."

Jackson huffed out a breath. "So I noticed things seemed pretty tense with Katie earlier. I hope things work out for you guys. She brings out a different side of you, one I haven't seen in a long time."

"She makes me happy," Bennett admitted.

"Good. Well, I need to get back to Ridley and let her know how the baby is doing. Since she lost so much blood they don't want her on her feet just yet so she's sending me for updates on the baby. If I take too long, I wouldn't put it past her to try to come down here on her own."

Bennett was about to answer when he heard his name being called from the other end of the hallway. They both looked over to see Grant walking down the hall. He was obviously on duty because he was wearing his white coat and carrying a patient's chart.

"What's this I hear about a new Alexander man in the family?" Grant put out his hand and pulled Jackson into an exuberant hug. "Happy for you, Jack."

Jackson beamed. "There he is. Look at my boy."

Grant peered through the glass. "That's a beautiful thing." He glanced over at Bennett. "Glad to see you here. I've been meaning to come by and check on those stitches."

Jackson frowned. "Stitches? When did you get stitches?"

Bennett waved away the concern. "Long story. Go report back to Ridley. And kiss the new mom for me."

Jackson waved as he went. Grant held out his hand to motion toward one of the empty exam rooms.

"Let me just take a quick look. I wasn't exactly working under ideal conditions so I've been a little concerned."

Bennett followed him into the exam room, trying not to breathe too deeply. He didn't want to stay any longer than necessary but if he didn't appease Grant, his cousin would just annoy the hell out of him later. He might as well let him check the wound and reassure himself that it was healing properly.

Oblivious to his distress, Grant set the chart he was holding down and washed his hands in the small sink against the wall.

"So I saw your girl here earlier. I was surprised you weren't with her then."

Bennett had already rolled up his sleeve so Grant could access the wound that he'd been keeping clean and dry. His cousin carefully pried off the three large bandages covering the cut.

"Yeah, I would have been here earlier but ... Well, that doesn't matter anymore. Things are fine now."

Grant was quick but thorough as he checked the tender skin around the cut. He shook his head in dismay. "Disgraceful. I can't believe you waited so long. If I'd been able to close this right away there wouldn't even be a scar," he muttered.

Bennett rolled his eyes. Grant was one of the East Coast's top plastic surgeons so he was sure it was torture to his professional pride to see a wound leave a scar unnecessarily.

"Anyway, I hope you aren't having girl troubles already with the fiery Katherine. I liked her. She's the type that doesn't let you get away with any shit."

Bennett glared at his troublemaking and all-together too handsome cousin. It hadn't escaped his notice that Grant had *really* seemed to like Katie. It probably wasn't often that he met a woman willing to tell him off.

"Whatever. Is my arm going to fall off or what?"

"It's fine. It's not perfect, which is what it would have been if you weren't so stubborn but there's no sign of infection and it's healing well."

Grant smeared something that Bennett hoped was antibiotic ointment over the scar, then added fresh bandages and covered the wound lightly.

"Anyway, I hope things work out with Katie. Because if you let a woman like that get away, you deserve to lose her. Maybe even to your younger and better-looking cousin." Grant grinned, flashing perfect white teeth. "Women like that don't come around all that often."

Bennett was still more than a little annoyed at how much attention his cousin was paying to Katie. "I'm surprised to hear you say that. I figured you'd be the more the merrier type."

Grant stiffened. "Can I tell you something?"

"It's never stopped you before."

"You're the smartest dumbass I know. I'm not trying to steal your girl. I'm hoping you won't be as dumb as I was."

Bennett shifted, suddenly feeling guilty. His cousin was for once being sincere and he'd reacted out of jealousy. "Grant, I'm sorry–"

"Whatever's going on with the two of you, fix it. Whatever she needs, be that. It's really that simple," Grant interrupted. "Or you might find yourself with a little competition."

Bennett sighed. Just when he was getting used to seeing the softer side of Grant, the arrogant side he was used to reemerged. "I'm starting to wonder why I talk to you."

Grant washed his hands again. "Because it gets lonely being the only brilliant one. I get it." After drying his hands on a paper towel, he reclaimed his clipboard from the bed and left.

His cousin might be arrogant but he was also pretty damn smart. Katie had said they'd talk and she just needed some time but that didn't mean he couldn't be useful in the meantime.

She'd arrived with Ridley in the ambulance so she didn't have her car. It was likely that she'd be here for quite some time, possibly even overnight. But maybe she'd need a ride home in the morning. If so, Bennett planned to be the one taking her home.

Whatever she needed, he would be there.

———

EARLY THE NEXT MORNING, Katie walked out of Ridley's hospital room starving and in desperate need of sleep. She had told Ri that she could stay longer but it seemed she wasn't needed.

As soon as she heard her twin was in labor, Raina had flown straight home. With her twin sister and Jackson there, Ridley was back in her comfort zone. Katie was both relieved and sad that she was no longer needed. Because helping out her friend had been the perfect distraction from thinking about Bennett.

Bennett who had kissed another woman at the first opportunity.

As if she'd conjured him by her thoughts, Bennett pushed off of the wall across from Ridley's room. Katie stopped, startled. Had he really been waiting out here the whole time? Then she noticed that he was wearing different clothes and carrying a paper bag.

"What are you doing here?" Her question came out crankier than she'd intended, mainly because she'd been awake for what felt like three days and was in desperate need of food and a shower.

"Waiting for you," he replied. He held out the paper bag.

Katie took it tentatively and then almost dropped to her knees in gratitude when she saw that it contained a breakfast sandwich and a bottle of apple juice. Now she really felt like a bitch for sniping at him when he was just trying to do something nice.

"Thank you. I really needed this."

Bennett held out his arm for her to precede him down the hall and Katie was happy to oblige. She cracked open the bottle of juice first. It was still cold so she could only guess he'd purchased the items in the hospital cafeteria.

"How long have you been waiting in the hallway?" she asked.

Bennett inclined his head back towards the room. "Not long. Jackson texted me so I'd know when to come pick you up."

Katie should have known. Jackson probably thought he was helping her out. She couldn't fault him. He didn't know that she'd been hoping to avoid his oldest brother for a little longer. After such a long and exhausting day, she wasn't ready to hear about his sexual experimentation with his first love.

"I'm not sure that was a good idea. We didn't leave things at a good place."

"I know. But you needed a ride home. When you need something, I'll be there. Always."

Intense hazel eyes fixed on hers and Katie could barely breathe. How had she thought this would get easier? There was never going to be anything easy about knowing that she wasn't Bennett's first choice. Could she really accept a relationship where she had to compete with the memory of someone else? It had been bad enough dealing with Don's wandering eye but with Bennett it would be worse because he wasn't a jerk. With time and distance, she could admit that she hadn't really been devastated at Don's betrayal. Furious and humiliated, yes. But she hadn't really even been all that shocked.

But Bennett ... Katie had to work hard to swallow over the sudden lump in her throat. He was a fantastic human being and it would hurt like hell to know he preferred someone else.

They were silent the entire ride over to his place. She checked her phone for no reason other than to give her something to do besides stare at him. Julia had texted her a picture of all the kids finger painting last night so she knew they'd had fun. For the first time, she had nowhere to be.

No one who needed her.

"Did you get any sleep at all last night?" Bennett asked just as he pulled into the driveway next to his barn.

Katie shook her head. She climbed out of the truck and followed him inside. It was weird to be back after taking a week off. She hadn't realized just how much she'd missed being here. It drove home how different things were without Bennett in her life.

He took her hand and led her upstairs. Considering how they'd left things, she should probably stop him but then he gave her a look and she clamped her lips together.

"Get comfortable. I'm going to tell you about my weekend and then you're going to take a nap."

Amused by his uncharacteristic show of bossiness, Katie went over to the chest of drawers and pulled out one of his long T-shirts. Too tired to even care that he was watching her every move, she shed her clothes and pulled the shirt on. Bennett pulled back the covers on the bed so she could climb in. He took off his own T-shirt and jeans and then climbed into the bed next to her wearing just his boxers.

He turned his head to look at her. "First, I'd like to apologize for the way I handled things with your ex-husband. I didn't give you the chance to explain what I saw that day. That's something I regret."

Katie nodded. "Thank you for saying that. I would never do that to you. Don was drinking that night and I just didn't want him driving drunk and possibly hurting someone."

"I was jealous," Bennett admitted. "He was bragging about how he'd tired you out the night before and I couldn't see anything past that."

Katie was quiet for a moment, thinking about her own reaction to hearing that he'd kissed Olivia. "I was jealous when you told me you kissed Olivia."

Bennett turned over so he was facing her. This close, the space between them seemed even more intimate. Even though she was still filled with lingering doubt and insecurity, Katie felt like she could tell him anything in that moment.

So she hesitantly added, "I know you said that the kiss didn't mean anything. But when you said that Olivia is in love with someone else, it felt like it did when Don cheated on me. Like I'm not really the one you want, just the one who's available."

Bennett listened, his eyes on her face like he wanted to absorb the words straight from her mouth. "This is one of those times when I need a translator. Because what I meant to say was Olivia is in love with someone else and I'm thrilled about it. Because I'm in love with you."

Her heart squeezed so hard that Katie let out a little startled puff of breath. This whole time she'd been ready to hear stammered excuses or rationalizations about why his kiss with Olivia didn't matter. She'd expected him to deny it was a real kiss or claim that he'd been surprised and hadn't meant to kiss her back.

Not that he'd kissed another woman and decided he loved Katie. Anything other than he'd chosen Katie as the one he truly wanted.

"You're not saying anything. Please tell me I haven't ruined things between us." Bennett placed his hand over hers. The warmth of his touch brought her out of her state of shock.

"No. You haven't ruined things between us. I was just surprised. I wasn't expecting you to say that. That you still love me."

His eyes softened. "You should get used to hearing it. I plan on telling you for a very long time."

Katie held in a sigh as his head lowered. When he placed his lips on hers, she melted beneath him. She'd missed this so much. Bennett had a way of making her feel like she was the only thing he needed.

When he tried to pull back, Katie wrapped her arm around his neck to hold him there.

"Aren't you tired?" Bennett asked.

Katie pulled him closer and kissed him again. "Not *that* tired."

BENNETT ALLOWED Katie to pull him down closer so she could steal another kiss. He was happy to let her take whatever she wanted from him. He settled on top of her, allowing his full weight to press her into the mattress. Katie responded with a soft, satisfied sigh that made Bennett smile.

Then she reached down and cupped his hard length and he stopped breathing.

"You are going to kill me."

Her husky chuckle sent even more blood below his waist. Her slender fingers moved over him gently, stroking him through the thin fabric of his boxers. Bennett wasted no time getting her T-shirt off. She stretched beneath him, her full breasts bobbing temptingly in front of his face.

"How the hell did I get so lucky?"

The smile that crossed her face lanced through him like a blade. She probably thought it was just flattery but Bennett truly wondered why a vivacious creature like Katie was attracted to him. But he certainly wasn't going to argue the point. Sometimes you got lucky and that's how she made him feel.

Like he was finally the lucky one in the family.

Katie tugged at the edge of his boxers, pushing them down over his ass. He sat up long enough to kick them off before he came back. The first contact, skin to skin, made them both groan.

"I missed you so much," Katie whispered in-between soft kisses to his neck, jaw, and finally his lips again. "I survived being left behind before but I won't be okay if this doesn't work between us, Bennett. This is so much more."

She sighed and shook her head, like she couldn't figure out how to finish the statement. But she didn't need to. Bennett understood her completely. She was telling him not to start this if he wasn't ready to finish it. Not to play with her heart because she was in this thing all the way.

Which was exactly how he felt, too.

"I'm going to show you, over the next few days, weeks, months, that this is it for me. You, Katherine Mason, are it for me. So get ready to be courted."

Her answering laugh was filled with wonder and hope. "Courted? Wow. I can't wait to see this. What does courting look like?"

Bennett slid one hand under her back, holding her in place so he could trail kisses over her neck and shoulders. Her breathing was getting faster as he moved lower.

"It looks like dinners out and nights in. Spending time with Hunter and Matthew so they can get to know me." He raised his head from where he was currently hovering over her breasts. "It means proving to you that I'm here to stay. That I'm serious about us being together. It's showing you what our life together can be."

Her eyes glittered. "I'm scared how much I want that."

Bennett pressed his face between her breasts, listening to the beat of her heart. Katie wrapped her arms around his back, holding him against her. He was overwhelmed with the love and protectiveness he felt in that moment. He vowed right then and there that he was going to show her love was nothing to fear.

Just then she surprised him by locking her heels behind his back and rolling them over. She settled on top of him, rocking her hips over his erection. Bennett moaned at the contact and her eyes went dark and sultry. Then she reached down and caressed his hard length, positioning him so he could slide deep.

Her eyes closed as she took him inside, the look on her face one of sublime pleasure. Bennett wanted to remember it forever, the moment she let herself go, trusting him to catch her.

They moved together, her hips riding him until they were in perfect sync. He watched her, taking in every inch of this woman he loved, wanting to imprint the image on his brain. He couldn't look away. He wanted to drink up the sight of her.

"You are so perfect. And all mine."

Her eyes met his at the softly growled words. Then her mouth fell open when he reached down to adjust her hips. She shuddered at the extra stimulation, her inner muscles clenching desperately.

"*Oh god.*" He couldn't hold back, even though he wanted this to last forever. It was too good, being held in her tight heat while she looked down at him with slumberous eyes. He stroked her faster, wanting her to go first.

He would always put her first.

Katie cried out helplessly as her orgasm took hold, dropping her hands to his chest to stabilize herself while she rode out the waves of pleasure. Bennett kept his eyes on her the whole time, the sight of her coming so intensely arousing that it brought him down with her. He moaned as his own orgasm coiled low and then unleashed, wringing every last bit of strength from him.

Katie collapsed on his chest, panting softly. He grabbed the sheet and threw it over them both. He was suddenly exhausted after a night spent worrying over whether she would forgive him. He patted her back gently, reminding himself that she was there with him and would be there when he woke up.

She must have felt the same because she rubbed her face against his chest and sighed. "I'm so glad you came to get me."

"Me too. Now sleep, sweetheart. I know you're tired."

As she drifted off, Bennett knew that she was still worried about a multitude of things but he vowed to show her that the promises he'd made to her were solid.

He fell asleep with visions of how he wanted the next few months to pan out. Now that he had his mission, he wouldn't rest until he'd achieved his objective.

To show Katie what it meant to be truly and completely loved.

twenty-one

One month later...

BENNETT WATCHED Katie wiping down the counter in her kitchen. He'd offered to help but she'd shooed him into the living room where Hunter and Matthew were watching television along with Chris and Jase. Katie was babysitting so Ridley and Jackson could have a little break. Jackson had described baby Zane as being able to sleep while simultaneously screaming his head off so the new parents were both exhausted.

Although Bennett wasn't sure what his little brother was talking about because Zane was sleeping in his arms just fine.

"I can't believe it. You got him to sleep." Katie appeared at his elbow, looking down at the sleeping baby in awe. "How did you do that?"

Bennett shrugged, not wanting to speak aloud and possibly wake up Zane. Moving carefully, he walked up the stairs and into the guest room Katie had set up for the baby. She'd set up the crib Matthew had used since she'd never gotten rid of it, and Bennett approached it with all the caution he'd use when handling liquid nitrogen.

Katie had followed him and she tiptoed forward to lower the side of the crib for him. Slowly, carefully, Bennett settled the sleeping baby on his back in the middle of the crib. He'd been so nervous before tonight that he'd read up on infant safety so he already knew not to cover the baby with any blankets or sheets. Instead, he raised the side of the crib and let out a sigh of relief when it latched silently.

With a triumphant smile for Katie, he walked back into the hallway. She closed the door behind them.

"Well done, Mr. Alexander. I'm impressed. It takes a special touch to put a cranky baby to bed."

Bennett was pretty impressed with himself. It took a lot of trust for Jackson and Ridley to allow someone to care for their children and he knew that it was the highest of compliments that they trusted Bennett with their son. Katie's presence had a lot to do with that, he knew, but it was still an honor. And one that had him thinking.

He pulled Katie into his arms. "Do you ever think about having more kids?"

Katie froze and he could feel the tension in her body. He didn't allow her to pull back and eventually she relaxed, resting her head on his chest.

"I do. Sometimes. I always wanted a big family but then after a while I stopped wishing for that."

Bennett held her tighter. Over the last few months, he'd been relentless in his mission to court her. It was an old-fashioned concept but then again, he was an old-fashioned kind of guy. He wanted Katie to know how serious he was about working toward a life together so he'd worked hard to insinuate himself into every aspect of her life. From helping out with the kids, to bringing her flowers and little gifts to show her his feelings, to encouraging her to go after her own dreams, which recently included working part-time with a local mid-wife.

His goal was to show Katie that he loved her wholeheartedly and that her happiness was important to him. Soon it would be time to show her exactly what it meant to be the owner of his heart. Waiting for the perfect moment was getting harder and harder. Because if his Katie wanted children, then damn it all, he wanted to give them to her.

"What about you?" Katie asked. "Do you want children?"

"Absolutely. As many as possible."

Katie laughed softly. "That's a little scary. How many are we talking here?"

Bennett figured this was one of those times when blunt honesty might not be the best route. He was pretty sure that if he said he wanted five that she'd run away screaming. So he exercised his newfound diplomacy skills that Katie had been helping him develop over the last few months.

"I'll be happy with whatever happens as long as it's with you."

She patted his chest. "Good answer, babe. You're getting good at this. Sorry if I was a little intense. It's a bittersweet thing for me. After all, I've been blessed with two amazing kids but I failed at the most important part, finding a father who would appreciate them."

It wasn't the right time to reveal the next steps in his *make Katie happy* plan just yet but he couldn't let her walk away after she said that. He captured her chin gently, forcing her to look up at him.

"You haven't failed. You *have* found a father that will

appreciate them. No matter what happens with Don, I will always be there for them."

Katie's eyes went soft and liquid. She blinked rapidly. "Thank you, Bennett. You have no idea what that means to me. And to them."

"It means just as much to me. There's nowhere else I'd rather be. I love them, too."

Part of the reason he hadn't asked Katie the question he was dying to ask her yet was because he knew she was secretly waiting for him to get bored and go. She hadn't figured out yet that he wasn't going anywhere.

She hadn't figured out yet that for Bennett, she was home.

As difficult as it was, he could wait until she was ready. He'd been raised by two people who never gave up on each other. That's what he wanted with Katie.

He just had to be patient.

They walked downstairs hand in hand to find the boys trying to make popcorn in the microwave. Even as Katie released his hand to rush forward and deal with the kitchen catastrophe, Bennett was silently counting the days until he never had to let her go.

———

Three months later...

SOMETHING TICKLED the side of Katie's face and she batted it away. Only a few moments later, the tickling sensation resumed only this time on the sole of her foot. Her eyes popped open.

Bennett sat on the side of the bed holding a single red rose.

"Hey. Sorry, did I sleep too long?" She'd come upstairs to take a nap in the loft because she'd almost face-planted into one of the worktables downstairs while recording the results of their latest soil sample test. Working part-time with a local mid-wife had been so rewarding and had given her a new purpose in life. But it was definitely taking its toll on her.

Lucky her other boss was so accommodating, Katie thought with a smile. Bennett had been nothing but supportive of her taking on something new, even though it had cut into their time together. It was something she'd had to get used to, having a man who cared as much about her personal fulfillment as his own.

Bennett leaned over and kissed her soundly. "It's almost seven o'clock."

Panic took hold. "*Oh my god.* The kids! I wasn't there to meet the bus."

He tapped the end of her nose, interrupting her meltdown. "It's okay. I met the bus and brought the boys back here. They're currently with my mom making apple pies."

Katie whimpered in relief. She'd been so tired lately but she'd never missed picking the kids up after school. Bennett had recently started coming with her to pick them up and they'd all come back to the farm. The kids loved having so much room to play and they'd both become accustomed to Bennett taking an interest in their lives.

He'd taken them both to the fields so they could help him spread the first batch of his new soil on the test area he'd chosen. Hunter in particular had loved seeing all the different crops. Katie wouldn't be surprised if he took an interest in farming when he got older. Bennett would be thrilled. It had been both difficult and heartwarming to watch her sons fall in love with Bennett the same way she had.

"That was so nice of her. Your mom has been a lifesaver these last few months."

Bennett smirked then. "She's trying to give us as much time alone as she can."

Katie smacked his arm playfully. "Your mother is not trying to give us naughty time."

He rubbed his nose against hers. "Don't let her fool you. My mom is not so innocent. I'm grateful for that because there's something that I want to show you."

There was a strangely intimate look in his eye so Katie didn't ask any questions. She just stood and allowed him to lead her downstairs. Her shoes were by the front door and she slipped them on and followed him out to his truck. He held the door for her as she climbed up. After he rounded the front of the cab, he climbed up next to her, sending her a brief, excited glance.

Katie just shook her head. What was he up to? She couldn't understand why anyone had ever thought he was boring just because he was brainy. Bennett was actually quite spontaneous and loved to try new things. They'd gone to the beach to try surfing, which had been a major fail for both of them, but also to the planetarium in Virginia Beach for a special presentation by one of his friends. He often would have an idea and then jump right to it. Over the last few months, she'd learned to just go along with his sudden schemes.

When they pulled up to an empty field, Katie glanced over at him curiously. "Where are we?"

Bennett blew out a nervous breath. "Home, hopefully."

Confused, Katie turned to look at the empty field again.

Now that she was looking closer, she could see little orange flags marking the boundary of the lot. There were no other houses around it but she could see another house behind it in the distance.

"This is ... yours?"

He nodded. "Come on. I want to show you something."

She climbed down and waited as Bennett retrieved something from the back of the truck. He came toward her and held out his hand, a large roll of paper under his arm. They walked forward until they were roughly in the middle of the lot. Katie shaded her eyes and looked around. She could see a river in the distance.

"Is that the river you showed me before? The boundary between the Alexander land?"

"Sure is. If you keep going that way—" He pointed ahead to the line of trees. "—you'll run right into Mom and Dad's land."

He took the large scroll from beneath his arm and unrolled it. Katie could see at once that it was architectural plans.

"For a few years now, I've had my eye on this parcel of land. It was owned by some distant relative up until last year when I bought it. I've been working on plans for my dream house for quite a while. Now I want to show it to you."

Katie knelt next to him to view the plans. "This is amazing. But this is a lot of house for one guy. You really planned to build this all along?"

He pointed to one section on the plans. "I wanted a lab. And I also wanted an attached greenhouse here. But recently I called my architect and had him make some changes."

Katie peered closer and could see that on the plans he'd written words in pencil. *Master bedroom. Playroom for the kids. Hunter's room. Matthew's room. Katie's office.*

Nursery.

She put a hand over her mouth. Her eyes filled with tears, and she blinked trying to clear her vision. Part of her was scared to blink because she was afraid to believe in what she was seeing.

"A nursery?"

When she looked over at Bennett, Katie gasped. He knelt next to her on the ground, holding out a black ring box.

"Katie, I brought you here to show you what I see in our future. A life filled with new adventures and endless discoveries. Waking up together, falling asleep together, laughing every day. Together."

"That's what I want, too."

Her heart felt like it would bounce out of her chest when he flipped the ring box open to reveal a stunning round solitaire on a simple gold band. Bennett took a deep breath, like he was gathering his courage and then took her hand gently.

"I love you, Katherine Mason. I want you to keep me on my toes, tell me when I lose track of time, and read me outrageous books at night."

Tears slipped down Katie's cheeks. "Maybe I'll read you one of those inappropriate books," she joked.

"I hope so. Be as inappropriate as you want. We don't have to follow anyone's rules but our own." He squeezed her hand. "Now I need to ask you a question. One I've wanted to ask you for so long. Will you marry me?"

She held a hand over her mouth, trying to hold the happiness in. "Yes! There's nothing I want more."

He smiled tremulously and then took the ring out of the box. She held out her left hand and watched as he slipped it over her ring finger. It settled against her skin like it was meant to be there.

"It's beautiful. I love you so much. Sometimes I can't believe this is real."

Katie wiped at her eyes, completely overwhelmed. She'd gone from feeling like she didn't know what she was supposed to do with her life to knowing without a doubt that she was exactly where she was meant to be.

Bennett stood and grabbed her, swinging her around until she laughed from sheer joy. When he set her on her feet again, she rested her head against his chest. He rested his head on top of hers.

"This is real. And it's forever."

epilogue

One year later...

BENNETT ADJUSTED the lapels of his tuxedo and tugged at the knot of his tie. He wasn't a man given to worry over his appearance but even he had his vanity.

He stepped next to his brother Elliot and looked in the mirror. He was startled by the transformation. He'd always considered his appearance to be adequate but the guy reflected in the glass was more than just adequate. He looked distinguished. More than that, he looked happy. Bennett leaned closer and observed the flush on his cheeks and the sparkle in his eyes. It wasn't a surprise since the past year had been the best of his life. Life with Katie was even better than he'd hoped. They had so much fun together.

And today he would make her his wife.

He glanced over at Eli, who was wrestling with his own tie. A lot had happened over the past year. Kaylee had given birth to a beautiful baby girl named Grace Elizabeth. It was so strange that all of his brothers had become fathers before he did. He smiled. Considering the secret Katie had yet to tell him, Bennett figured he only had to wait about seven months before he joined the fatherhood club. He wasn't going to tell her that he'd figured it out, though. She would want to tell him in her own way and he wanted her to have that.

Eli yanked at his tie again exasperated, and Bennett finally took over, tugging on the fabric gently and repositioning it. "Thank you for allowing us to share your day."

Once he was done, Eli looked in the mirror and smiled.

"It's no problem. Hell, you were going to be standing up there as my best man, anyway. You might as well get married, too."

Bennett smiled. Once the family had heard about his proposal to Katie last year, his mother in particular had been almost woozy from excitement at the thought of two weddings. It was Kaylee who'd suggested that they share the day to minimize the stress and worry of planning things twice over. Bennett had been unsurprised but thrilled with how completely Katie had blended right into the family. His parents already referred to her as one of their "daughters."

Suddenly, he just wanted to see her. His mother had banished them to his lab to get ready, since they weren't supposed to see the brides before the wedding. But Bennett figured they'd broken plenty of rules up to now, what was one more? He pulled out his phone and texted Katie. She responded immediately.

"I'll be back," he told Eli.

His brother nodded knowingly. "Tell Katie I said hi. And don't let Mom see you."

Bennett snickered. They were two grown men still

tiptoeing around their parents like they were worried about being grounded. He hoped they never changed.

Katie was waiting for him on the back porch when he walked across the grounds toward the main house. It was hot outside but she wore a thick robe. Glancing behind her, she stepped off the porch and ran toward him. He grabbed her up, both of them laughing as he dashed back toward his converted barn with her in his arms.

Her face was pressed against his neck so he could feel her laughter.

"Hurry before Julia catches us. She's been freaking out all morning about something going wrong."

Bennett carried her into the lab and set her on her feet. Eli was still upstairs in his loft so they were alone.

"This is where it all started," she commented.

"I know. It's hard to believe. Now I have everything I've ever wanted. You love me and we're getting married. The only thing that'll make this better is the day I have a little mini-me or mini-you running around."

Katie turned to him. The expression in her eyes was one he hadn't seen before. She placed a hand over her abdomen.

"I wasn't going to tell you yet but I can't keep it in. We'll have that little mini-person next spring. I'm pregnant." He thought he'd done a good job of playing surprised but Katie narrowed her eyes. "You'd already figured it out, hadn't you?"

"Maybe. I do notice everything about you. Such as when you're no longer drinking alcohol and suddenly are even more curvy and beautiful than usual."

"The perils of having a brilliant husband. I can't get anything by you." She sighed happily.

Bennett pulled her into his arms and held her close, resting his hands over her still flat stomach. "Thank you."

"For what?" She looked up at him, love shining from her eyes.

"Not running away when you found out the real reason I hired you. Having patience when I zone out or get so involved with my research that I forget what day it is or that the trash hasn't been taken out. For reading to me every night and smiling at me every morning."

"That's no hardship, Bennett. I'm smiling because you make me so happy. I'm smiling because I love you."

"I know. That's why I'm thanking you. For loving me as I am."

Katie kissed him softly. "Don't tell Ridley I said this, but I'm so glad she pushed us together. Otherwise I'd be back at my old house, going to sleep alone every night and wondering if I'd ever love any man again."

Bennett understood. He'd often had similar thoughts, thinking of how different his life would be if not for one fateful family dinner.

"It may not have been just Ridley's work that put us together. You know I'm not a religious person. I guess I've always been skeptical of things I can't see or test with the scientific method. But I sent up a wish one night." He smiled thinking of it. "I felt so guilty doing it."

"Why?"

He shrugged. "I already have so much; it felt excessive that I wasn't happy already. But I knew that if I could wish for just one thing, it would be my perfect match. My other half. And the next month, there you were."

Katie's smile was shy as she pulled him down for another kiss. "Here I am. And I'm not going anywhere."

His phone ringing startled them both. When he pulled it out of his pocket, his mother's face was on the screen.

Katie winced.

"Actually, on that note, I am going somewhere. Back to the house before your mom freaks out. See you at the altar, handsome."

She kissed him lightly on the cheek and hurried out the door. Bennett stuck his head out to watch her progress. She was met at the back door by his mother. He ducked back inside before his mother could see him.

Only one more hour to go ...

———

"ARE YOU READY, KATHERINE?" Her mother reached over and made a minute adjustment to the placement of the crown of white roses on her head. For once, Katie didn't mind her mother fussing over her. It was nice, actually.

The last time her mother had walked her down the aisle, it hadn't felt like this. She'd been nervous and her mother had been apprehensive. It turned out they were both right to have reservations but Katie didn't regret it at all. She'd gained her two amazing children and a lifetime's worth of experience about what kind of marriage she *didn't* want.

Katie glanced over at her mother who was positively beaming with pride. This time they were both excited. Her mother had been just as charmed by Bennett over the past week of her visit as everyone else in her family. He'd decided to call her 'Mama Sheila' and treated her with the same reverential respect that he gave Julia. Katie wouldn't have thought it possible but she'd fallen even deeper in love with her shy, awkward fiancé after watching how hard he'd worked to make her mother and siblings comfortable.

Her sister, Mari, in particular was a huge Bennett fan. Katie still laughed thinking about her loudmouthed sister's response to seeing the smorgasbord of perfection that were the Alexander brothers. She'd been blushing furiously the whole time as Katie introduced her to everyone.

Then she'd winked behind Bennett's back and pointed at his butt. Katie had almost choked trying to keep her laughter in.

Their brother, Nelson, had rolled his eyes at their antics before inviting Bennett out for a drink. They'd come back that night half drunk but in great spirits. Her brother had finally said that Bennett was "all right" which in Nelson-speak was about as good as it got.

"Are you two ready?" Tiana, the ever-perky wedding planner hovered beside them. At Katie's nod, and then Kaylee's, she gave them both a thumbs up before speaking into her earpiece.

A few moments later, the sound of the iconic wedding march played through the sound system. Katie clutched her mother's arm tighter and took a deep breath.

Sheila patted her arm comfortingly. "You have nothing to be nervous about. You got it right this time, baby. You really did."

Kaylee walked out first on the arm of her father. Katie watched as they made their way up the white runner leading to the altar.

Leading to the future.

Once Kaylee took her place next to Elliott at the altar, the wedding planner motioned for Katie and her mom to start. She took a deep breath and then walked out. All the eyes on her were intimidating until she got close enough to see Bennett.

From that moment on, all she could see was him.

Her mother hugged her and then set her hand in Bennett's. He squeezed her hand gently before bringing it to his mouth for a gentle kiss. They walked up the two steps to the altar where Kay and Eli were waiting.

The minister cleared his throat. "Dearly beloved ... "

All through the ceremony, Bennett held her eyes, sometimes making faces that caused Katie to blush because she knew it meant he was thinking something dirty. They watched with affection as his brother and Kaylee were led through their vows before it was time to say their own.

The minister looked at Bennett. "Repeat after me. I, Bennett Mark Alexander, take you, Katherine Anne Mason..."

Bennett repeated the sacred words in a strong, clear voice. They'd opted for the standard vows because he'd been stressed about forgetting what he wanted to say. But even though she'd heard the words before, Katie would forever cherish the memory of Bennett reciting those iconic words to her and the unbelievable thrill of saying them back to him.

After the exchange of rings, the minister faced the assembly of family and friends with a huge smile. "And it is with great pleasure that I present to you, Elliot and Kaylee Alexander and Bennett and Katherine Alexander. Gentlemen, you may now kiss your brides!"

There was an explosion of cheers and whistles but Katie couldn't hear anything. Her entire world condensed to the moment Bennett's lips met hers. She didn't close her eyes, wanting to see and commit to memory every moment of this special day.

Bennett ended the kiss with a little nuzzle against her nose before he opened his eyes. "I love you, Katie."

"I love you too, Bennett." She held on to the lapels of his tuxedo, wishing they were already alone but then suddenly he was pulling back and the noise of the crowd permeated.

They turned to face their family, hands entwined and hearts full. Eli and Kay stood next to them with their arms around each other's waists. Katie immediately noticed Ridley and Jackson in the front row clapping and cheering. Next to them, Mark and Julia beamed, looking as proud as any parents could. Behind them Olivia sat with her boyfriend, King. They'd had dinner a few nights ago and Katie could already tell she'd found a new friend.

A sharp whistle cut through the air and Katie's eyes swung to the opposite side of the yard where her family was. Mari was wiping away tears, arm in arm with their mother. Her husband Dennis was beside her, clapping heartily. Nelson whistled again, before pumping his fist in the air.

Everyone was happy.

Bennett grinned down at her. "Our family can get a little crazy. Are you ready for this, Mrs. Alexander?"

It was ridiculous how much she loved hearing that. Especially since this time around she had no doubts that this was the name she'd carry for life. As she looked into her new husband's eyes, the entirety of their lives flashed through her mind: birthdays, anniversaries and several babies with her dark skin and his hazel eyes. A lifetime of joy and pain, successes and failures, and a bond that would transcend it all.

"I am now," she whispered back.

————

AS THE MUSIC changed to something slow and heartfelt, Mark Alexander held out his hand to his wife. As his wife looked up at him, her eyes reflected the same love as when they were newlyweds over thirty years ago.

"Dance with me, my love?"

Julia had been running around all day, seeing to this and that, heading off disasters and doing whatever was necessary to make sure her two oldest sons had the perfect wedding. He'd helped as much as possible but the bulk of the credit went to Julia. But now that the cake had been cut, the bridal bouquets thrown, and the newlyweds seen off in a shower of rice and well-wishes, his responsibility was making sure that his lovely wife enjoyed the event she'd worked so hard on.

"I thought you'd never ask." Julia accepted his hand and together they walked out to the dance floor.

The music flowed over them and Mark pulled his wife into his arms. She settled against him with a happy little sigh. It had been a truly beautiful day. It was also a bittersweet day as a parent. He looked around the land that had been passed down through generations of Alexanders and saw the results of a life-time of hard work and community. Family, friends and every-thing in between was gathered together to celebrate the start of a new life for his two oldest sons. And Mark couldn't help feeling a sense of accomplishment.

"We did it, my love. All of our boys are married and happy with wonderful families of their own."

Julia patted his chest affectionately. "Did you ever think that all of this would come from flirting with your little sister's friend while on summer break?"

Mark chuckled at the memory. He'd suspected as soon as he saw Julia that she was something special. And he'd known for sure when she'd put him in his place with her sharp tongue and fierce determination.

"I was smart enough to recognize a priceless gem when I saw it. Pretty good for a young country boy from Virginia, I'd say."

As he spun her around, Mark caught sight of his brother on the other side of the dance floor. He'd called his brother the same day he'd told Bennett he would and they'd come to a tentative truce of sorts. When Stewart caught his eye, he nodded respectfully and then glanced away.

And Mark made a decision.

"I'm going to go say hello to Stewart and Lily."

Julia raised her head in surprise. "You are?" When he nodded, she beamed at him. "That's wonderful. I'll come with you."

Hand in hand, they walked across the makeshift dance floor to where Stewart and Lily danced, looking slightly uncomfortable. Lily caught sight of them first and tapped her husband on the shoulder. Steward turned and froze when he saw them approaching.

"Hello, Stewart. Lily, it's lovely to see you again," Julia greeted them both.

Mark squeezed her hand in appreciation. Considering their history, she had plenty of reason to hold a grudge but that wasn't his wife's way.

Lily held a hand to her mouth in surprise and glanced at Stewart. "Hello. Thank you for inviting us."

"Of course. Why don't we go say hello to Mama and Papa Alexander and let the boys talk?" Julia said, referring to Mark and Stewart's parents, in town from Arizona for the wedding. She held out her arm and Lily took it gratefully.

Once alone, Mark and Stewart eyed each other awkwardly. Since he was the one who'd initiated the conversation, Mark pointed toward his nephew. "I heard Grant was profiled in *The Virginia Chronicle* for his volunteer work on burn victims. You and Lily must be so proud."

Steward relaxed slightly. "Yes, we're very proud of him. He works too much, which worries Lily, but he's doing great things."

Mark nodded. "We messed up along the way but our kids came out pretty great."

Stewart laughed. "I can't argue with that." He hesitated before he extended a hand to Mark. "Hopefully we'll do better going forward. Agreed?"

Mark accepted his hand gratefully. "This is going to be a new era for the Alexanders. I have a feeling great things are coming."

They turned to see Lily and Julia motioning to them from across the yard. Mark had spent some time with his parents in the week before the wedding but he knew they were excited to see him and Stewart getting along.

"Let's go make Mom and Dad happy."

Stewart followed along as he started across the yard. "So all of your boys are married now. Maybe you and Julia can give us some pointers on how to get ours to settle down. It'd be nice to have some grandchildren."

Mark smiled at that. It was a great thing that they'd made peace with each other of course. But his nieces and nephews might not think so once they understood what having their aunt and uncle back in their lives would mean. He met Julia's eyes as they got closer.

"Don't worry, big brother. Once Julia hears that, I don't think you'll have to wait too long."

I hope you enjoyed *Just One Thing*!

Bonus Material: Everyone's favorite anti-social brother, Bennett, has been invited to a bachelor party. If you think Ben's awkward now, imagine how he'll react in a strip club! To get your bonus material, join my VIP list!

Keep reading for a special excerpt of Olivia's book.

BAD KING

Thane Kingsley's parents just put a gold diggers target on his back. But if all they want is a wedding, he can do that.

Who Wants to Marry a Billionaire?
Must be completely inappropriate.

KING COULDN'T STOP STARING at her mouth.

He took another swig of whisky, relishing the smooth burn as it traveled down and settled in the pit of his stomach.

She sat up slightly and smiled at him, a wooden smile that

didn't reach her eyes. He'd seen that particular look plenty of times on his mother's face when his father was droning on about something or other.

"You've already decided you're going to say no."

Surprise flickered in her eyes before she glanced away. Her fingers wrapped around her glass but there was nothing left but ice.

"Look... King. I don't want to be rude but I have a feeling whatever you're going to ask me probably isn't something I want to do."

"Oh really? You don't like parties? Or eating exquisite cuisine? Or shopping for clothes and shoes that you don't have to pay for? The job comes with a clothing allowance."

She dipped her head. "Go on. Not that I'm interested or anything."

King pressed his lips together to stifle a grin. "My parents have decided that I need to settle down. I'm the CEO of the family business and as a result, I haven't had much time to meet anyone."

"They're probably just worried about you," she said.

He grimaced. "That may be the case. But they've also decided that they'll hand control over to my little brother if I don't settle down. My little brother who at this very moment is probably out drinking, sleeping with anything on two legs and generally being as much of a spoiled brat as possible."

Angel didn't say anything but he could tell she was listening because she'd angled her head closer to him. It was impossible not to notice how long her eyelashes were or how the tips of her long, wavy hair brushed her lower back. She'd changed into street clothes but he could still see her sweet curves even beneath jeans and a leather jacket.

"So, you need me to pretend to be your girlfriend? Come on. That only works in the movies. You don't think your parents will find it suspicious that you suddenly have a girlfriend? They're going to know you're just pretending to placate them."

"I know."

Her mouth puckered into the most adorable little pout. Damn he was going to enjoy this. His parents would be appropriately scared off by her smart mouth and would leave him, and his position at Kingsley International, alone. Meanwhile, he was going to enjoy having that smart mouth all over him. He'd never been so happy about his parents meddling before.

"Okay, maybe I'm just tired or perhaps there actually was vodka in the cranberry juice but I don't get the point of this. Why bother having me pretend to be your girlfriend if your parents are going to know what you're doing?"

He couldn't resist anymore so he tapped her softly on the end of the nose. She gasped softly and a faint flush covered her cheekbones.

"Because, my sweet angel, my parents know me well. They aren't expecting me to fall in love. They just want me to marry for appearances sake. My parents aren't in love either. My mother's family had some corporate holdings that my father's family was interested in. So they married and now Kingsley International is one of the biggest banking and investing firms in the world."

"That sounds very cold."

"They seem happy enough. But apparently not so happy that they keep their nose out of my business. So here's the deal. I have a meeting next month with some important European investors. I've spent years preparing for this deal. There is no way I can let them pull me off now and stick Colin in there." He winced at just the thought.

"Who's Colin?" Her question brought him back to the matter at hand.

"My little brother. I love him but he'd fuck it up and then I'd have to spend another five years cleaning up the mess by the time my father comes to his senses. I have worked so hard for this. Everyone thinks I got my position just by virtue of my last name but my father made me prove myself every step of the way. I've been at his knee since I was a child learning the ins and outs of our business. While everyone else was partying, I was studying finance and economics, preparing for when I'd finally be old enough to take over. This job is all I have."

He stopped talking to find her watching him, stunned. Embarrassed by how much he'd just revealed, he cleared his throat.

"The point is, I don't have time for this. So let's just play the game for a few weeks and keep my parents happy. You'll get to shop, eat and basically do whatever the hell you want on my dime the entire time. It's a pretty decent deal."

She made a face. "Are you really going to pretend you don't have a long list of girls who'd be more than happy to wine and dine on your tab?"

Uncomfortable, he took another swig of his drink. How could he explain things without sounding like even more of an entitled jerk than what she already thought?

"I've had girlfriends, sure. But this is just a short term thing."

She snorted. "Of course. Wouldn't want any of them getting the wrong idea. They might actually think you *gasp* liked them! How inconvenient."

"Did you just say gasp? As in, actually say the word out loud?"

"Did you just say you can't ask any of the girls you already know because it would be hard to get rid of them afterward?" She pantomimed putting her fingers down her throat.

Oh yeah, his father was going to shit a brick when he brought her home.

"I didn't actually say that but if we're being blunt, then yes. Giving someone false hope doesn't seem like the kindest thing to do."

She shrugged. "Well, I guess that's true. But it doesn't mean that I'm participating in this nonsense either. Good luck!" She stood and straightened her jacket.

"I'll pay you ten grand for the month," he blurted out.

Her mouth fell open. "How much?"

Normally an expert negotiator, King couldn't believe he'd just thrown a number out there with no forethought. She was already going to hose him in clothing and spa charges so he hadn't been planning to offer any kind of salary. After all, what woman wouldn't jump at the chance to buy all the clothes, shoes and whatever other shit women bought on someone else's credit card?

"You heard me. Are you in or what?" It came out more aggressively than he'd intended but he was still grouchy about being put in a corner.

The bartender leaned over, interrupting their tense stand-off. "You ready to close out, Livvy?"

She pulled her eyes away from his and handed over some cash. "Yeah, I'm done Jeb. Keep the change."

"You got it." The bartender glanced over at him so King pulled out his wallet and handed over the first credit card his fingers touched. "Charge her drinks to my tab. Keep the cash for yourself."

The bartender didn't look impressed at his largesse but took the card.

She crossed her arms. "Okay."

"Okay," he echoed. "You'll do it?"

She nodded and pulled out a small business card from the inner pocket of her jacket. "Here's my card, my cell number is on the back. Let me know when you need me. Don't worry about the clothes. I've got that covered."

She turned and he reached out before he thought, panicked at the thought of her leaving without him. He wanted to walk her to her car and make sure she was safe, a completely alien feeling, but the bartender still had his card so instead he stood there patting her arm like an idiot.

"He called you Livvy."

Her lips curled up. "You didn't really think my name was Angel, did you?" She stuck out her hand. "Olivia."

He shook it. "Olivia. I'll call you tomorrow, Olivia."

She winked. "I'll answer."

People moved out of the way as she walked though the crowd, as if they too could sense the power in the swing of her hips. There was something hypnotic about the way she moved. It made him think he could enjoy watching her do anything and not just the dirty things he'd been unable to stop imagining the entire time they were talking. He'd love to watch her dance when she thought no one was watching, or sing in the shower or wiggle that perky little behind while she brushed her teeth in the morning. The door to the pub swung shut behind her and King groaned.

"You don't look so good." The bartender held out his card, watching him with a knowing smile on his face.

"I'm not. I'm completely fucked."

Bad King is Available Now at mmalonebooks.com/badking

TANK: BLUE-COLLAR BILLIONAIRES

Three things I know about the woman of my dreams: she's quiet, loves animals, and *hates* me

I am not her type. She's into three piece suits and pocket protectors not bodyguards in military boots. I've never been the kind of guy you take home until a sudden inheritance flips my life upside down. Suddenly I have brothers I've never met and my only peace is when I'm with Emma.

Between picnics on the beach, and accidentally adopting a naked rescue cat, with this girl nothing goes according to plan. But when she's in danger, I'll do anything to protect her, even if she's got secrets that might just change everything.

Find out more at mmalonebooks.com/tank

TANK

She's not here.

I'm in my lawyer's office for the third time this month, squashed into a hard wooden chair that's too small for my six foot five inch frame. It still feels weird to say that, *my lawyer*, like I'm some kind of big shot now or something. But it's true. I have a lawyer and an accountant. I also have a huge stack of money sitting in a trust with my name on it.

Shifting as much as I can in the narrow seat, I avert my gaze from the brunette currently sitting behind the secretary's desk. She's beautiful but she's not *her*. She looks like she'll faint if our eyes meet one more time, although to be fair I have been glaring at her for the past ten minutes. There's not much else in the room to look at.

There's an older woman with a cane and a small white dog in her purse that yaps every time someone enters or leaves the room. A middle-aged man in the corner mumbles under his breath while working on a crossword puzzle. A guy in a suit sits a few feet away typing into a laptop.

Waiting rooms are not my favorite places. No matter how hard they try to be comfortable, they never get it quite right. Inevitably they are either too cold or too warm. The piped in music is too loud or it's eerily silent. Everyone is staring at everyone else and pretending not to. Since I'm usually the biggest one in the room, you guessed it. Most of the attention is directed at me.

There's only one reason I've been voluntarily coming here for the past few weeks to sit in uncomfortable chairs all while paying for the privilege.

To see *her*. The one person that makes all the noise in my head subside.

And now she's not even here.

The outer office door bursts open and a gust of cold air sweeps through the room, stirring the little dog into a yapping frenzy.

"I'm sorry. Sorry." A young woman rushes past, a flurry of blond hair and apologies, and places her bag on the floor behind the secretary's desk. I sit up straight, watching. The brunette smiles at her with genuine affection. They whisper back and forth before the other woman gets up and walks down the hallway leading to the offices.

The blonde glances over at me before tucking a few of the

stray hairs around her face behind her ears. It takes her a few minutes to get settled. She moves a few things around on the desk and then pulls a bottle of water from her oversized bag. She's doing an admirable job of appearing busy and engrossed in whatever's on her computer screen but a few minutes later, she looks at me again.

Usually this kind of thing annoys the hell out of me, but for some reason, with her, I don't mind. Maybe it's the madcap cloud of blond hair or the big, wounded gray eyes. I'm not sure what it is, but there's something about this girl. Something that keeps me coming back week after week. I think it's because she never smiles.

"Don't worry I'm still here."

She lets out a surprisingly crude snort. "Like I could miss you. And I wasn't looking for you."

"Okay, okay." I lean back and make a show of spreading my arms over the backs of the chairs next to me. I'm a big dude and I have a wingspan like a giant. Her eyes follow the movement but when she sees me watching, she turns up her nose a little and goes back to her typing.

I chuckle a little. She doesn't like me much and for some reason, it amuses me. I stare at her openly because I know when she notices she'll do that little huffing sound again. She's a pretty little thing. Elegant. The kind of girl who clutches her pearls when I get too close. The nameplate on her desk reads *Emma Lynn Shaw*. Even her name is prissy as hell.

Despite that, there's something about her that I find compelling.

The phone on her desk rings and she answers, her voice a soft whisper in the quiet room. She nods and then places the phone carefully back on the hook.

"Tanner Marshall?" she calls out, looking around at the other people in the waiting room.

The little dog gives an irritated yip. No one else even looks up. Finally her gaze lands on me. Chuckling, I walk over and stand right in front of her desk. I've been here every Monday for the last five weeks. Surely she knows who I am by now. She also knows that I hate to be called by my legal name. I've told her to call me Tank every time. I've also asked her to dinner every time.

Then again, she looks like the kind of girl who wouldn't remember a guy like me.

"Is he ready for me?"

"Yes. Just go straight through."

Instead of walking down the hallway, I lean against the wall next to her desk. "So, I have to eat dinner again tonight. Just like last week. And the week before that. It's a pesky recurring event, this dinner thing. I'm assuming you're familiar with it?"

"I am aware of it, yes. Sometimes I go wild and have dessert, too. But you know what I like the best?" She leans closer like she's imparting a secret. "Eating it alone."

I wink at her. "One of these days you're going to realize how much you're missing out on."

"One of these days. Not today."

"Ouch. You're brutal for such a tiny thing." But I've achieved my objective. She's almost smiling.

"Mr. Stevens is waiting for you." She gestures toward the hallway again. Her eyes are gleaming as she turns back to her computer. She types a few words and then looks up at me from the corner of her eye.

"Thank you, Emma." I use her name deliberately just to see her blush again. Patrick's office is the first door on the hallway.

When I push it open, he looks up. "Come on in, Tank. Have a seat."

I wave away his offer. "You can just tell me. Did he agree?"

Patrick looks slightly uncomfortable. "He didn't, did he? Then there's no point in wasting any more time."

"I didn't meet with your father. He sent his right hand man. Mr. Jonathan Boyd."

This news doesn't surprise me. "He couldn't even be bothered to deal with it himself? I'm sure he outsources everything. He probably has someone to wipe his ass when he needs it, too."

Patrick sighs. "I understand that your father isn't ... well." He rifles through the stack of papers on his desk. "All these meetings haven't been entirely unproductive, however. I've gathered quite a bit of information that we didn't have before."

He looks up at me. I cross my arms but I don't leave. He's got me interested and he knows it. "What do you mean?"

"Your father's estate is larger than I was originally led to believe. The amount he's given you so far is merely a drop in the bucket."

"He gave me and Finn both half a million dollars each. He's rich. I got it."

Patrick clears his throat. "All he's asked for are weekly meetings, an hour each time. Every week you show up, he'll put money in your trust fund. From what I understand, your father is very ill. He doesn't have a lot of time left. You have very little to lose and everything to gain."

"Look, I'm not completely heartless all right, but I haven't seen the bastard in almost twenty years. He left us high and dry and he's been off gallivanting around Europe ever since. This money would have been nice when we were growing up and Mom was working her ass off trying to keep us fed."

"I understand that, Mr. Marshall. However, your father wasn't playing around that whole time. He was making his fortune in coal and steel and investing in green energy solutions. His lawyer indicated that if you should agree to meet with him, then the money you'll inherit will be ...substantial."

"I don't want anything from him. He wasn't there for us in life and I don't want shit from him now that he's on his deathbed and feeling guilty."

"Well, as an incentive, he's authorized another distribution into your account of five hundred thousand. That money comes with no strings attached. If you agree to his terms, you'll receive even more. Congratulations, Mr. Marshall. You just became a millionaire."

"What the hell?" I put out a hand and use the wall to steady myself. I'm not sure what I'm supposed to feel. Grateful? Instead I just feel vaguely dirty.

Patrick hands me a folder. The first page has been flipped up to reveal a new letter from my father's law firm.

"Mr. Boyd has asked if I can help notifying the others. Your brother Finnigan was the only one who responded. You wouldn't happen to know where they are, would you?"

Others?

I have no idea what he's talking about and it obviously shows on my face because Patrick points to the list at the bottom of the page. "Your father has plans to split his empire equally amongst his sons."

"I only have *one* brother. Finn."

Patrick looks stunned for a moment. Then he yanks out the chair in front of his desk.

"Perhaps you'd best take that seat now, Mr. Marshall."

Find out more at mmalonebooks.com/tank

acknowledgments

There are so many people who were instrumental in helping this book come to life. Writing the same characters for the past few years has been an honor and a challenge, but one that I wouldn't have even attempted without the encouragement of the Alexander fans. Thank you all so much for reading, reviewing, sharing and just loving my "family" as much as I do.

I have to thank my husband for countless things. Cooking a million dinners, ignoring the sound of my fingers clacking on a keyboard while you're trying to sleep and for loving me in spite of my constant daydreaming and cranky moods when my characters aren't cooperating. Loving a novelist isn't easy but you are the model of a romantic hero.

For my sister, I love you, firecracker! The best thing Mom and Dad ever did for me was decide to have you. Our do-nothing vacation is coming soon, I promise!

Also I have to say a heartfelt thank you to the amazing Nana Malone. Meeting you at conference that day was definitely fate. This book wouldn't exist without your encouragement :) You can't get rid of me now! Mwa-ha-ha! The world isn't ready for us.

reformed con artist and a perfect little princess don't belong together. But I still can't leave her alone.

Zack : She's my brother's ex. Off limits. But she needs a nude model for her show so I'm taking one for the team. Turns out she needs more than just my picture...

Luke : My online BFF is the only hacker better than I am. Then I'm asked to consult on a hacking case for the FBI and the hauntingly beautiful suspect seems to know a lot about me. Things I've only told one other person...

Bad Business (The Kingsleys)

Contemporary Romance

Bad King: My parents just put a gold diggers target on my back. But if all they want is a wedding, I'll find the fiancee of their nightmares. *Who Wants to Marry a Billionaire? Must be completely inappropriate.*

Bad Blood : I'd do anything for my best friend's little sister. Until she asks for the one thing I can't give. One night. No rules. ***RITA® Award Winner!***

The Alexanders

Contemporary Romance

One More Day : "Good girl" Ridley has always attracted bad guys. Now she's on the run and has nowhere to hide. So when Jackson Alexander mistakes her for her twin, she decides to do something she knows is wrong. *She lies.*

The Things I Do for You : Nick Alexander finally has what the woman of his dreams needs. He'll give Raina a baby if she gives him what he wants. *Her.*

All I Want: The only gift Kaylee wants is for Elliott Alexander to stop treating her like she's invisible. When her car skids out of control on Christmas Eve, she's forced to reach out to the only man she trusts to save her. **(VIP List only)**

All I Need is You : When the man she loves leaves town after their steamy kiss, Kaylee Wilhelm is done. But when she's targeted by a stalker, Eli is the only one who can protect her.

Just One Thing : Bennett Alexander is a bona fide genius but he still can't figure out how to "get the girl". So he hires a dating tutor. What could go wrong? Other than falling for his teacher, of course.

One More Chance : Now that Ridley is expecting, everything is different. All she needs is for Jackson to pretend that he finds her as sexy as he used to, even if it's not true. But with a little advice from her meddlesome twin, she has a plan to seduce her own husband.

* Join my VIP list for FREE books *

newsletter.mmalonebooks.com

about the author

M. Malone is a RITA® Award winner and a NYT & USA Today Bestselling author of completely inappropriate romantic comedy. She lives with her husband and their two sons in the picturesque mountains of Northern Virginia even though she is afraid of insects, birds, butterflies and other humans.

She also holds a Master's degree in Business from a prestigious college that would no doubt be scandalized at how she's using her expensive education.

instagram.com/minxmalone

BB bookbub.com/authors/m-malone

patreon.com/minxmalone

amazon.com/author/mmalone

tiktok.com/@minxmalone

www.ingramcontent.com/pod-product-compliance
Lightning Source LLC
Chambersburg PA
CBHW010347170726
48284CB00011B/2818